THE TAKEDOWN

EVIE HUNTER

Boldwood

First published in Great Britain in 2024 by Boldwood Books Ltd.

Copyright © Evie Hunter, 2024

Cover Design: Colin Thomas

Cover Photography: Colin Thomas

A CIP catalogue record for this book is available from the British Library.

Paperback ISBN 978-1-83518-092-1

Large Print ISBN 978-1-83518-088-4

Hardback ISBN 978-1-83617-839-2

Ebook ISBN 978-1-83518-085-3

Kindle ISBN 978-1-83518-086-0

Audio CD ISBN 978-1-83518-093-8

MP3 CD ISBN 978-1-83518-090-7

Digital audio download ISBN 978-1-83518-084-6

Boldwood Books Ltd
23 Bowerdean Street
London SW6 3TN
www.boldwoodbooks.com

1

'Come on, guys. Drink up now.' A harried barmaid sent pleading looks at her remaining clientele, none of whom took a blind bit of notice. 'Have a heart. It's late and some of us need our beauty sleep. Ain't you got no boats to go to?'

'Ah, Sophie love, you're such a nag,' slurred a deckhand whom Freya vaguely recognised from a yacht moored close to the one she was working on.

The rest of the crews in the still busy bar and those spilling out onto the pavement where all the tables were occupied in a quaint, cobbled side street off the marina in Antibes in the South of France appeared oblivious to Sophie's plight.

'Is it always this raucous?' Freya asked the mechanic seated a little too close beside her.

'You've caught it on a quiet night, darlin'. Come back at the weekend and it'll be standing room only.'

Freya glanced at the drink in front of her – the same drink that had remained untouched for the past half-hour – and withheld a sigh. Already the glamour of working on a superyacht had started to fade. Not that she'd gotten into it in search of actual glamour, or because she harboured a desire to see the world from the decks of a floating gin palace. Her reason was far more fundamental and went by the name of revenge.

'Not all it's cracked up to be, is it?'

The voice close to Freya's ear made her almost jump out of her skin. 'Don't do that!' She clutched a hand over her heart. 'You scared the life out of me.'

'Sorry.'

She looked up into the handsome face of Greg Larson, captain of the *Perseus*, all chiselled features, dark hair and moss-green eyes – the sort of distraction she had not expected and could definitely do without. She had joined the crew for a specific reason that had nothing to do with macho captains who were better looking than they had any right to be. Not that she needed to worry about Larson coming on to her. In the unlikely event that he tried it on, Freya knew that Sandy Drew, the ship's catering manager, would stake a prior claim. For reasons that Freya failed to understand, Sandy had taken a dislike to her the moment she'd stepped on board and had made her feelings apparent in a dozen annoying little ways ever since. Freya wanted to tell her to save her energy. She most definitely didn't have designs upon Greg. Sandy was welcome to him.

She glanced up, felt Sandy's hostile gaze boring into her from across the bar and sighed. Turf wars over a man were definitely not on her agenda and for that reason, she wished Greg would leave her alone. She really didn't want to get into a spat with Sandy or draw the attention of the rest of the crew towards her. If she was to stand a prayer of achieving her objectives, then she needed to fly beneath the radar.

She glanced at the expensive yachts moored in the marina with their fancy radar domes glistening even in the dark and grinned. Yep, she needed to fly beneath the whole lot of them.

Quite literally.

'You're not a drinker?' Greg nodded towards her untouched drink. The ice had melted and condensation ran down the outside of the glass, spilling over the edges of a drip mat and leaving a puddle of icy water on the table.

Freya shrugged. 'Need to make a good impression.'

'Ha!' Greg threw back his head and laughed. 'If you're worried about the boss, don't be. He speaks to me because he has to but the rest of you will be invisible. Trust me. The guy's from a different planet to us mere mortals.'

'I guess the rich can do as they please.' Julien Falcon, self-made man and owner of the *Perseus*, Freya knew for a certainty, definitely could. And did. He rode roughshod over the feelings of anyone who got in the way of his blind ambition. He used people to get what he wanted and then discarded them like trash without a backward glance. He got away with it because no one had the balls to fight back. He was simply too powerful to be touched, or so Freya had repeatedly been told.

'What's he like?' Freya asked.

Greg screwed up his features but still managed to look disarmingly handsome. 'Make up your own mind,' he said. 'He'll be here tomorrow. Probably. I'd hate to cloud your judgement by expressing my personal views.'

In other words, Greg valued his job and wasn't about to speak out of turn. Just like everyone else she'd discussed Falcon with, Greg was putting his own interests first. Even so, Freya got the impression that he neither liked nor respected the man who employed him. She also figured that Falcon would probably resent Greg, who had a responsible job and one that Falcon couldn't hope to emulate, even if he did pretend to steer the ship himself when safely out at sea – and when the autopilot ensured that no steering was necessary. Ergo, Falcon couldn't do without Greg. Even so, the yacht's captain was probably forced to jump through hoops of the owner's making, just so that he, Falcon, felt like he was in charge.

Freya had seen that attitude more times than enough in her line of work and knew that those with the most to prove tended to pull rank. She was absolutely sure that Falcon would be no exception.

'What do you mean, "probably"?' she asked, returning her wandering attention to Greg. 'We're ready for him to come tomorrow.'

Greg laughed. 'Doesn't mean he'll actually arrive. Falcon is a law unto himself. Even so, you're right. If this lot get too wasted, the chances are he *will* turn up this time and I'll get it in the neck if half his crew are hungover. Come on, guys.' Greg barely raised his voice but still managed to catch the attention of the dozen members of *Perseus*'s crew scattered about the bar. 'Let's call it a night.'

Drinks were downed in long swallows and the

crew obediently stood up, some more steadily than others. Sandy materialised at Greg's side and sent Freya a moody look. Greg, Freya noticed, barely glanced at her as she clung tenaciously to the captain's side when the crew made their way back to the yacht.

Freya had always thought of yachts as small, flimsy things with canvas sails that got buffeted about in the unpredictable English weather and whose crews absolutely always endured a salty water soaking. The *Perseus* was something else entirely. Freya looked up at the sleek structure as they approached it, three decks lit up like a Christmas tree, the gentle hum of generators barely audible about the gentle lapping of the water against the hull. There were even lights illuminating the helipad on the aft deck, as though Greg expected Falcon to fly in at night. Perhaps he would. Nothing would surprise Freya about the man's excesses: his determination to flaunt his wealth.

The two crew members left on watch pressed a button and the passerelle was lowered on a silent hoist. The crew, raucous a few minutes previously, boarded quietly, their training kicking in. Freya said goodnight to her colleagues and made her way below deck through the crew's corridor, akin to the servants' entrance in grand English houses, she often thought.

All the twenty-strong crew were housed below decks, with the exception of Greg, who had his own quarters in the wheelhouse. As the new hostess, at least Freya qualified for a single cabin, albeit small but with the added advantage of her own bathroom. Apart from Greg, she was the only member of the crew who didn't have to share. The deckhands, she knew, were four to a cabin. Despite the fact that even the crew cabins were air-conditioned, she imagined it must be stifling and cramped for them on their down-time and could understand why they took the opportunity to let their hair down in port.

Tired but too wired to sleep, Freya got ready for bed and lay on it, staring at the ceiling, wondering if the elusive Julien Falcon would appear the following day in a clatter of helicopter rotors and, more to the point, if he would recognise her. She was counting on the fact that he wouldn't and so Greg's view that his crew were invisible had been encouraging. She fully intended that Falcon *would* discover her identity, but in her own time and in her own way.

She was drifting off to sleep, lulled by the gentle swaying of the massive boat and the creaking of the lines that secured it to the pontoon, when her phone vibrated.

'Hey,' she said, smiling when she saw her friend

Jasmine's name on the screen. 'You're up late. What's going on?'

'Just wanted to make sure that you haven't done anything rash.'

Freya smiled. 'Me? Rash? I think you have the wrong person.'

Jas's rich laughter echoed over the airwaves. 'I know you, Freya, far too well.' She sighed. 'I suppose there's no point in telling you that... well, that there's no point in going after Falcon. I feel as bad as you do about what happened, you know I do, but he's untouchable and will squash you like an irritating fly if you confront him. So please don't. The past can't be changed.'

'I've told you before, I just want to get a feel for the man.' Freya crossed her fingers to negate the lie. Jasmine was the only person who knew why she'd taken this job and would also know that she had more than a 'look-see' in mind. But she wasn't ready to share, mainly because she was making it up on the fly.

'What's his boat like?'

'A palace.' Freya gritted her teeth as she spoke. When she thought of the luxurious salon and palatial master suite, paid for by deception, all her old grievances rose to the fore, reinforcing her determination to right a few wrongs.

Somehow.

'When's he due to arrive?'

'Not sure. He has a habit of pleasing himself. Everything is ready for him, food cooked every day and wasted because he doesn't show.'

'Sounds typical.' Jas sighed when a baby wailed in the background. 'Duty calls,' she said.

'Give my lovely godson a big kiss from me.'

'Your lovely godson has decided that sleep is for wimps.'

Freya laughed. 'He takes after his mum and is too busy to waste time sleeping.'

'Keep in touch and DO NOT do anything rash.'

'Did you just talk to me in shouty capitals?'

Jas chuckled. 'Whatever it takes.'

'Love you. Now go read stories to my baby boy.'

'Love you too.'

Freya lay awake long after Jas hung up, watching the shadows cast by the lights in nearby Juan-les-Pins harbour dancing on the walls of her cabin. The rational side of her brain knew that Jas was right. When it came to one-sided fights, her ambition to bring Falcon down made David's struggle with Goliath seem entirely plausible.

'What am I thinking?' she asked aloud.

She reminded herself of the damage that the man

had carelessly done to her family and many others besides and knew that she wouldn't be able to live with herself if she didn't at least give it her best shot. After all, she'd beaten a big field of applicants and been appointed to this position at a point in her life when she had almost given up on the idea of retribution. It seemed like a sign.

She set her alarm to wake her at three in the morning; the witching hour when even the crewman left on watch would be dozing on the aft deck. She knew because she'd checked them out several times. No matter who was on duty, they weren't alert and posed no threat. They were looking for signs of unusual occurrences off the yacht, not on it. Tonight though, she wouldn't be checking the lie of the land but doing what she'd taken this position in order to achieve. If Falcon did arrive tomorrow then she wouldn't get another opportunity.

Freya yawned and eventually fell into an uneasy sleep, wondering if tomorrow would be the day when she finally came face to face with the man who had ripped the heart out of her family.

* * *

'What do you make of the new hostess?'

Greg looked up from the charts he was studying in the wheelhouse and suppressed a sigh at the sound of Sandy's voice. She clung more tenaciously than the barnacles that didn't get to attach themselves to *Perseus*'s hull for long before they were ruthlessly antifouled.

'Not my department,' Greg replied shortly. 'Why? Don't you like her?'

Greg regretted asking the question and thereby initiating a discussion. Sandy didn't need any encouragement.

'I hoped I might get the position.'

'You're a chef.'

'Doesn't mean I wouldn't make a good hostess. Freya doesn't have any experience of working on a yacht. I do. I understand how things are done.'

'If you wanted the position, why didn't you apply for it?'

'The boss indicated the last time he was on board, and the last hostess quit in a tearful strop, that the job was mine. Didn't realise until it was too late that it had been advertised and that I would need to actually apply.'

Greg glanced up at Sandy and knew she was sulking, her feelings hurt, perhaps accounting for her antagonistic attitude towards Freya. 'You shouldn't have taken Falcon's word as gospel,' he said. 'You know how unpredictable owners can be. You haven't been on board for long, but long enough to understand the score. He probably forgot what he said the moment he said it. Either that or he was playing you.'

'Yeah well, I don't suppose this one will last for long. Anyway, I'll know better next time, especially if you put in a good word for me.'

Greg held up a hand. 'Falcon's people do the hiring and firing and never ask for my opinion. Take my advice: stick to what you do best, wow the boss's guests with your culinary inventiveness and make yourself indispensable to him by that means.'

Sandy, far from being discouraged by Greg's off-hand tone, wandered further into the wheelhouse and glanced at the lights reflected in the water from the other superyachts moored up in one of the most prestigious marinas in Europe. There to be seen, admired and drooled over by the hoi polloi. Some of them didn't leave their moorings for months at a time.

'Do you think she's pretty?'

'Do I think who's pretty?' Greg knew full well whom she was referring to and resisted the urge to tell Sandy to grow up.

'Freya of course. No one knows anything about

her. It seems odd that she was appointed, is all I'm saying. There's something off about her.'

'She mentioned that she was housekeeper at a country estate for several years and that she has a BA in business management.'

'Boasting about her qualifications?' Sandy sneered.

'I had to extract the information from her.'

'Why did she leave such a prestigious position?'

Greg threw up his hands. 'How the hell should I know? Ask her if you're curious. I don't suppose there's any great mystery surrounding her career move.'

'Why are you working with paper charts?' she asked, in an abrupt change of subject. 'You have all these up-to-the-minute gizmos,' she added, waving a hand in the direction of the controls. 'Paper is outdated.'

'A good skipper always has a backup,' Greg replied impatiently, pointedly returning his attention to the charts in question. 'The gizmos you refer to could all fail whereas paper never lets you down.'

'Where are we going?' She peered over his shoulder. 'Croatia? Isn't the water too shallow for a boat of this size?'

'Yep. Which is why I need to be well prepared.'

'Wonder why he wants to go there. It's not exactly poser central.'

'That's most likely why.' Greg tutted when he miscalculated. 'He's a small fish in a big pond of ostentatious wealth in this port, whereas...'

Sandy shrugged, seemingly disinterested in a conversation that she'd instigated. 'Yeah, I hear you.'

She didn't take the hint when Greg again tried to concentrate and instead prowled around the wheelhouse like a caged lion. 'If I'd been given the hostess's position, at least I'd have my own cabin. Brenda snores fit to wake the dead.' She glanced meaningfully at the closed door to Greg's cabin, situated at the rear of the wheelhouse. But if she was hinting that she wanted a look-see then she was wasting her energy. Greg had absolutely no intention of getting stuck in a bedroom with Sandy and now bitterly regretted the drunken fumble they'd had on shore a week or so back. A fumble that she'd instigated and that Greg had been too wasted to stave off.

Big mistake! He knew now that she hadn't taken it nearly as casually as he had. He'd tried to steer well clear of her since then, but she was either too thick-skinned or too determined to get the message.

'Do you know, Freya went through the kitchen accounts with a fine-tooth comb earlier today and made me feel like I had to justify every last euro spent.'

Greg glanced up. 'Well, don't you?'

Sandy shrugged. 'Izzy always took my word for things. She didn't resort to counting the boxes in the storeroom.'

'Presumably there were no discrepancies,' Greg said, suspecting that there had been, 'so why are you getting so hot under the collar?'

Another shrug. 'I like to feel that I'm in charge of my own domain.'

'We all have to answer to someone.'

'You don't.'

Greg threw his sextant aside and looked up at her. 'Go to bed, Sandy. I need to work and you're distracting me.'

'I wanted to talk to you about something.'

'Not now!'

'Oh okay, I know when I'm not wanted.' She jutted her lower lip like a child on the verge of throwing a tantrum. 'It'll be interesting to see if the boss does grace us with his presence tomorrow and what he makes of Miss Uptight if he does.'

'Night.' Greg waved to her over his shoulder and breathed a massive sigh of relief when he heard the door to the crew quarters close behind her.

Instead of returning to his charts, Greg wandered out onto the enclosed deck that circled the wheel-house, an area from which he often navigated by the stars during night passages. Unlike being in fashion-able ports where nothing was ever completely silent, being at sea at night when everyone else on board was asleep, was peaceful like nothing Greg had ever known before.

He leaned on the railing, pondering upon Sandy's take on the new girl, Freya. He would never have ad-mitted it to Sandy, but her introspection had intrigued him. Most people liked nothing more than to talk about themselves but whenever he'd asked Freya about her reasons for taking the job, she always changed the subject.

Something else he'd never have admitted to Sandy was that he thought her stunning. She had an elegance about her and a soft manner of expression that he found mesmerising. Her looks would have gone a long way to getting her the position, he knew. Falcon liked to employ the beautiful people, at least front of house. Sandy wouldn't stand a hope in hell in that regard. Her round face and heavy hips ruled her out. Not that the need for a shapely body and pretty face would ever find their way onto a job description but male chauvinism, at least insofar as the Falcons of this world were concerned, had yet to go out of style.

Freya was friendly with the others but, as in the bar earlier, never let herself go completely. He'd been watching her and knew that she'd had no more than a couple of glasses of wine the entire evening. Everyone else had been far too self-engrossed to notice.

A bark of laughter from another yacht echoed through the air, sending Greg back to his charts. But his concentration was shot. It was late and he really ought to get some sleep. Sod's law, if he didn't then Falcon would turn up with his retinue at first light and demand to get under way immediately.

Greg heartily disliked Falcon. He'd heard enough rumours about his shady background to accept his own judgement of the man. Even so, he wanted to keep his job and so needed to be at the top of his game. Falcon knew absolutely nothing about boats but owned this one and so could do what he liked, hiring and firing at will. What he liked more than any-thing else was to throw his weight around to impress his hangers-on.

Chances were, once Greg had sorted out how best to navigate the shallow, Croatian waters, Falcon would change his mind about their destination, simply be-cause he could. It had happened before.

His eyes grew heavy and the lines on the charts blurred. His head nodded forward and just for a moment, he gave in to tiredness. When he opened his eyes again and glanced at his watch, he swore voraciously.

It was after 3 a.m.

Greg got up, stretched and headed for his cabin. But first he did a turn around the wheelhouse deck, perched high above the water line, just as he did every night. Even the surrounding yachts were mostly quiet now, with just the occasional raised voice to shatter the peace. The stars were putting on a show and Greg paused as he identified as many of the constellations as he could.

Then a flash of artificial light reflecting spasmodically, a bit like a torch being switched on and off immediately below caught his attention. Tiredness forgotten, he was now fully alert. It was coming from this boat, from the owner's study to be precise, and wouldn't have been visible from any other part of the yacht except for the bridge where Greg happened to be standing.

'What the fuck...'

Greg scratched his head and went to investigate. He slipped down the stairs from the bridge and paused outside the study's door. He heard a smothered oath come from within as drawers were quietly opened and then closed again just as softly. It was a female member of the crew rifling through Falcon's private things and Greg had a pretty good idea who it must be.

He flattened himself against the panelling in an adjoining corridor when Freya's footsteps, light on the wooden floor, approached the door. She closed it gently behind her and headed for the crew quarters. Greg stuck his head round the corner but quickly withdrew it again when she paused and looked round. Had she heard him, or somehow sensed his presence? He inhaled, unsure why he was the one hiding when he'd done nothing wrong. He let out a long breath when he heard the door open. He emerged from the shadows in time to see her disappear though it, wondering what she'd hoped to find and, more to the point, what he should do about it.

'Freya Addison,' he muttered. 'Who are you and what are you looking for?'

2

Freya returned to her cabin, breathless and dispirited. She had taken an almighty risk and for what? She'd found absolutely nothing of any interest. *What had she expected?* she wondered as she slid between the sheets and waited for her heartbeat to return to normal. Sensitive material, if he'd been stupid enough to keep it, would be on a computer somewhere, heavily encrypted, or else lodged with a solicitor. There was a locked drawer in that study that had called to Freya. She'd been sorely tempted to break into it but was held back by her lack of knowledge on the lock-picking front.

She hadn't been able to shake the feeling that

someone had seen her. There had been a dim light coming from the direction of the wheelhouse but there were always lights on in the boat's hub. It didn't follow that anyone was actually awake. Besides, if they had seen her, surely they would have challenged her. Her position as a maritime housekeeper, for want of a better description, gave her carte blanche to go wherever she liked on the yacht. But if anyone had seen her furtively enter the owner's study at the dead of night, it would throw up legitimate questions that she would much prefer not to provide answers to.

'Stupid, Freya, stupid!' she muttered as she aggressively thumped her pillows, searching for sleep that she knew would be a long time coming.

She sat bolt upright again when it occurred to her that Greg could well have been burning the midnight oil. He had mentioned something earlier about the problems of sailing a large yacht in shallow, Croatian waters and the amount of planning that would be required to ensure that they didn't run aground.

But if he'd seen or heard her, surely he would have challenged her, she reasoned once again. He was the only member of the crew with greater authority than hers and the buck stopped with him. The ultimate responsibility for safety and security on board was his and he took his duties seriously. She liked and respected Greg and would much prefer not to get on his wrong side. She hadn't given up a position that she loved and taken up servitude on a floating gin palace just to fall at the first hurdle.

If Greg had seen her then the chances were that he'd tell Sandy since they appeared to be an item. Sandy had made it clear that she resented Freya and wouldn't hesitate to drop her in it if she caught her stepping out of line.

Freya knew that Sandy was cooking the galley's books. Freya, despite her dour frame of mind, giggled at her mental metaphor. One glance at Sandy's accounts was all it had taken for someone with Freya's experience to realise that Sandy was claiming to have cooked extensive meals, sufficient for the owner and a dozen guests, every day. True enough. Wasteful though it might appear, those were Sandy's orders. But Freya also knew that she cooked half as much as she claimed, presumably selling the excess expensive ingredients on and lining her own pockets.

Part of Freya approved of the temperamental chef's determination not to needlessly waste food, and to profit from her thrift. Freya wasn't about to grass her up. She had much bigger fish to fry. She chuckled once again at the nature of her mental perambulations which appeared to be stuck on food. In Sandy's shoes, she would have gone out of her way to befriend Freya, thereby reducing the likelihood of Freya exposing the scam. Perhaps she thought she was too clever to be caught and that Freya was too thick to notice anything amiss.

Now that was downright insulting!

Anyway, Freya knew she would have to watch the woman. She seemed to have reached the erroneous conclusion that Greg had a personal interest in Freya and resented the competition. She was wrong. Greg had never made a move on her and Freya would rebuff him if he did. She had a specific reason for being on the yacht that had nothing to do with romantic aspirations.

'Ah well,' she said aloud. 'Sandy's the least of my problems.'

Freya eventually fell into a deep sleep but woke with the dawn. She could hear the crew on the yacht next to theirs preparing to get under way. They worked quickly and quietly but sound carried over water and she could hear them quite distinctly, communicating in French too fast for Freya to understand.

She yawned, feeling as though she'd barely slept. A headache threatened. Sighing, she pushed back the covers and headed for the shower. Ten minutes later, she was dressed in her crew uniform of navy shorts and polo shirt with the boat's name embroidered across the back. She winced at her reflection. Navy was not her colour. It drained her complexion and made her look as tired as she felt. She pulled her hair back into a ponytail and dabbed a little concealer beneath her eyes. A swish of mascara and pale lipstick and she looked as good as she was ever likely to.

Her first duty of the day was to ensure that everything was in readiness for the owner and his guests. Although he had so far failed to materialise when expected, Freya sensed that today, he *would* actually show his face. She checked the master stateroom and then all the guest suites. Everything was pristine.

'Morning, Gloria,' she said to a fellow crew member when she emerged from a storeroom clutching a box of cleaning supplies.

'Morning, Freya,' the girl replied cheerfully. 'I reckon they might actually fetch up today.' Gloria rolled her eyes. 'It will be entertaining, you mark my words. The type of people who the boss brings on board have to be seen to be believed.'

'I hear you. Oh well, let's try and ensure that they don't find anything to complain about.'

'Ha! Good luck with that one. Falcon always finds

something. It makes him feel important to lord it over us mere mortals.'

Freya liked Gloria's infectious good humour and although she probably ought to have taken her to task for criticising their employer, she let it go. Anything she could learn about the man to help her quest for retribution would be welcomed.

'Sounds like I'm in for a treat.'

'You and Greg are the one's who'll get it publicly in the neck. Falcon does not believe in taking people to task in private.'

Freya took her turn to roll her eyes. 'Is that why no one stays in this job for long?'

'Possibly.' Gloria waggled a hand from side to side. 'But there's generally a big turnover in this profession. You've probably cottoned on to the fact by now that it's not nearly as glamorous as people think.'

'Amen to that. Endless cleaning,' she said, glancing out the window to where two crew members were wiping down the stainless steel guard rails; a job that was necessary every day to prevent the salt air from causing corrosion. Freya didn't have to worry about that side of the operation. It was Greg's domain. The interior of the boat was hers and she was determined to make a good first impression upon a man whom she had never met but thoroughly despised.

'Anyway, let's get some breakfast, then we can fine-tune our preparations.'

The crew mess was crowded by the time that Freya and Gloria joined the throng. Greg was there, eating a plate of eggs standing up with his backside perched against a ledge. He glanced at Freya and nodded but there was none of the usual friendliness in the gesture. Sandy was nowhere in sight. The conversation, unlike the rowdiness in the bar the night before, was muted and restricted to business.

Freya forced down cereal and a mug of strong coffee, saying little, preoccupied and anxious. Greg kept glancing at her, adding to her nervous anticipation. She pretended not to notice and avoided talking directly to him. If he had seen her last night then he was clearly intent upon making her sweat before confronting her.

His tactics were working far better than he could possibly know, as attested by the fact that the hand holding her coffee was unsteady. If anyone noticed, she hoped they would put it down to nerves. Thankfully, there was an air of anxious anticipation in the crew mess that hadn't existed before. Everyone seemed to share Gloria's opinion that the owner would finally appear that day and were intent upon ensuring that everything was, quite literally, shipshape.

'We off on our travels today then, skipper, do you reckon?' one of the deck hands asked, voicing Freya's thoughts. 'I ain't never been to Croatia. What's it like?'

A loud clatter of approaching helicopter rotors drowned out Greg's response. Everyone abandoned their breakfast and ran to assume their posts.

'Game on,' Greg muttered in Freya's ear as he passed her on the way to the door.

Freya felt a fluttering of nerves as she put aside her empty mug and followed in Greg's wake. She was conscious of Sandy standing in the doorway to the galley, glowering at her. Freya ignored her as she made her way up to the main salon, checking instinctively to ensure that nothing was out of place as she went. Thankfully, the daily delivery of fresh flowers had arrived and Gloria had already perfected a beautiful arrangement in the centre of the massive table. She had placed another on the aft deck, where the owner and his guests would gravitate in order to see and be seen.

Freya had only worked in the glorified world of super yachts for a month but she already knew that it was all about one-upmanship. A competition between the ultra-wealthy to outdo one another. Those with a real interest in yachting purchased far more modest vessels and crewed them themselves.

The noise as the helicopter landed on the pad situated on the upper rear deck was deafening. The downdraft from the rotors threatened to dislodge anything not anchored down. Freya snatched up the flowers from the aft deck and moved them into the salon. She closed the door and waited for the rotors to stop turning before opening it again and returning the flowers to their previous position.

A bark of high-pitched, feminine laughter offended Freya's ears seconds before the woman responsible for it appeared from the side deck, clutching the arm of the man whom Freya despised. The woman was no more than twenty, less than half of Falcon's age, and tottered unsteadily along on four-inch stilettos. Freya glanced at Gloria, who gave a miniscule shrug to imply the woman's behaviour was par for the course. Walking on teak decks in anything other than deck shoes or bare feet was a big no-no and one of the first and most important rules of boating that had been drummed into Freya. Stilettos were the worst offenders but Falcon clearly didn't give a flying fuck if his teak was damaged. He wasn't the one that would have to repair the damage and footing the bill wouldn't make much of a dent in his bank balance.

Another couple appeared in the wake of Falcon. The man, Freya knew, was Eddie Bairstow. He was the same age as Falcon and the two were joined at the hip. Falcon was the concepts man; Bairstow made it happen. The woman on Bairstow's arm was closer to his age but still not much older than Falcon's date. Both men were married but clearly their wives weren't included in this particular excursion. It was Freya's understanding that the fragrant Mrs Falcon almost never set foot onboard.

Freya took a moment to examine Falcon. It was the first time she'd seen him in the flesh and she felt a momentary shiver travel down her spine. She thought she'd prepared herself for the moment and hadn't expected such a violent reaction at the sight of him. He was slightly below average height for a man, no more than five-ten. His hair was in full retreat but he was still handsome and the air of swaggering authority that he exuded reminded her that she had taken on a powerful and dangerous adversary.

'Larson.' Falcon shook Greg's hand without breaking stride. 'And you are?' He paused when he reached Freya and gave her person an insulting once over.

'Freya, your new hostess,' Freya replied in a neutral tone, swallowing down the bile that rose at the back of her throat.

'I see.' He continued to look hard at her, as though trying to decide where he knew her from. 'Let's hope you prove to be better at your job than your predecessor.'

Falcon's lady friend glanced at Freya and quickly looked away again. Clearly, the woman thought her too old to be any threat. To emphasise her point, she carelessly threw the jacket she'd carried over her arm onto the nearest chair. Freya showed no reaction and the woman – little more than a girl – was the first to look away.

'Another four people will be here within the hour,' Falcon said, raising his voice to be heard above the noise of the departing helicopter. 'We'll get under way as soon as they're on board, Larson.'

Greg acknowledged his orders with an inclination of his head. He looked impossibly handsome in navy shorts that showed off muscular thighs and long, tanned legs. He had a good four inches over Falcon and was at least a decade younger than his boss. Seeing them side by side, there was only one man who stood out and it was not the yacht's owner. Falcon frowned, causing Freya to wonder if he resented being outshone by his captain. If that was the case, Freya wondered how he'd kept his job for more than a year. Good skippers were in short supply, apparently, but even so...

Greg's white shirt with the gold epaulets denoting his position as captain seemed a little over the top to Freya. She assumed it was Falcon's idea, who probably regretted it since Greg carried it off with elan, making Falcon look shabby by comparison. Even the gold digger on Falcon's arm had trouble tearing her gaze away from Greg.

'Oh, Jules!' the female in question squealed. 'This is a palace. I love it!'

She glanced up at the glazed dome rising high above their heads and sighed, clearly thinking she'd finally made it. Freya reckoned she'd be in for a disappointment. She knew from her research that Falcon had been married to the same woman for twenty-five years. He was a serial player, but the other women never lasted for long. Presumably his wife either didn't care about his womanising or chose to ignore it, instead pursuing her own charitable interests.

'Go and get changed, Chelsea,' Falcon said, giving her backside a hefty pat: the type of pat that would have earned him an elbow in the ribs if he'd tried it on Freya.

Predictably, Chelsea giggled and sashayed down

the steps that led to the cabins. Freya was conscious of Greg watching her with unnerving stillness as she preceded Chelsea and showed her to the master stateroom. Chelsea handed Freya her oversized handbag to carry and wobbled on her heels when a passing boat caused the *Perseus* to rock on her mooring.

'This way,' Freya said, opening the door to the stateroom and standing back so that Chelsea could enter first.

'Ooh! This is heaven.'

Possibly, Freya thought, *but was it worth what she would have to do for Falcon to earn her passage?*

'Where're my bags?' Chelsea demanded to know, appearing to recall that she was the guest of honour.

'They will be unpacked as soon as they arrive,' Freya said. 'Is there anything you need now?'

'A glass of fizz would hit the spot, love.'

'I will arrange it.'

Freya sent someone else to serve the required champagne and returned to the salon in time for the arrival of the remaining four guests. They had been delivered by taxi rather than helicopter. Two middle-aged couples with whom Falcon undoubtedly wanted to do business, hence his hospitality. The men all remained in the salon, where Freya served drinks. Gloria conducted the ladies to the respective staterooms and attended to their needs. She would have an easier time of it, Freya suspected, than she herself had had with Chelsea, who had done her level best to ensure Freya remembered she was the hired help.

As though I would choose to involve myself with these people.

She unobtrusively served drinks and canapés as the men talked business. As Freya had hoped would be the case, she might as well have been invisible since they spoke freely in front of her. The men whom Freya had clocked as prospective lambs to the slaughter, Mike Parker and Jason Pyke, banged on for a while about the luxurious yacht as they swilled Krug on the aft deck, standing with legs braced against the gentle rocking motion.

'This is the life,' Mike said. 'Wouldn't mind a bit of this myself.' He was glancing at two scantily clad females on an adjoining yacht as he spoke and all the other men laughed.

'Easy enough to arrange,' Falcon said.

'I don't hunt when my wife's around,' Mike replied. 'Can't do that to her.'

'Don't bring her next time,' Eddie suggested with an easy smile.

'Hold that thought,' Jason muttered, glancing in

the direction of the cabins where their wives were establishing themselves.

Falcon let the conversation flow but Freya was uncomfortably aware of his gaze constantly coming to rest on her, his expression quizzical. She ignored him as she conducted her duties with unobtrusive efficiency.

She was glad when the sound of the powerful engines throbbing caused all the men to step onto the foredeck as the crew efficiently let the lines go and winched up the anchor. Freya cleared away the discarded glasses and ensured there was no lingering sign of the men's presence on the aft deck.

As the yacht smoothly and slowly cleared the marina, the women joined the men, settling themselves on the thickly cushioned sunbeds and slathering lotion on their limbs. Chelsea and Bairstow's date – Freya had heard her called Barb – wore miniscule bikinis that left nothing at all to the imagination. The wives were more modestly dressed in one-piece swimsuits but infinitely more elegant in Freya's opinion.

Leaving the women to their sunbathing, the men returned to the body of the yacht, presumably to change. A deckhand showed the guests to their staterooms, leaving Freya momentarily alone with Falcon.

'Have I seen you somewhere before?' he asked.

Without an audience, he dropped the affected attitude and seemed almost human.

Almost.

But Freya knew what a ruthless individual he was and wouldn't be swayed by the artificial charm.

'Not as far as I'm aware,' Freya said, taking more time than was necessary to straighten a cushion that had moved when the yacht hit a slight swell in the entrance to the marina.

'I never forget a face. Especially a pretty one.'

God! Could he get any cornier?

'We move in different circles.'

If he expected her to address him as sir then he'd have a long wait. Just being in the same room as such a callous individual made Freya's skin crawl. *What had made her suppose she'd be able to face him without giving herself away?* she wondered. She had assumed that he wouldn't recognise her, but he already appeared to suspect her motives.

'It doesn't have to be that way.' He sent her a quizzical look. 'You're different to the usual type that work on this tub. There's something about you. An elegance. A sense of true style that I appreciate. Why did you take this job?'

'Who wouldn't leap at the opportunity to see the world in luxury?'

'It's not for everyone.'

Freya wondered why he couldn't be himself, talk to people like they were individuals rather than underlings, all the time. That wouldn't make what he'd done right but it might make it easier for others to like him for himself rather than for his wealth.

Anything was possible.

'Perhaps that's why there's such a high turnover of staff.'

Falcon shrugged. 'I wouldn't know about that. I leave the hiring and firing to others.'

'Do you do a lot of firing?'

'I expect people to live up to my expectations.' He fixed her with a probing look. 'And I have very high standards.'

'Oh, Jules baby, there you are.' Chelsea tottered into the salon, having exchanged her stilettos for equally high wedged sandals. She sent an accusatory glance Freya's way. 'I wondered what was keeping you. The sun's waiting and so am I.'

'Well then, come and help me change.' He slung an arm around Chelsea's slim shoulders. 'We'll dine at seven,' he said curtly to Freya, his game face back on.

Freya watched them go. Falcon was mauling Chelsea's backside and she was roaring with laughter, egging him on. Falcon looked back over his shoulder and something Freya couldn't quite interpret flitted through his expression. Interest? Suspicion? It was impossible to be sure.

She lowered herself into a chair and closed her eyes the moment her employer was out of sight, feeling discomposed and disadvantaged. Had he been one step ahead of her all along and approved her appointment to such a prestigious and highly sought after position in order to make a point? It seemed unlikely, or so she tried to convince herself. The man didn't do subtle. He would credit her as being nothing more than an irritating distraction and would have had Eddie get rid of her before the yacht had left its mooring if he had recognised her.

She had imagined their initial meeting a hundred times, but it hadn't turned out the way she'd expected and had wrong-footed her. What was it about her that he found so fascinating? Why had he even bothered to spare her the time of day? Every member of the crew agreed on one thing. Their boss simply never interacted with the hired help and yet he had gone out of his way to talk to her on equal terms. Getting close to him had been her objective, even though she hadn't intended for the closeness to be personal, so she ought to feel a sense of achievement.

She felt only fear and renewed determination.

There was no danger of him making a move on her with the vigilant Chelsea on board. Getting closer to him without the intimacy becoming physical might just be her way in though. *Anyway, what other choice did she have?* she wondered as she hauled herself to her feet and went to tell Sandy about the dinner arrangements.

3

Greg waited for the last of the lines to be let go and then used the thrusters to move *Perseus* sideways from her berth. Clear of the dock, he navigated out of the marina, watched by a crowd on the quayside whose admiration of the sleek yacht would doubtless further bolster Falcon's already overinflated ego. The owner stood on the aft deck with his retinue like lord fucking muck, ignoring the envious glances but doubtless revelling in the reaction to his ostentatious display of wealth.

Standing on the flybridge deck immediately outside the wheelhouse gave Greg a better view of the chaotic marine activity. Half the idiots who bought boats had absolutely no conception of the rules of the sea. Tenders and small craft cut across Greg's path; a channel marked by buoys that was supposed to be used only by vessels entering or leaving the marina. And yet it was littered with day boaters, oblivious to the presence of the displacement hull of a three-storey, sixty-metre yacht bearing down on them.

Greg gave five sharp blasts of the yacht's horn. It was standard marine procedure to remind fools such as the one attempting to raise a sail in the middle of the navigation channel to get the hell out of the way. The would-be sailor glanced up but stayed where he was, drifting aimlessly as he faffed with a tangle of rope and canvas.

Greg rolled his eyes, thought of all the paperwork involved if there was a collision that wouldn't be his fault and tweaked his controls at the last minute. He avoided the small boat but ensured that it was rocked perilously by *Perseus*'s wake. The yachtsman had now definitely seen him and shook a fist at Greg as he windmilled his arms and just about managed to avoid being hurled into the sea by the surge created.

The harbour was deep, having been dredged to ensure that superyachts wouldn't be put off by the em-barrassing possibility of running aground from stop-ping by and paying the outrageous mooring fees. Greg glanced behind him at millions of pounds worth of fancy yachts that were probably put to sea at most for three months of the year. The sea was in Greg's blood, he'd learned to sail almost before he could walk, but what he did now was akin to driving a racing car. Every modern navigation aid was at his disposal: radar, depth finders, fish finders, electronic route planners combined to make him almost surplus to requirements. Once they were clear of the marina, he could set the autopilot and there would be nothing for him to do other than to keep watch.

No challenge. No sense of achievement. No satisfaction.

But satisfaction of the marine variety wasn't what had lured him into the world of superyachts, determined to be appointed captain of his particular vessel. Greg had a specific reason for having tolerated Falcon's mercurial moods for over a year and the time was rapidly approaching for him to make his move.

He heard raucous laughter as the owner and his guests moved to the comfort of the sun deck now that they were out of sight of their audience and no further posing was necessary. At least not for the benefit of the hoi polloi.

'Enjoy it while you can,' Greg muttered beneath his breath.

With a path eventually clear of obstacles, Greg

navigated around the headland and out into the open sea. He set the autopilot for a course to Ibiza, Falcon's first destination, and returned to the wheelhouse.

'All good, skipper?' Alex, Greg's second in command, asked.

'Give or take the odd idiot.'

'I noticed that sailor almost take an early bath.'

'I was so tempted.' Greg laughed. 'I ought to be used to it after all these years but the antics of some of them still manage to surprise me.'

'Well, at least the weather looks set fair,' Alex said. 'We should have a calm trip to party island.'

'That's a shame.'

Both men laughed. In rough weather, seasoned crewmen took bets on how long it would be before owners and their guests felt the effects of being at sea.

'Hold her at fifteen knots, Alex, and we'll make the crossing in twenty-four hours.'

'Will do.' Alex scratched his head. 'Why does a man of Falcon's age want to be seen in Ibiza? It's for the young and foolish.'

Greg shrugged. 'And for the rich willing to throw their dosh about. There's no such thing as an ugly rich man. You know that.'

'Yeah, I guess, but it's a crying shame. Having all that money and not doing good with it, I mean.'

'Yeah, it sucks.'

Greg walked to the back of the wheelhouse and looked down on the sun deck one floor below, where Falcon and his retinue were spread over the sunbeds, already on the champagne. He caught a glimpse of Freya as she refilled glasses, then retreated to pick up a book that Chelsea obviously wanted and was too lazy to fetch for herself. She had originally snapped her fingers at Freya, who ignored the gesture, waiting until Chelsea voiced her demand. Greg could hear Chelsea's whining tone, even over the rumble of the engines, and was impressed by the professional manner in which Freya dealt with her antics.

As though sensing him watching her, Freya glanced up. Their gazes met momentarily but she quickly looked away again. Greg sucked air through his lips, wondering what her purpose had been the night before in Falcon's study and if she'd realised that he'd seen her. That would explain why she'd avoided him ever since.

They had gotten along well in the month she'd been on board. Greg had come to enjoy her intelligence, her lively wit, her willingness to muck in and the fact that she didn't take life too seriously. She was new to the boating world but a quick study, willing to listen to what her more experienced crew mates told her and take their advice on board. Quite literally.

So the question remained and continued to nag at Greg: why had she searched Falcon's study? What had she hoped to find? Was she avoiding Greg so that she wouldn't have to explain herself or was he seeing shadows on a cloudy day? It could well be that she was being kept on her toes by Falcon and his retinue and wanted to make a good impression. She was evasive when asked why she'd left her previous job. Not that Greg would ever tell Sandy that he was curious about her circumstances too. Everyone had a right to privacy.

Greg strolled back to the controls.

'I'll take first watch,' he told Alex. 'Relieve me in three hours.'

Alex gave a mock salute and disappeared.

Left with nothing better to do other than to look out for other boats or unexpected hazards, Greg's mind returned to the subject of Freya. He liked her but wasn't about to let her interfere with the smooth running of his yacht. If Falcon found out she'd been snooping then Greg would get it in the neck for allowing it to happen. The ultimate responsibility for everything and everyone on board was his. He would have to make time to speak privately with her and do it today.

Had his own ego taken a nosedive because she was avoiding him? he wondered. Greg shuddered, hoping he wasn't that shallow. Given the hoops they all had to jump through prior to taking to sea, was his imagination getting the better of him? If he hadn't known about her nocturnal activities then occupied with his own responsibilities, he probably wouldn't even have noticed her evasiveness.

What he had noticed was Falcon clocking her and clearly liking what he saw. Greg hadn't been surprised. Falcon was an all-out womaniser and there was something about Freya's innate elegance and self-contained way of conducting herself that had caught Greg's eye the first moment she'd stepped on board. Clearly, she'd made a similar impression upon Falcon.

Greg cursed. He couldn't be distracted, and it was none of his business anyway, but the thought of Falcon getting his greasy hands on Freya brought bile to his throat. Perhaps Freya would repel his advances. Greg shook his head and dismissed the possibility out of hand. Falcon always got what he wanted and anyone who stood in his path, he had good reason to know, got swept aside like an irrelevant irritant. He probably conducted his private life in a similar man-

ner, assuming that his wealth would override all obstacles and that a member of his own crew couldn't
possibly resist his advances.

'Coffee, skipper?'

Greg turned at the sound of Sandy's approach.
She'd climbed the steps to the wheelhouse with sur-
prising stealth.

'Thanks,' he said.

'When will we get to party central?' she asked,
leaning a hip against the control console.

'Mid-morning tomorrow, most likely.'

'At least I know that they'll have to dine on board
tonight and not change their minds at the last minute.
Do you have any idea how disheartening it is to have
my efforts repelled in favour of tortilla and chips?
Makes me wonder why I bothered to work so hard to
establish my reputation.'

'You'll have your opportunity to impress tonight.'

'Ha! Fat chance.' She handed Greg his coffee.
'Falcon only ever complains.'

Greg shrugged as he sipped at his drink. 'What do
you want me to say?'

'You ask me, Falcon's got his sights set on our new
hostess.'

Greg glanced at Sandy, whose eyes gleamed with
barely suppressed spite. 'I'd have thought he'd got his

hands full with his latest squeeze,' he said in an indifferent tone, suppressing his misplaced unease.

'You know Falcon. He plans in advance.'

Greg said nothing and instead checked his instruments. But Sandy didn't take the hint and continued to linger. 'There's something about Freya that doesn't sit right with me,' she said.

'You clearly don't like her, but I fail to see what she's done to you. Boats are too small for crew members to bear grudges.'

'Yeah well, she thinks she's better than us.'

'Grow up, Sandy!' Greg said impatiently.

'She's got you thinking with your prick too, I see.' Sandy's expression turned petulant. 'Well, don't come crying to me when she shafts you.'

When Greg didn't respond, Sandy stomped off, this time with the heavy tread of the disappointed.

'What the hell was that all about?' he asked aloud.

But he knew. Sandy was possessive, had picked up on Greg's interest in Freya and drawn erroneous conclusions. It was as good a way as any to get his point across, he supposed. The yacht's chef could no longer be in any doubt that Greg didn't want a relationship with her, but Sandy clearly wasn't the type to take no for an answer. He'd seen the spiteful side of her character now and wondered what trouble she might cause in an effort to restore her damaged pride. There was, he knew from experience, no accounting for the actions of a woman scorned.

He reminded himself of his reasons for having taken this job and the patience he'd exercised since so doing. Freya clearly hadn't given up a lucrative career in private house management in order to see the world as a glorified housekeeper. If he'd had any doubts then catching her snooping the previous night was enough to eradicate them.

'I'm gonna have to confront her,' he said aloud.

* * *

'Not quite what you expected?' Gloria asked with a sympathetic smile as she and Freya, kept busy by the ceaseless demands of the owner and his guests, crossed paths in the passageway that led to the galley.

'Why aren't they roaring drunk?' Freya asked, nodding towards yet two more empty bottles of Krug that she was taking to the glass bin.

'They'll fall asleep just before dinner and Sandy's efforts will go to waste,' Gloria predicted. 'Either that or they'll turn up an hour late, the food will be spoiled and then there'll be hell to pay in the galley.'

'Thanks for the warning,' Freya replied, shuddering.

'You look a bit green around the gills,' Gloria said, peering more closely at Freya. 'Sea sicknesses?'

Freya shrugged. 'I guess so.'

'Bloody hell! This is calm, love. God alone knows what you'll be like if we hit a swell.'

Freya shuddered. 'Don't want to think about that.'

'Look, take an hour off. I'll deal with the punters. I was like you when I started out but you do get used to the motion. Go and sit on the aft deck and stare at the horizon. It helps, trust me.'

'Well, if you're sure. I don't like to leave you to take all the flack.'

'Don't worry. I'm used to it. It's water off a duck's back. Besides, can't have you throwing up over the fragrant Chelsea.' Gloria chuckled. 'Only imagine the mayhem that would cause.'

'It's almost worth doing it, just to see,' Freya replied, smiling apologetically when her stomach rumbled ominously. 'But thanks, if you're sure, I will take a break.'

'Eat something. I know you'd rather not, but a slice of toast would help.'

Freya waved a hand over her shoulder and walked away. Toast was out of the question, mostly because it would mean asking Sandy to sort it and she wasn't about to show any signs of weakness in front of a woman who seemed determined to make her life difficult.

She poured water from the cooler in the crew corridor into a plastic glass, then took Gloria's advice and made her way to the aft deck. The owner and his buddies were sprawled over the foredeck and no one would bother her here. She took a seat and stared at the horizon, immediately conscious of her queasiness diminishing. Protected by the overhang from the deck above, she enjoyed watching the sun, now high in the sky, beating down and turning the water a dozen different shades of turquoise.

A gull, wings outstretched, came to briefly land on the railing in front of her, and then took off again with a loud squawk. The breeze was deceptive, she knew, and if Chelsea and the others remained exposed to the sun for too long and without applying sufficient sunblock, then they would live to rue the day.

Freya chuckled at the thought as she closed her eyes, lulled by the gentle motion of the boat. She felt almost human again, now that she wasn't running around like a blue-arsed fly, at Chelsea's beck and call. And more to the point, now that she didn't have to endure Falcon's hungry gaze following her every move.

His interest in her was a problem. She hadn't expected to be noticed by him and had fully intended to fade into the background while she tried to decide how best to achieve her objectives.

'Damn!' she muttered.

'Talking to yourself?'

Freya's eyes flew open and she inwardly groaned when an unsmiling Greg loomed above her.

'Doesn't everyone?' she asked. She had managed to convince herself that he hadn't seen her leaving Falcon's study the night before, otherwise he would have tackled her on the subject there and then. She realised now that with Falcon's arrival, there hadn't been an opportunity, but clearly there was something he wanted to discuss with her.

He sat beside her, his eyes hidden behind sunglasses, making it impossible for her to read his expression. 'Feeling motion sickness?' he asked.

Freya rolled her eyes. 'Is it that obvious?'

'I've seen it too often to misinterpret the signs.' He finally cracked a smile. 'Oh, and Gloria mentioned something when I passed her a moment ago. Here.' He produced an unopened packet of salty crackers. 'It'll help. Trust me, I'm a captain.'

Freya took the packet from him, opened it and nibbled on a cracker. 'Thanks,' she said belatedly.

'No worries. It'll pass within twenty-four hours – the queasiness, that is.'

'Good to know.'

She said nothing more but instead crunched on a second cracker. Greg seemed perfectly content with the silence, whereas it made Freya feel uncomfortable for reasons that had nothing to do with the motion of the boat.

'We'll be passing through the Gulf of Lion a bit later,' he eventually broke the silence by saying. 'Might get a bit choppy, so make sure you eat something before then.'

'Aye, aye, Captain,' she replied with a mock salute.

'Glad to get some respect,' he said flippantly. 'So,' he added after a significant pause. 'What were you looking for and did you find it?'

Freya was on the point of pretending not to know what he meant. Then she turned to look at him. He had pushed his shades onto his head, taking a thick lock of black hair away from his disconcertingly intelligent eyes in the process, and his gaze bored into her face. She knew then that... well, that he knew what she'd done but had not said anything to anyone else. She appreciated his discretion but wasn't sure she could depend upon it continuing if she feigned ignorance.

'Ah, so you did see me.' She let out a long breath. 'Well, at least I'm glad that it was you.'

'You haven't answered my question.'

'I can't.' She looked directly at him, and then shook her head firmly. 'It wouldn't be fair to draw you into my war.'

'Who are you at war with?'

'Don't be so obtuse!' She exhaled sharply.

'I don't know what your grievance with Falcon is about.' Greg allowed a significant pause. 'But I can guess.'

She turned to give Greg her full attention, her eyes wide with the dawning of realisation. 'You,' she said softly. 'He's shafted someone close to you as well.'

4

Julien Falcon watched an assembled throng on the quayside gushing over his yacht as it left Antibes. Being the recipient of so much envy never got old but today, it didn't give him the satisfaction he usually took away from the experience; a tangible reminder of how far he'd come and how much he'd achieved in a relatively short space of time. People called him lucky, but Julien knew he'd made his own luck through a ruthless determination to use the brains he was born with to rise above his humble origins. No one ever remembered the person who came second.

About the only advantage of growing up in poverty that Julien could think of was that it gave any person with an ounce of ambition in his belly a burning desire to get out of it.

And stay out.

Julien might have had to cut a few corners and flirt with the letter of the law, but bankers did that every day of the week. Far from being prosecuted, they were rewarded with massive bonuses.

Julien's success had come at a heavy cost. His own kids were a case in point. All three of them had enjoyed the best education that money could buy. They'd never travelled any way other than first class and... well, never wanted for anything, much less known what it was like to go hungry. They rolled their eyes whenever Julien mentioned the disadvantages he'd had to overcome as a kid. They had been spoiled and were screwed up as a result. He blamed Bridget; his wife's only job had been to run his house and raise his kids, keeping them on the straight and narrow. Not a lot to ask but had she done it?

Had she fuck.

His elder son was in rehab, for the third time. The younger had almost killed himself driving Julien's Porsche too fast. He was currently in a wheelchair and might never walk again. And Bethany, his daughter and the apple of his eye, had fallen pregnant at fifteen.

Fifteen!

It defied belief. Kids nowadays were taught all about birth control whilst still in nappies, or so it seemed. But did they practise safe sex? Did they hell! It had been different in Julien's day. They knew how not to get a girl in trouble. Julien wasn't sorry that Bethany had miscarried, but she'd been screwed up ever since, blaming Julien for the loss of the brat. He'd caused her stress apparently by losing his rag when he found out about her condition and beating seven shades of shit out of the snotty kid who'd knocked her up.

Unbelievably, he'd almost got his collar felt for his trouble. He still fumed when he thought about the old bill knocking at his door, making accusations. The amount of his hard-earned dosh that reached the pockets of law enforcement ought to have made him untouchable. He'd had to have a quiet word and no charges were forthcoming, but that wasn't the point.

Julien had threatened to withdraw the generous allowances he gave all three of his kids but he hadn't actually done it. It wasn't worth the fight with Bridget. His wife kept her head down for the most part, not caring what Julien got up to between the sheets, just so long as it wasn't with her. She had her charities, her circle of friends and free access to Julien's bank account. He had neither the energy nor the desire for a divorce and was happy with the status quo. If he was free and single, then the Chelseas of this world would have expectations he had no desire to fulfil. The attractive women his money ensured a steady supply of were for display purposes only and definitely not the type he'd like to marry.

He glanced at Chelsea, her curves such as they were on full display, and knew she'd let him do whatever he felt like doing to her. Willing women were ten a penny and the fun had gone out of the chase years before. But he still did it because it was what men in his position did and his cronies envied him. He hadn't had to work to get what he wanted from any female since making his first million, which was probably why he was getting bored.

His gaze fell upon the new hostess as she poured champagne and attended to Chelsea's constant needs with quiet dignity, and a dormant desire stirred in his groin. She was elegant, self-contained, and seemingly unimpressed by Julien's stature as a man of means. He knew that she wouldn't give out as willingly as Chelsea or her predecessors, which made her a challenge. He'd never tried it on with any of his crew members before now; demarcation lines had to be respected. But for this one, he might well make an exception, he thought, watching the elegant sway of her hips and her long, tanned legs as she moved about the deck. His cock swelled of its own volition. That hadn't happened for a while. With Chelsea et al, it required a little chemical intervention in order for him to be able to perform nowadays.

For the first time in a very long time, a woman had gained his attention without making the least effort to put herself forward. Julien made a mental note to look up her record and felt some of the now customary lethargy falling away as he relished the prospect of the chase.

* * *

Greg swallowed as he absorbed the full force of Freya's incredulous look. He hadn't intended to give himself away. He didn't think that he had but she was astute and so denial would be futile. Besides, if they had a common cause, it would be better if they didn't get in one another's way. In other words, to coin a childhood phrase, he was here first.

'Yeah,' he said simply. 'Something like that.'

Freya nodded decisively. 'So I was wasting my time last night.' She rested an elbow on her knee and her face on her clenched fist, looking glum and dispirited. 'If there was anything to be found, you would have found it by now. It was a long shot anyway. That said, I had no idea you had an axe to grind too.'

'Care to elaborate?'

She sat upright again and shook her head. 'I asked first.'

'You don't trust me?'

'I'm slow to trust nowadays. No one is what they appear to be.'

'If I was on Falcon's side, I would have told him that I caught you snooping and we wouldn't be having this conversation.'

'Perhaps you're trying to find out why I have a grudge against him so that he can shut me down,' she shot back.

'Okay.' Greg held up his hands in a defensive gesture, having reached the only decision possible under the circumstances. 'I was born and brought up around boats. Cowes on the Isle of Wight was the sailing capital of the UK back then and I loved everything to do with it, even in the bad weather. Especially then. Pitting my wits against the elements made me feel alive. Invincible.'

Freya nodded. 'I think I can understand that, seasickness notwithstanding.'

'My dad taught me to sail in a dinghy when I was five.'

'Blimey!'

'I took to it like a duck to the proverbial apparently and Dad and I went on to compete in regattas, just the two of us, when I was barely into my teens.'

'Your dad means a lot to you. It shows in your expression every time you mention him.'

'Battling the weather, getting it right, is a bonding experience. You have to trust one another. So yeah, he taught me a lot, not just about the sea. Although he did teach me to respect its mercurial moods, I guess.'

'You speak of him in the past tense.'

Greg's expression closed down. 'That's because I found him hanging in the boatshed ten years ago.'

Freya covered her mouth with her hand. 'Shit!' she said quietly through her splayed fingers.

'Yeah, that about covers it.'

Greg looked away from her, unable to withstand the sympathy in her eyes. He had never spoken about his gruesome find to anyone other than his family and the police at the time. Since then, he'd compartmentalised. It was the only way he'd been able to function; to withstand the injustice. The senseless waste of a good man's life.

'How old were you at the time?'

'Twenty-five. I was working in Edinburgh but had come home unexpectedly. Mum told me Dad's depression had gotten worse so I thought I'd surprise him. Take him out sailing. He always said it was impossible to be depressed out on the water. Too much else to think about.'

'I assume he killed himself because of something that Falcon did.'

Greg sent her a sideways look. 'Intuitive,' he said. 'Sorry,' he added, holding up a hand in apology. 'You don't deserve my sarcasm. None of this is your fault. It's just that... that I find it hard to talk about.'

She nodded. 'Yeah, I can identify with that.'

Greg allowed a protracted silence which Freya made no effort to break. 'Falcon had made his first few millions ten years ago and wanted to get into boating. He wasn't in a position to buy a tub of this size and so he asked my dad to design and build a forty-foot gin palace for him. Said he'd heard of him by reputation and wanted to have the best. Flattered him, I suppose.'

'Your dad did both, design and build, I mean?'

'Yep. It was his passion. Bespoke craft for the discerning gentleman was his mantra. There was a waiting list for his services but, of course, Falcon bamboozled Dad into letting him jump the queue.'

'Surely Falcon could have bought a used boat from one of the well-known designers for a fraction of the cost?'

'He could but then it wouldn't have been unique. Or new. Falcon wanted to stand out, show off to the world that he could afford not to follow the crowd.'

Freya puffed out her cheeks. 'Yeah, that I can believe.'

'Well anyway, Dad drew up designs. Falcon kept changing his mind about what he wanted but they eventually agreed upon a specification and it went into production. Dad told him how long it would take but Falcon was in a hurry; kept pushing and withholding payments until Dad agreed to reduce production time.'

'Oh God! An accident waiting to happen.'

'Long story short, the boat hit heavy weather shortly after its launch. Falcon was at the helm but didn't have much experience, especially in bad weather. He lost control and the boat was thrown against a shallow rocky outcrop around the Needles. It took on water and the bilge pumps couldn't keep up with the inflow. They had to abandon ship. Falcon had friends on board and a child got swept into the sea during the evacuation, losing his life.'

'That's awful,' Freya said, touching his arm, 'but not your father's fault.'

'He didn't see it that way. Insisted that he should have stuck to his original production schedule and not been bullied into cutting corners. There was an inquest, of course, but Dad wasn't called to give evidence and no blame was attached to him.'

'Or to Falcon either, I'm guessing.'

'In the UK, you don't have to have any qualifications to take to the helm, which is bat shit crazy, if you ask me, and as dangerous as a learner driver being let loose on a busy motorway unsupervised. Anyway, the accident was blamed on the weather. It's my understanding that Falcon offered a big payout to the parents of the dead child, gave the father a lucrative position in his company and all was forgiven.'

'He bought his way out of it.' Freya screwed up her features. 'Somehow that doesn't surprise me.'

'It's the way he operates. There's no situation that can't be fixed with an influx of cash. Money's his god.'

'But your father never forgave himself.'

'Nope. As I say, he went into a deeper depression and refused to get medical help. I should have stayed at home. I knew mum wouldn't be able to reach him and that I was the only one who stood a cat in hell's chance of doing so.'

'You don't have siblings?'

Greg shook his head. 'I'd qualified as an architect and took a job with a firm in Edinburgh, just about as far away as I could be, but not intentionally. The job market was tough, and it was the best offer I'd received. Mum and Dad both urged me to take it, and so I did.'

'If this was ten years ago, why have you taken so long to go after Falcon?'

'Mum made me promise that I wouldn't. She said he was too powerful and that she didn't want to lose me as well as Dad. But she went into a deep funk herself after that. She lost her vibrancy and was never the same. And it's all that bastard's fault,' Greg added, jerking a thumb in the direction of the sun deck.

'I hear you,' Freya said softly.

'I kept tabs on him, watched him getting richer and more powerful and felt so fucking useless.' Greg splayed his legs and focused his gaze on the teak beneath his feet. 'There was nothing I could do to make him face up to what he'd done.'

'And all the time, the injustice gnawed away at you like acid.'

He looked up finally and held her gaze. 'You get it, don't you?'

Freya nodded emphatically. 'Better than you could possibly know.'

Greg reached across and gently squeezed her hand, but his gaze remained focused on the sea. He barely heard the laughter coming from the sun deck but for the first time since setting foot on Falcon's tub, he felt briefly at ease with himself. Perhaps there was something to say for letting it all out to someone who understood, he reasoned.

'It helps to talk about it?' He shrugged. 'Who knew?'

'Not me. No one who hasn't been there would understand so who would you talk to?' She looked directly at him. 'I'm guessing that your mother passed away, which meant you were free to pursue a career change.'

He gave a brief smile. 'Yep. Pretty much. I inherited Mum and Dad's house, which I sold. The memories would have haunted me. So, I returned to my first love.'

'The sea?'

'The sea. I took all the necessary exams, qualified as a delivery skipper and enjoyed the long voyages.'

'Delivering boats from one part of the world to another without the owners on board.'

'You've got it. It was like... I don't know, like I was drifting with no clear destination in mind. I couldn't settle. The injustice of Dad's death never left me. Then, I saw Falcon advertising for a skipper and knew it was what I'd been waiting for.'

She nodded. 'Did he know who you were?'

'Oh yes. He didn't interview me himself, of course. Eddie does all the heavy lifting and he recognised my name, told Falcon and I knew I'd get the job.'

'Falcon's way of making amends.'

'Pretty much. He thought that by employing me, he could make my resentment go away, just like he paid the family of that poor drowned child to get over their loss.' Greg kicked at the deck. 'He has no fucking idea!'

'So, what's your plan? You must have one,' she added when Greg failed to respond.

'I've kept in touch with the detective who investigated Dad's suicide. I told him why I thought he'd done it and who was responsible but he said that Falcon hadn't broken any laws so he couldn't touch him. He implied that he wouldn't have been able to, even if he had done wrong.'

'He's up close and personal with senior policemen.' Freya scowled. 'I'd always suspected as much.'

'Yeah well, I speak with Detective Sergeant Milton once a year. He was a humble DC when Dad died. I used to bug him all the time but eventually realised I was being a jerk. There was nothing he could do to help me. I just wanted to feel that I was being proactive by not letting the matter drop. Anyway, I did ring him when I took this job and he asked to meet me, off the record.'

'I'm intrigued.'

'We met in an out of the way pub in Southampton, all a bit cloak and dagger. Anyway, he told me that Falcon is suspected of running an investment scam. Several complaints have been made by people who've lost their investments, but Milton and his colleagues have been given instructions from on high not to pursue the matter.'

'The senior officers who are in Falcon's pocket?'

'That's what Milton's governor thinks but obviously it's sensitive. The chief inspector, who Milton ultimately reports to, gave Milton permission to talk to me, as I say, off the record when Milton told him I'd taken this job.'

'They want to see if you can run down anything definitive about Falcon's illegal actions?'

'And about anyone in the police service who Falcon's bribing to look the other way.'

'Blimey, they don't want much, do they?'

Greg shrugged. 'I'm guessing that your vendetta is equally implausible.'

'I think it's safe to assume that,' she replied with a wry smile.

'Tell me. Perhaps we can join forces.'

5

Following Greg's revelations, Freya was slow to respond. He kept his gaze focused on her profile but didn't say anything to try and persuade her to open up, probably sensing that she still didn't entirely trust him. Prestigious positions as skippers on super yachts were hard to come by. Would he really risk his by gunning for the owner? If they could somehow make Falcon answerable for his dubious activities then the yacht would presumably be the first sacrifice, taking Greg's job with it.

She wanted to tell him not to take her doubts personally. Experience had taught her not to accept anyone at face value.

'Seems Falcon scatters bodies in his wake,' she

said, fixing Greg with a speculative look and making up her mind to level with him. What was the worst that could happen? He could rat her out to Falcon, she supposed, and it would be her who found herself unemployed. Even so, she already knew that her chances of taking him down alone were virtually impossible, so she had to take the risk. 'My younger sister, Polly, got caught up with him.' She kicked at the deck with her bare toe. 'Now she's gone.'

'He killed her?' Greg stared at her, his mouth gaping open. 'What the hell! Was nothing done about it?'

'He didn't kill her with his bare hands, but he might just as well have done. He got her started down the wrong path and so was responsible for what happened to her.' Freya impatiently dashed at a tear with the back of her hand, preventing it from trickling down her cheek. 'Polly was three years younger than me and strikingly beautiful.'

'You were close?'

'Yes, but were very different in our outlook. She had a casual disregard for discipline. A real wild child in a household that was ruled with a rod of iron. Looking back, I suppose that two such strong willed people as my father and sister were bound to clash. It was a disaster waiting to happen. Even so, no one could have foreseen quite how tragic the outcome would actually be... although I should have.'

'You blame yourself, I can tell, but it wasn't your fault.'

'I was her big sister. She looked up to me, we shared everything, until she hit her teens and then... well, she became secretive, rebelled against everything and created havoc inside the house and out of it. She wanted to have fun, and no one was going to stop her. Our father tried once too often to ground her. She got fed up with having her wings clipped and told me she was leaving.' Freya threw up her hands. 'I didn't believe her so didn't even try to talk her out of it. Anyway, she climbed out of a window and never came back.'

'And fell in with Falcon, I'm guessing.'

Freya was glad that Greg didn't try to sympathise. He probably understood that sympathy served no useful purpose. The past was done and there was no way to alter it. He probably also understood the burning desire for revenge that had never left her.

'Spot on. Well, not with him personally but Eddie Bairstow noticed her in a club one night. Falcon was there in a private room and Polly was invited to join the party.' She paused. 'That was when she experienced cocaine for the first time.'

'Shit!'

'Falcon played with her for a while, a bit like he's playing with Chelsea now, which is what makes my blood boil, watching him operate and not being able to do anything about it. Nothing has changed for him. It's as though Polly never existed, and he carries on wrecking lives with callous disregard for the consequences.'

'How do you know all this if Polly left home and never went back?'

'She kept in touch with me but swore me to secrecy. She said she knew what she was doing. Falcon was the opportunity she'd been waiting for. He could open doors for her. She wanted to be a model, you see, and had the figure and looks to make it happen. Besides, I didn't know where she was living. She only ever sent me messages and would have changed her number if Dad tried to intervene. She was eighteen, above the age of consent and an adult in the eyes of the law. The police wouldn't do anything to find her. They pointed out that she'd left a note and called just once after she'd gone to assure our mum that she was safe. They didn't have the resources to look for someone who didn't want to be found, despite the fuss that my dad made.'

'I can well imagine.'

'Against my better judgement, I didn't tell my dad that we were in contact. I regret that now even though I know it wouldn't have done any good. If Dad had traced her to one of Falcon's clubs, he wouldn't have got past the door. He would have made a scene and... well, it wouldn't have ended well for him. Or for Polly. Falcon's bouncers took no prisoners and Falcon didn't like having unnecessary attention drawn to him.'

'What happened?'

'Polly was one of Chelsea's many predecessors but she had an addictive personality, wanted to try everything that was trendy and got hooked on recreational drugs. Her way of keeping slim because her ambition to become a model had not waned. I think Falcon stoked those ambitions by telling her she had what it took. Anyway, nothing I said could persuade her that Falcon wasn't her ticket to fame and fortune. She got mad if I uttered one word of criticism against him and said I was too straitlaced to understand.' Freya swallowed. 'But I could see what he was doing to her. She became impossibly thin to the point that she became gaunt. I know because she sent me pictures of the "new" her and was proud of her gamine look. When I couldn't reach her any more, I knew the drugs must have taken hold.'

'Wasn't that the time to tell your parents where she was?' Greg asked gently.

'I didn't know! Really, I didn't. All I knew was that she was hooked up indirectly with Falcon. He'd dropped her by then, of course.' Freya spread her hands in frustration. 'Besides, if Dad had known that she was an addict, he wouldn't have tried to send her to rehab. He would simply have washed his hands of her, which is more or less what he'd done anyway. He was old school, wouldn't tolerate disobedience in either of us, and never accepted that times had changed since his own childhood and that his strict rules had driven Polly away. He was a post-war child and said that a lack of parental discipline nowadays was wrecking the country.'

'How did Polly die?' Greg asked.

'An overdose. She was found in one of Falcon's brothels. He'd set her to work when he got tired of her. Instead of coming to me for help when she hit rock bottom, she did whatever she had to do to get her hands on her next fix.' Freya shook her head, and this time didn't bother to wipe the tears away. 'It's all so tragic and that bastard's to blame for making her think he was her knight in shining armour.' She blinked back the residue of her tears, lifted her head and set her chin in a line of stubborn defiance. 'He has to pay for what he did, if only to save others like Chelsea finishing up down the same route. Stupid though Chelsea is, she doesn't deserve that. No one does.'

'So you took this job in the hope of what exactly?'

Freya sighed. 'I wish I knew,' she admitted with a wry smile. 'Dad died a year ago. I don't think he ever got over what happened to Polly and blamed himself for failing to control her. Mum and I have discussed Polly's situation countless time since then. We never did when Dad was alive. Mum was frightened of him, and I'd lost all respect once he washed his hands of Polly, so I stayed away.'

'You gave up a promising career to come and work on this tub. Why?'

'I kept an eye on Falcon's activities, his public ones anyway, and this boat was all over his online profile. A bit like you jumping at the opportunity to skipper it, I suppose, in the hope of gaining retribution. When I saw an advert for a hostess, it seemed like providence.' She spread her hands. 'So here you find me, hoping to dig up evidence that he runs illegal girls out of his massage clubs. That he runs a brothel at all, come to that, and forces girls into the oldest profession, a bit like he did Polly. And he *did* take illegals on; Polly told me that much before she herself was forced onto the game.' Freya sighed. 'All very tenuous, I know, but I had to take this job and try to dig something up on him.'

'He won't keep those sorts of records and certainly not on this boat. Take it from one who knows.'

'There's a locked cabinet in his study.'

Greg just smiled and shook his head.

'You've had a look?' she asked.

'There's nothing to see that would interest us. He's not stupid.'

'Us?'

'Well, we're both here with a common aim. It would make sense for us to work together.'

'So you already suggested, but Sandy won't like that.'

'Sandy?' He looked genuinely perplexed. 'What's it got to do with her?'

'She seems to think, or to imply anyway, that the two of you are an item.'

Greg shook his head. 'Never,' he said mildly.

'Well, okay, wishful thinking on her part notwithstanding, how can two heads be better than one? I'm willing to think about it. God alone knows, I have nothing better to suggest. It was stupid of me to think that anything would jump out at me once I was on board.' She rolled her eyes. 'I assumed he'd turn up with a young woman, so at least I was right about that. I was hoping to get chatting with her, seeing what insights that might throw up about Falcon's current operation but... well, Chelsea likes lording it over me. I think it's safe to assume that we won't become besties any time soon.'

'She feels threatened by you.'

Freya laughed. 'Don't be daft. I have absolutely no interest in Falcon. Besides, he likes them young and I'm a good ten years older than Chelsea.'

The boat hit the wake thrown up by a distant tanker and lurched to one side. Freya's stomach lurched right along with it. She clasped a hand over her mouth, hoping that her breakfast would stay put.

'Look at the horizon,' Greg suggested.

She did so and then felt more in control again once the sea settled back to a calmer state.

'You have caught Falcon's attention but don't encourage him,' Greg said. 'I don't want you following in your sister's footsteps. There has to be a better way.'

Freya shook her head. 'He covers his tracks too well, I can quite see that now.' She sighed. 'I was stupid to think that I could... Anyway, tell me about the investment scheme that drew vulnerable punters in.'

'Cryptocurrency.'

'Ah.' Freya nodded. 'Everyone seems to be jumping on that particular band wagon these days.'

'Right. Falcon was the brains behind a fund set up in Monaco, I'm reliably informed. And Falcon *does* have brains, and street cunning, so don't underestimate him. Monaco's a glamorous setting that implies respectability and had those with more money than sense wetting themselves to become involved.'

'When something seems too good to be true, it almost always is.'

'Right, but a convincing and charismatic salesman who gives the impression of having money to burn—'

'Which might explain why there's so many pictures of him online on this yacht.'

'Anyway, he got careless and his fund was investigated when compliance rules weren't followed. There was a huge hole in the books and investors took a big hit. The fund was shut down and the majority of punters lost their capital. But, and here's the clincher, the missing funds have never been found.'

'You assume they found their way into Falcon's coffers.'

'Don't you?'

'In that case, why wasn't Falcon arrested?'

'Why do you think?'

Freya nodded. 'Friends in high places? He was

warned about the investigation and helped himself to the funds before they were frozen.'

'Right. Friends who probably frequented his clubs. Besides, the fund was run by a shell company and Falcon's identity only came to light after a lot of delving. He had no direct connection and none of the people working for the fund even recognised his name. It would have been impossible to prove his involvement but I'm guessing that's how his extravagant lifestyle is funded. There were rumours that he was down to his last few million, and that wouldn't last five minutes, given all his expensive toys.' Greg glanced up at the yacht's structure to emphasise his point.

'He cashes in on other people's stupidity?'

'That about sums it up.'

Freya allowed a moment's reflection. 'If the police know he's behind the scheme then there must be other ways to prove it, independent of their efforts. Ones that even the policemen in Falcon's pocket can't ignore.'

'Possibly.'

She sat forward and sent Greg an expectant look. 'Okay, so how do we go about it?'

'Well, it just so happens that Mike Parker, one of Falcon's guests here right now, was heavily involved with the fund.'

'Ah.' Freya's heart rate quickened. 'So why hasn't he been arrested?'

'He might very well be. At the moment, Falcon's influence is keeping him out of jail. I'm guessing that if his collar is felt then Falcon will take good care of his family and ensure that he emerges from prison a very wealthy man, *provided* he keeps his mouth shut.'

Freya nodded. 'The ostentatious display of wealth on this boat is his way of showing Parker that he can afford to be generously inclined towards those who display their loyalty.'

'But Bairstow will let him know in many not-so-subtle ways what to expect if he cuts and runs.'

'Hmm. Parker is between a rock and a hard place.'

'Pretty much.'

'But surely, if he tells what he knows to the police then not only will he avoid prison himself but Falcon and Bairstow will be banged up. Parker will be safe.'

Greg shook his head. 'It doesn't work like that. Falcon has too many fingers in too many pies. Other men, who'll be worried about their involvement with him if anyone decides to squeal, will take drastic action to protect their interests.'

'In other words, if Parker went to the police, then his life expectancy would be vastly reduced?'

Greg nodded, his expression grim. 'These guys are

no boy scouts. Besides, the investment fund is complicated. There's no guarantee that Falcon's connection to it will ever be proven. His expensive lawyers will have made sure that there are lots of layers of names behind the company running the investment and Parker knows that. Parker is claiming to be an innocent investor but he's worried, which I guess is why he's been invited along on this trip: the carrot and stick approach.'

'Eddie Bairstow is here because... well, because Falcon doesn't sneeze without him being on hand to offer him a tissue.' Freya frowned. 'But how is the other guy, Jason Pyke, involved?'

'He and Parker are partners in a more legitimate investment fund. I guess, a bit like Falcon and Bairstow, they're joined at the hip.'

'And if anyone delves a little deeper into the fraudulent crypto fund, they'll likely dig up Pyke's name too.' Freya paused to consider what she'd just learned. 'It would explain the tension I noticed on the sun deck earlier. I thought it was just the wives disapproving of Chelsea and Bairstow's squeezes being on such public display. Anyway, perhaps their disapproval is about something else altogether.'

'The disapproval coming from the wives is likely

to do with the bimbos. They won't know anything about the fraud.'

'Makes you wonder why the wives were invited along, in that case.'

'Watch Falcon. He'll charm them over the following days, demonstrating to their husbands just how easily he can manipulate them.'

Freya gaped at him. 'Surely not.'

And yet even as she spoke, Freya wondered why Greg's prediction held the power to shock her. She was well aware that Falcon was capable of just about anything. More to the point, the ladies lapped up the attention.

'Falcon is a hard individual. Nasty. There's nothing he wouldn't do to ensure his own security. The women and children exempt bit, if it ever was a code amongst the bad guys, certainly doesn't exist in Falcon's world.' He touched her hand. 'After the way he so callously destroyed your sister, you hardly need me to tell you that.'

Freya swallowed and nodded, getting a better idea now of just how ruthless Falcon could be. It frightened her and yet also made her more determined to stop him from hurting others in the way that he'd hurt Polly. 'I hear you.'

'I'm hoping that the guys will discuss the elephant in the room sooner or later. That must be why they've come on this trip. Presumably, Falcon insisted that they bring their wives, perhaps to convince whoever's keeping an eye on them that it really is a pleasure cruise. Either that or, as I suggested earlier, as a more sinister reminder.'

'How were you planning to hear what was said between the men? Your place is in the wheelhouse. You'd be a bit obvious lingering in the salon, or outside Falcon's study.'

'I hadn't worked that part out,' Greg admitted with a rueful grin. 'My police contact suggested listening devices, which is highly illegal from law enforcement's perspective, and anyway, nothing picked up on them would be admissible in court. Besides, I have a feeling that Falcon might sweep his office to ensure that it isn't bugged. He's too fucking wily for me to take that risk.'

Freya nodded, having already worked out that much for herself, and feeling demoralised before they'd even started to bring him down. 'Frustrating.'

Greg gave a half-smile. 'And then some.'

'All things considered, it's just as well that I blend into the woodwork. No one will blink an eye if they see me hanging about. There are benefits to being invisible.'

'Oh no! No, no, no, no, no!' Greg held both hands towards her, palms first, as though warding off an attack. 'Surely what happened to your sister is enough for you to realise how ruthless Falcon is.'

'I am not a child! Besides, you don't get to tell me what to do. And anyway, I have to serve at mealtimes, talking of which,' she added, glancing at her watch, 'I should be setting up the table for lunch. My point is, I have a legitimate reason to linger, *and* I have eyes and ears.'

'I hear you and I can't stop you, but it doesn't mean that I have to like it.'

'Oh for goodness' sake, what century are you living in?'

Greg smiled at her fit of pique. 'If you want to help, a safer way would be for you to befriend Parker and Pyke's wives. Get chatting to them when they're on their own, which I'm guessing they'll try to be. The men will be doing whatever men on an expensive yacht do and they won't want to mix with Chelsea and Bairstow's date. What's her name?'

'Barb.' Freya wrinkled her nose. 'She's not as in your face as Chelsea but there's still not much to choose between them.'

'I've seen her with Bairstow before. She's lasted a bit longer than the others. There might be real affec-

tion there on both sides so steer well clear of her. Her
loyalties will lay well and truly with her meal-ticket
and anything you say will get straight back to him.
Talking of names, won't Falcon recognise yours?'

Freya shook her head. 'We never met.'

'Even so, Polly might have talked about her big
sister and Freya isn't a common name. If you look like
her...'

'Addison is my mother's maiden name.' She
smiled at Greg, attempting to hide the fact that he
could well be right. She had always known that but
considered it to be a calculated risk. 'I'm not completely clueless.'

Greg chuckled. 'Evidently not.'

'Anyway, it seems it will have to be the wives if I'm
to have any hope of getting useful information,' she
said, not bothering to add that the moment the men
closeted themselves together, she would find a way to
listen. 'You suggest that they won't know anything
about their husband's dealings, but I don't buy that.
Women always know more than they let on and often
more than they want to know. They obviously don't
want to be here and so just perhaps they'll unwit-
tingly give me something.'

Freya wasn't sure that she believed that the
women would talk to her about their husbands' pri-

vate dealings with Falcon, even if they did disapprove, but she wasn't ready to make that admission. Not to Greg. Not to anyone. She felt relieved to have found an ally in Greg but she wasn't about to let him take over. They were in this together and if he couldn't live with that then she'd do things her way.

She smiled at him and turned to leave.

'Later,' she said.

6

Julien felt as though his complex business arrangements were slipping beyond his control. It was an alien concept, anathema for a control freak of his ilk. It made him want to punch a hole in the superb walnut lining the walls of his study, where he'd retreated for a few moments respite from the endless prattle coming from the mouths of Chelsea and Barb. And from putting on a show of strength in front of his underlings. Not that any such display ought to have been necessary given what he had done for them, but when the going got tough, people, Julien had good reason to know, had short memories and questionable loyalties.

There was an awkward atmosphere on the sundeck, the cause of which he couldn't quite put his finger on. Pyke and Parker were edgy, understandably so, and the sanctimonious bitches they'd married didn't help matters. How dare they turn up their long noses at his date! Didn't they understand that without him, they'd still be working checkouts to make ends meet? Oh, they enjoyed the high life right enough and were quick to flirt with him when he turned on the charm, but when it came to younger competition, they got judgemental.

It wasn't yet noon but Julien poured himself a hefty measure of Napoleon brandy from his tantalus and downed half of it in one swallow, feeling the rich burn as it trickled down his oesophagus and settled in his belly, calming him. Julien had learned as a young man never to lose control. He'd be the first to admit that he had a bit of a temper on him and if he let it get the better of him, things never ended well.

He could sense that Parker's nerves were teetering on a knife edge and that he wanted to bail. Too late for that – hence this cruise, a reminder of what he'd be giving up and, more to the point, what retribution he could expect if he got cold feet. Julien had seen a fierce ambition in Mike Parker when he'd met him a decade before, labouring on Julien's building site. It was the infamous pink newspaper, the *Financial*

Times, sticking out of his back pocket that Julien had noticed. He struck up a conversation with the labourer, realised that he had a fierce intellect that had slipped past the guard of his teachers at a failing comprehensive, and a natural talent for playing the stock market hampered only by a lack of funds with which to speculate.

Julien gave him an opportunity to look after his investments: small at first until Mike proved his worth. And look where he was now, all thanks to Julien trusting his own instincts. Okay, so the crypto fund had taken a hit. That couldn't have been foreseen and Mike would have to take the fall in the event that the old bill pushed for a conviction. His wife Maureen had enjoyed the spoils and knew how to spend Mike's money. She'd be well looked after if Mike had to do a stretch and the school fees for their two indulged offspring would be taken care of as well. Mike had known the score from day one. He'd never complained when Julien cut corners and pointed out a few shortcuts that were on the dodgy side of legal himself. It was too late now for him to get cold feet.

Thinking matters through ought to have reassured Julien. He held all the aces but even so, his feeling of deep unease endured. He drained his glass and considered a refill, deciding against it. He needed to remain sharp. He sometimes wondered why he still strived to improve his circumstances. He had everything a successful man could ever wish for, particularly the envy of his friends. He chose not to dwell upon his dissatisfied wife and screwed-up kids.

Julien threw himself into the chair behind his desk, noticing through the portlight on the aft side of the cabin the shapely legs of his new hostess as she walked along the side deck. There was something about her elegance and sense of self-containment that had struck a chord with him. He was convinced that their paths had crossed before but couldn't for the life of him think where they'd met. Despite the fact that attractive women were ten a penny in his life now that he could afford to treat them like royalty, this one would not have escaped his notice.

He pulled up her application for the hostess position and glanced through it. She had a good track record managing a large country house. It was open to the public several days a week and she claimed responsibility on her CV for keeping it profitable. Julien leaned back in his chair and rubbed the side of his index finger across his lips as he thought the matter through, wondering why she had given up such a lucrative position to work on his tub. Perhaps he'd ask her but that would suggest a degree of interest in an employee that would send out all the wrong signals. Besides, he was unsure if he'd get an honest answer out of her and would prefer not to force her into a lie.

'Someone needs to play referee with those women,' Eddie said, entering the room and throwing himself into a chair. 'Sorry to say this but Chelsea's being a right bitch and stirring everyone up.'

'Yeah well, let her enjoy herself. She'll be history after this.'

'She needs to keep her trap shut. I told you that when you first picked her up. She has ambitions and sees you as her meal ticket.'

Julien leaned back and rolled his eyes. 'Don't they all.'

Eddie was the only man on this planet who could speak his mind to Julien and get away with it. They went way back, and Eddie knew where all the bodies were buried, figuratively speaking. He was the only person alive whom Julien trusted absolutely. He would never grass him up and would personally wring the neck of anyone who even thought about going rogue.

Eddie kept his violent tendencies under wraps nowadays, but Julien knew that he still enjoyed dishing it out, sometimes going too far. More to the point, Julien's associates knew it too. Eddie had developed a semi-sophisticated persona, as had Julien, but underneath it all, they were still street brawlers who'd pulled themselves up by their own endeavours and didn't take shit from anyone.

'Mike's on edge,' Julien said. 'He needs to be reminded what's at stake if the shit hits the fan.'

'Let's talk to him together after dinner. Him and Jason both. They need a little reminder about where they've come from and who's responsible for the upturn in their circumstances.' Eddie cracked his knuckles, clearly relishing the prospect. 'You could do worse than turning it on for Mike's old lady. You know she's got an eye for you, and it won't do no harm for Mike to see it too. It might even curb Chelsea's excesses if she realises that she has competition for your affections.'

Julien grunted. 'What I can make, I can break.'

'Yep. Something like that.'

'What's the latest from our tame policeman? Any chance of the investigation into the Monaco fund being dropped?'

'Unlikely.'

'Fuck! Why do I pay Garner so well if he can't put a lid on it?'

'Out of his hands, or so he insists. In fairness, there are crypto technical advisors attached to just about every major force in the country nowadays, which is why I suggested cutting and running before they caught up with us. Garner did tip us the wink about our being under the spotlight, so he did something right.'

'Yeah, I know you made the right call, Ed, and I'm grateful. It's easy to get carried away and let the profits keep on rolling in when it's so simple.'

'Garner reckons that the filth can't keep up with the crypto schemes and they would drop the investigation into ours, but for the fact that it crosses international borders *and* more to the point, because your name came up. You know they've been looking for a reason to feel your collar for years.' Eddie grinned. 'Mine too. I feel a bit like a star of the most wanted variety.'

Julien grinned. He could always depend upon Eddie to make light of things and cheer him up. 'Send Garner a little reminder of the hold we have over him. A picture of him with sweet little Polly should do the trick.'

'Consider it done.'

Speaking Polly's name out loud chased away Julien's brief moment of light heartedness. She had been something else: special. She had style, class and ambition but he'd let her get away. Ironically, his son had been on a downward, drug-induced spiral at the time and gone on the missing list. Julien had tracked him down and got him back into rehab.

Again.

But it had taken time and he'd neglected Polly in favour of familial priorities. He hadn't realised that she'd taken to the nose candy quite so enthusiastically and that she'd become addicted so quickly. He thought she had a determination to succeed and would understand how to keep the drugs recreational, without their getting in the way of her plans for a modelling career that Julien had agreed to sponsor. He could have opened doors for her, got her what she wanted and basked in reflected glory when she made a name for herself.

He might even have left his wife for her, and none of his other women had come close to making him think the unthinkable. Polly's frailties had been a timely reminder and he reckoned now that he'd had a lucky escape.

Even so, he still thought about her and the way she'd been before she became an addict. Twice her age, she'd made him feel young again. He put her on a pedestal but she kicked it away and disappointed him. She'd got what she deserved. She'd let him down in the worse possible way, made him look vulnerable in front of his friends because they all knew that he'd come dangerously close to falling in love with her.

Julien himself hated drugs and never touched them but he also knew that they had a place in the world that he aspired to inhabit. They were a means to an end. He hated what they'd done to his son and hated even more the fact that they'd destroyed Polly. She'd gone from being vibrant, intelligent and driven to becoming a pathetic junkie who couldn't even keep herself clean, begging him on bended knees for just one more fix before she checked herself into rehab.

Julien had been repulsed at her lack of self-control and so set her to work in his club as a punishment. She'd lost all self-respect and would do absolutely anything that the punters asked of her. Things she would never do for Julien, he recalled, bile rising in his throat. She wasn't like the Chelseas of this world. She had standards, or did have before she lived for nothing other than chasing the fucking dragon.

He didn't blame himself for what happened to her. Everyone was responsible for their own actions. In the early days, he'd warned Polly, but she'd brushed his concerns aside, assuring him that she had it under control.

Ha!

If nothing else, the episode had taught Julien a

timely lesson. There was no one he could depend upon, with the exception of Eddie, and he'd not make the same mistake again. A mistake that had almost cost him his freedom. He'd let his guard down in front of Polly before she became a lost cause, thought he could trust her, and she knew stuff about his operations that few others did. The old bill found her turning tricks for him and tried to get her to rat him out. She'd have done it too if she'd thought there'd be a steady supply of drugs in it for her. She'd gotten to the stage when she couldn't think beyond her next fix.

That was why she'd had to kill herself, even though it had almost killed Julien too when he'd given Eddie the order.

Julien had trained himself not to think about Polly and what might have been because, fuck it, he still gave a damn. Even so, thinking about her now made him realise why the new hostess looked so familiar. She was the spitting image of Polly. Julien closed his eyes and threw his head back, trying to recall if Polly had mentioned a sister. She never spoke about her family much, other than to complain about her father being from a different age. He hadn't pushed her, aware that she didn't want to look back. He hadn't wanted her to either. He only wanted her to think about him. He was the centre of her universe, she looked up to him with adoration in her eyes in the early days, and that was just the way that he wanted it to stay. It stoked his ego and made him feel invincible.

He'd ask the new girl if she and Polly were related. Or perhaps not. If she'd somehow found out about his links to Polly, he would prefer not to talk about it. Loose lips and all that.

'Come on then, Eddie. Let's put on a show for our adoring audience,' he said, standing.

'Show time,' Eddie agreed, following him from the room.

* * *

Freya checked in the galley to ensure that preparations for lunch were running smoothly, unsurprised when Sandy scowled at her and offered up a sarcastic response.

'I'll take that as a yes then,' Freya replied, retreating with her dignity more or less intact. No sharp objects had been thrown at her, so she'd look upon it as a win. What she would absolutely not let Sandy, let anyone do, was intimidate her. She was, loosely speaking, Sandy's boss and would not permit the chef's hostile attitude to prevent her from carrying out her duties proficiently.

Freya went to ensure that the table on the after deck on the upper level had been laid out properly by Gloria. As she made her way along the side deck for that purpose, she could hear voices coming from Falcon's study. The portlight was closed but she could still mostly hear what was being said. But she also realised she would be seen from inside and so didn't linger. Even so, that discovery had given her ideas.

'You've done this before, I can tell,' Freya said, smiling at Gloria when she reached her destination and observed the long table pristinely laid for lunch. The deep cushions on the chairs in stripes of red and blue had been plumped up and silver cutlery sparkled in the sun. 'I hope your efforts are appreciated,' she added, making a small adjustment to the floral arrangement in the middle of the table.

'Ready when they are.' One of Sandy's helpers, red in the face, puffed up to the deck and told them.

Freya rang the bell situated to one side of the table and stood back, ready to open wine and serve the platters. Gloria winked at her and took her place at the opposite side. A full five minutes passed and there was no sign of Falcon and his retinue.

'Should I ring again?' Freya asked. 'Perhaps they didn't hear the bell first time.'

'Oh, they heard it. Don't worry, this is normal. Sandy knows that. Anyway, lunch is cold so it's okay.'

Sure enough, the sound of chattering voices preceded Falcon leading his party up to the table. He paused to subject Freya to a prolonged scrutiny before smiling at her and taking his place at the head of the table.

'Come and sit with me, Maureen,' he said to Parker's wife, stopping Chelsea in her tracks since she'd been about to take the chair beside Falcon. 'Go and sit down the other end,' Falcon added, not even looking at his date.

Freya bit her lip. She didn't like Chelsea, but she didn't deserve to be put down quite so publicly. She watched the woman, still only a girl really, as she jutted her lower lip and stomped off to sit beside Parker. She had put a coverall over her bikini, but it was totally transparent and left absolutely nothing to the imagination. She tottered on platform wedged sandals that had to be four inches high and had swept her hair extravagantly over one shoulder in a tangle of wild curls. She was a very pretty girl and part of Freya wanted to grab hold of her the moment the yacht docked and send her back home where she belonged before she too became a victim of Falcon's making.

Don't be another Polly.

Then Chelsea snapped her fingers at Freya to demand wine and the desire to rescue her dissipated.

'People with breeding don't snap their fingers at the help, princess,' Falcon remarked from the other end of the table.

Chelsea blushed and sank a little lower in her chair.

Freya and Gloria served Sandy's seafood platter and Freya did the honours with the wine. She poured a generous measure into Chelsea's glass.

'Just let me know if you want more,' she said in a quiet aside. Chelsea blinked at her, the gesture barely visible beneath her oversized, lightly tinted shades.

'Er, thanks.' Chelsea looked bemused by the olive branch and took a healthy swig of her wine.

Freya watched her picking at her food, barely eating a thing. Her behaviour was so reminiscent of Polly that Freya wanted to weep. She felt helpless as she stood unobtrusively at the serving station, watching to ensure that everyone had everything they needed. And listening, always listening to the conversation. Chelsea alternately flirted shamelessly with a somewhat bemused Parker and then glanced sullenly down the table at Falcon, who ignored her.

Freya could see what he was doing, purposely bamboozling Maureen Parker with his legendary charm, just as Greg had suggested would be the case. There was definitely trouble in paradise, she decided, as evidenced by the heavy atmosphere and forced bonhomie. Falcon's guests seemed on edge and obviously didn't want to be here. Perhaps Freya could use their unease to her advantage.

Somehow.

She'd tell Greg later what she'd witnessed and see what suggestions he came up with. There had to be a way to exploit the situation.

'Aw, don't!' Chelsea's high-pitched laugh caused all heads to turn in her direction. 'You're terrible,' she added, swatting playfully at Parker's arm. The man himself looked like a rabbit caught in the headlights of an oncoming car, clearly unsure what it was that he'd done. Falcon simply laughed and returned his full attention to a flushed Maureen who was, by Freya's reckoning, on her third glass of wine.

'Netflix has nothing on this lot,' Gloria said in an undertone to Freya as she returned empty plates to the serving station.

'When will we get to Ibiza, babe?' Chelsea asked, looking down the table at Falcon and burping behind her hand. 'Whoops!'

'What's wrong with being at sea in luxury?' Falcon

asked, his tone challenging. 'Not good enough for you?'

'I only asked. Can we see where the captain drives the boat later?'

'Why?'

Falcon was clearly in an argumentative mood and Freya wanted to tell Chelsea that she'd be better advised to leave him be.

'My dad used to have boats,' she said, sounding a little desperate.

Falcon opened his mouth, presumably to deliver another put down. Freya glanced at him and miraculously, he closed his mouth again without speaking. Why Freya felt the need to protect Chelsea from his spite she couldn't have said other than perhaps she would have liked it if someone had been there at the vital time to look out for Polly.

None of the ladies took dessert but the men tucked into Sandy's cheesecake with gusto.

'You keep a damned good chef,' Parker said, accepting a second helping.

'I pay for the best and that's what I expect.' He allowed a long pause. 'From all the people I do business with.'

Parker's ruddy cheeks paled, and he appeared to Freya to sink a little lower in his chair. It validated, if any validation was necessary, Greg's opinion that Parker and Pyke had been invited on this cruise to ensure that they toed the party line. It was equally clear to Freya that Parker was feeling on edge.

A very worried man.

Perhaps she and Greg could think of way to make him see the light, face up to what he'd done and come clean to the authorities. It was equally clear to Freya that Parker was no ladies' man. Chelsea's attentions appeared to scare the shit out of him. What's more, he didn't seem too happy to see his wife being the recipient of Falcon's charm offensive.

And responding to it.

She wondered if Falcon had miscalculated when singling her out. In her experience, all men had a breaking point. Maureen Parker had looked after herself and although probably twenty years older than Chelsea, she was still attractive and Parker himself obviously adored her.

The meal broke up, bringing with it an end to Freya's speculations. She stood back as the owner and his guests stood up, talking about what to do that afternoon. Chelsea was unsteady on her feet and Freya guessed that situation wasn't brought about only by her unsuitable footwear and the motion of the boat.

'Think I'll have a little lie down,' she said, once

again burping. 'You coming, babe?' she asked, addressing the question to Falcon.

'Later,' he said, waving dismissively and returning his full attention to Maureen as the party returned to the sundeck.

'The plot thickens,' Freya muttered, as she helped Gloria to clear the table and prepare it for dinner.

7

Greg returned to the helm and stood on the deck surrounding the wheelhouse, legs braced against the motion of the yacht as he watched the activity on the deck below more avidly than he watched the sea, hidden from the view of those enjoying Sandy's efforts.

Feeling like a voyeur, Greg was surprised by the game that Falcon had decided to play so early into the cruise. It implied that he was indeed a worried man, afraid that he could no longer control Parker, causing Greg to wonder if it also implied a chink in his armour that he and Freya could somehow exploit. Maureen Parker's tinkling laughter was audible even above the sound of the engines. It was obvious to Greg that he would have no trouble in moulding the woman, who was clearly impressed by the luxurious yacht and its charismatic owner, into backing him against her own husband if it came to a battle of wills.

And Parker knew it.

There was a strain in the forced conversation, almost as though everyone was playing a part. Chelsea was drinking far too much, not eating at all, and rather desperately flirting with Parker. Her voice was loud, shrill, and she was making a bit of a fool of herself. From his vantage point, Greg noticed her place her hand on Parker's thigh below the table. The man looked horrified and shook it off.

He wondered if Freya could sense the tension too and if she'd be able to pick up more from the body language of those gathered around the table. He knew she would be listening avidly.

And watching.

Clever but ruthless, Greg thought, watching Falcon in action. He hadn't actually done anything that Parker could object to, but the implication would be clear to him. Toe the line, remember who your friends are, keep your mouth shut and all will be well in paradise.

Greg transferred his attention to a small yacht a good distance away on their port beam, wondering how he could put what he'd just seen on the deck below to his advantage. Divide and conquer perhaps? Parker had seemed ill at ease since first stepping aboard. On previous occasions when he'd seen Falcon and Parker together, they'd been tight.

'What you looking at?'

Greg turned round and glared at Sandy, who had once again crept up on him. 'Shouldn't you be in the galley?' he asked.

'Nah. My work is done.' She leaned on the guard rail and peered down onto the tops of the heads of the diners. 'Trouble?' she asked.

'Why should there be? Do you know something that I don't?'

'The atmosphere's a bit tense, I can tell you that much for nothing. The bimbo that Falcon's brought along this time is a bit up herself. Nothing new there, I guess, but the rest of his guests... well, the men any-way, look like they'd much prefer to be somewhere else which you have to admit is odd.'

'Not our problem. We're paid to take them wher-ever they want to go.'

'What's up with you, Greg?' She touched his arm, forcing him to look at her. 'You've changed. I thought we were friends. Did I do something to upset you?'

'No idea what you mean. We're colleagues and

friends but not bosom buddies.' Greg decided it was necessary to be cruel to be kind. Sandy was thick skinned and clearly not about to take the hint and give up on him.

'We were. We could have been.' She let out a long breath. 'Everything was cool until *she* spoiled it all.'

'Is there a point to all this, Sandy?' Greg permitted his irritation to show. 'We had a drunken fumble, but that's all it was. I thought you understood that and were good with it. Don't read more into it than was actually there. Relationships between crew members never end well.'

Sandy sent him a long, hard look through narrowed eyes glistening with spite and Greg knew then that it had been a mistake to let her down so harshly. She was vindictive and would take what he'd just said as a personal insult. Sandy had clearly misinterpreted Greg's friendship with Freya. It was a large yacht but still hard to find complete privacy anywhere except in the cabins. Sandy had probably seen him and Freya with their heads together and gotten the wrong idea.

Greg wasn't about to put her straight.

Even so, he'd need to find a way to put Freya on her guard because Greg wouldn't bet against a chef with hurt feelings and a set of sharp knives taking her spite out on the yacht's new hostess. It would be easy for her to make Freya's life difficult in lots of small ways, which was annoying. She and Greg had more important issues to resolve. They absolutely didn't need a vindictive female watching their every move and perhaps reporting back to Falcon in an effort to salve her wounded pride. Not that there was anything she could tell their boss, he reasoned, unless she picked up on their real purpose, which would be a disaster. They would need to proceed with extreme caution.

'I'm sorry you feel that way.'

Sandy's voice was harsh with recrimination as she left the wheelhouse and walked down the steps to the lower deck with a heavy tread.

'Shit!' Greg muttered as he made a slight adjustment to the yacht's course, thereby steering well clear of the vessel he'd noticed a little earlier.

He didn't see Freya that afternoon and, aware that Sandy had eyes and ears everywhere, deliberately didn't go in search of her. If she'd overheard anything useful at lunch, then she'd let him know as soon as she could.

* * *

Freya watched Chelsea tottering off in the direction of the master cabin. Her shoulders shook and she was visibly upset. Despite the dismissive manner in which she had treated Freya, she felt a huge amount of sympathy for the younger woman, horrified to think that Falcon could have publicly humiliated Polly in a similar manner. The man was cruel, he played with people's affections, and Freya wasn't about to allow history to repeat itself. She'd failed to save Polly, but she was damned if she'd permit Chelsea to self-destruct as well.

Chelsea was all show and no substance. She wasn't particularly likeable and certainly wasn't Freya's responsibility. She had largely brought her problems on herself, and Freya ought to let her sink or swim without interfering. She had far more important matters to resolve, she reminded herself, thinking of the reasons why she'd taken this job and what she and Greg hoped to achieve. But, she reasoned, if she befriended Chelsea, and the girl certainly needed a sympathetic ear right now, then perhaps she'd pick up something useful by that means. The girl was silly, but still had eyes and ears and didn't seem to be particularly discreet. There was a slim possibility that she might overhear something relevant and repeat what she'd heard to her new best friend – AKA Freya.

She gave Chelsea fifteen minutes to compose herself. If she didn't reappear during that period of time then Freya would go in search of her.

Caught up with her duties, it was more than half an hour before Freya was free to think about Chelsea again. Unsure if she'd left the master cabin, Freya paused outside its door and could clearly hear sobbing coming from within. Resolved, she tapped at the door and opened it before Chelsea had the time to compose herself.

The girl was perched on the edge of the huge bed, her hair a tangled mess, her eyes puffy from crying. She glanced up at Freya and scowled.

'What do you want?' she demanded in a semi-hostile tone. 'You've come to gloat, I suppose?'

Freya said nothing. Instead, she went to the cooler fixed into a cabinet, took a bottle of water and poured a glass, which she handed to Chelsea. 'Here, drink this.'

'What are you, my mother?' Chelsea's eyes glistened with antagonism. She was obviously thirsting for a fight – an outlet for her pent-up emotions. But it was hard to fight with a person who refused to rise to the bait. She sat beside Chelsea and took her trembling hand in her own, watching as she downed the water in two unladylike swallows.

'If I was your mother, I would have taught you better manners,' Freya said mildly, 'but actually, I came to offer some advice, if you want to hear it.'

'Advice?' The girl sniffed, put the empty glass aside and wiped her eyes with the back of her hand. 'Why would you want to help me?'

'Why wouldn't I?'

Chelsea blinked up at Freya as she reached for a tissue, blew her nose and dabbed at her eyes. 'You work for Jules. Did he send you to...' Her words trailed off. She clearly wasn't accustomed to other women befriending her and didn't know how to handle the situation. Chelsea was so competitive, so determined to make an impression with her looks and body that other females didn't register on her personal radar.

'No one sent me.' Freya smiled. 'I saw the way he treated you at lunch and could see you were upset.'

Chelsea opened her mouth, perhaps to protest, but instead subsided into a fresh bout of tears. 'I don't know what I did wrong?' she stuttered. 'He says he loves me... Well, he didn't say it precisely, but I could tell. He's always treated me like a princess, says he's proud to be seen with me. Then he treats me like dirt.' She shook her head. 'I just don't get it. What did I do wrong?'

'He's a married man,' Freya said softly.

'Not happily,' Chelsea snapped back. 'And his kids drive him mental. But I could make him happy, if he'd let me.'

'He's been married for a long time and you're not the first younger model he's taken up with.' Freya raised a hand to prevent Chelsea from interrupting. 'I know it's not what you want to hear but it's the truth, nonetheless. His affairs never last long and he always goes back to his family so don't get your hopes up.'

Freya knew she'd said too much when Chelsea scowled, her eyes reduced to malicious slits. 'You're jealous!' she cried, her voice rising in shrill accusation. 'You want me out the way so you can make a play for him.'

'I don't think you believe that for one moment.' Freya remained calm, waiting for the tantrum to play itself out and for Chelsea's common sense, such as it was, to reassert itself.

'But I've seen the way he looks at you.' Chelsea blinked back her confusion. 'I just don't get it. You're old. Well, a lot older than me and... well, if he wants you, why wouldn't you go for it?'

'I have no interest in Falcon as anything other than my employer. That said, I don't like to see the way he treats you. It's none of my business and if you don't want my advice then I'll leave you alone.'

'What advice?' she asked suspiciously.

'Don't cling so much, but don't flirt with the other men either. They're Falcon's subordinates and they'd never poach on his territory. It makes you look desperate and makes the men in question feel uncomfortable.'

'You just don't get it, do you!' she cried. 'I *am* desperate. Jules has made me certain promises. I've left home, given everything up for him and already he seems to be getting tired of me.' Tears trickled down her blotched cheeks, but she didn't notice. 'I just don't know what to do.'

'He's playing games with you, Chelsea. It's what he does. It amuses him to have people dancing to his tune. It makes him feel powerful.'

Another Polly, in other words, Freya thought with a sinking heart, her worst fears confirmed. She wondered how often he'd played this game and what he got out of ruining the lives of ambitious young women who believed all the bullshit he fed to them. God, how she hated him! Her own eyes briefly blurred with tears brought on by a combination of anger and regret. Anger at the way he manipulated; regret because she hadn't done more to save her poor, damaged sister.

'Perhaps that's true.' Chelsea nibbled at the end of

an impossibly long fingernail that almost certainly wasn't natural. 'But there's no way back for me. You sound just like my dad. He told me that if I went with Jules then I needn't think of going home again. He said Jules was using me. Jules laughed when I told him. He said he'd give me a home to be proud of and I believed him.' She looked impossibly young and impressionable now that Freya was seeing the real Chelsea beneath the makeup, the silly shoes and the scanty clothing.

She looked very similar to Polly.

The hope that sprang into her puffy eyes almost floored Freya as she imagined Polly reacting in an equally naïve manner to Falcon's empty promises.

'Now if that doesn't imply an intention to leave his wife,' Chelsea said on a note of desperation, 'then I don't know what does.'

'Despite everything, you miss your family.'

Chelsea shrugged. 'I'm the oldest of four. My mum and dad both worked full-time. In fact, Mum worked two jobs in order to make ends meet, always scrimping and saving, looking old before her time. She expected me to look after the others. I became more of a mother to them than she did, and it got to the point where I'd had enough. I wanted to have some fun. Dad got heavy not because he cares but because he was in danger of losing his unpaid skivvy. I mean,' she added, clearly wanting to talk about a situation over which she still felt highly incensed, 'it's not as if my sisters were my responsibility but Dad had a way of making me feel guilty if I complained.' She kicked one bare foot aggressively against the base of the bed. 'It just wasn't fair.'

'No. Quite often life isn't.'

'Well anyway, I wouldn't go back now even if I could because it would be the same old, same old, and I'd be held back from my ambitions because I'd have to cook and generally look after the others. I'm five years older than my closest sister, see, so it would all fall on me again.'

'What are your ambitions?' Freya asked, suspecting that she already knew the answer but hoping she was wrong. She held her breath as she waited for Chelsea to respond.

'Why, to be a model, of course.' Her tone implied that it ought to be obvious. 'Jules says I have what it takes.' She preened briefly before deflating again. 'He says that he can open all the right doors for me and make things happen.'

Freya's heart sank even as her hatred for Falcon and his slimy technique intensified. Polly clearly hadn't been an isolated case. The man made a habit out of exploiting young women with ambition, promising them the earth while he enjoyed the prestige of having them on his arm but never delivering.

He had to be stopped. Chelsea's presence on the yacht filled Freya with determination and fresh resolve. She looked upon it as a sign, even if a few hours before, she'd been doubting the wisdom of her impetuosity.

'He didn't behave at lunch as though you were the love of his life,' Freya said gently, thinking it necessary to be cruel to be kind. To water the seeds of doubt already germinating in Chelsea's mind.

'No, but that's just his way. He cares. I know he does.' She leaned towards Freya, her expression intense, covering her mouth to smother a burp. 'He can't possibly prefer that frumpy Maureen Parker over me.'

'Perhaps he wants something from her husband and so buttered her up in order to get her on his side.'

Chelsea frowned. 'But Parker works for Jules, so he has to do whatever Jules tells him to.' She looked totally perplexed. 'I don't understand. Why would he need to be persuaded?'

'I have absolutely no idea.' Freya realised that she'd pushed too hard, and that Chelsea wasn't quite as gullible as she appeared to be. 'It was just a thought. I sensed a lot of tension between them, that's all. I don't know the first thing about the world of business, but I suppose there must always be problems. Differences of opinion.'

Chelsea gave a negligent shrug, bored with a subject that didn't centre directly upon her, reminding Freya just how self-obsessed she actually was. 'You said something about advice,' she reminded Freya.

'I've said my piece. No man likes something that's too readily available. Back off, maintain your dignity. Drink less, is my advice.' Freya got up and poured more water for the girl, standing over her like a mother hen whilst she drank it down. 'You can't handle alcohol and it makes you do and say stuff that would be best left unsaid. Besides, it also dries out your skin and will make you blotchy.'

'Play hard to get?' She giggled and glanced at the bed they were seated on. 'A bit late for that.'

'Possibly.' Freya stood, wondering whether she'd helped or hindered the girl. Wondering too if she'd overplayed her hand. If Chelsea reported their conversation verbatim to Falcon, which there was every chance of her doing if Falcon bothered to ask her how she'd spent the last hour, then he'd smell a rat. 'Anyway, let me know if you need my help. I'm always here for you.'

Chelsea looked at Freya as she headed for the

door, her expression reflective. 'You're not so bad,' she said, sounding surprised. 'I'm sorry if I was unkind to you.'

'Don't give it another thought.'

'Why would you want to help me, though? You don't know me.'

'I knew someone like you once,' Freya replied, standing and moving towards the door. 'I couldn't help her, but I might be able to help you.'

8

Julien returned to the sundeck, lay on a bed with his hands behind his head and watched the sea. There was sod all else to look at. Cruising on a private yacht sounded glamorous but once you were out at sea, there wasn't much to do, other than to eat and drink. And Julien never let himself get wasted, at least not during the day and seldom at other times. He'd seen too many rash decisions made under the influence of alcohol. Fortunately, when he did over-imbibe, his tolerance levels were high. When colleagues and adversaries alike were slurring their words, he remained compos mentis and relatively alert. People became indiscreet when pissed and let all sorts of useful snippets slip. Julien had made a few bob by acting on what he'd heard.

Slurring of words made him think of Chelsea for the first time in over an hour. She wasn't a bad kid and in fairness, he did encourage her to strut her stuff, to show off her body and make *him* look good. He regretted the way he'd treated her at lunch now, but he'd had his reasons. Not that he could explain that to her and nor would he. Never explain and never apologise had always been his mantra. He'd make it up to Chelsea without admitting that he'd been a jerk.

Maureen was on the sunbed across from him, sending coy looks his way. Christ, did she really think he'd touch her with a bargepole? There was clearly no age limit for stupid. But still, it had gotten the message across to Mike, loud and clear. He knew that both Mike and Jason were waiting for him to broach the subject of the failed crypto fund. They'd be getting edgy because he hadn't said a word about it yet and it was their necks on the line if the investigators decided there was a case to answer.

And they *would* make that decision, Julien knew, because matters had spun out of his control. It was downright infuriating. He felt like he was drowning and his struggles to resurface were being thwarted at every turn. Mike and Jason had become subdued, not

offering up any useful advice on how to get themselves out of a hole that they had dug through a combination of incompetence and greed. It was them
who'd put him onto the scheme, assuring him that it
was bombproof, so they were the ones who could
fucking well take the flack.

Fortunately, Julien was cautious by nature and so
he'd made sure that his involvement with the scheme
was buried deeper than a politician's promise. The
regulators would be digging from now until the next
millennium if they wanted definitive proof of his par-
ticipation. And even if they did get lucky, Julien had
an escape plan.

Never leave anything to chance.

The yacht lurched as it hit a swell and Julien tried
not to show how much it affected him. He fought seasickness all the fucking time he was on board, but
he'd never make that admission to anyone. Any sign
of weakness would be pounced upon by his adversaries and somehow used against him. It was a valu-
able lesson he'd learned early on in his business life
and one which had stood him in good stead ever
since.

Not for the first time, he questioned the wisdom of
owning and maintaining this floating tub, even
though he knew why he did it. It was the ultimate sign

of success and made him the envy of his friends. Everything was about perception, which is why the Chelseas of this world were so vital to his image. He didn't care if people thought he was a sugar daddy; in fact, he welcomed the accolade. Only the seriously rich and influential could buy that type of adulation and he'd spent most of his life aspiring to membership of that exclusive club.

But now that he'd achieved it, he sometimes wondered why it had been so important to him. He thought of his wife and kids and the constant demands they made on his bank balance. They didn't care about him, never expressed any desire to see him simply for the pleasure of his company and if Julien did decide that he wanted them to toe the family line in a show of solidarity, he was well aware that his wife had to literally round them all up.

The fuckers hadn't given him any grandkids yet. They couldn't even manage that simple task. He really would have to stop paying their allowances soon. They were adults, for fuck's sake, and should be making their own way. It was something he should have done years before. They needed a wake-up call. Let them work for a living. That would soon make them realise what their old dad did for them. He knew it was one of the areas where his wife would have fought him tooth and nail and he had his reasons for wanting to keep her sweet, so he'd let the matter slide.

Feeling aggrieved and ready to pick a fight, Julien glanced at Mike and Jason, standing together against the guardrail at the stern of the yacht, talking in lowered voices. It was us and them nowadays, Julien realised. Battle lines had been drawn, both physically and mentally, but how those two tossers thought they could get one over on him and Eddie defied belief. They'd still be breaking their backs to earn a meagre living if Julien hadn't spotted their potential and pulled them up by the boot straps. Perhaps a little reminder in that regard was overdue.

With shades covering his eyes, the two men couldn't know that Julien was watching them. They kept glancing in his direction as they conducted their conversation, but it was impossible for Julien to hear what they were saying. Maureen had fallen asleep in the sun, her mouth gaping open, and her snores helped to drown out their voices. She looked her age and the thought of taking her to bed repulsed Julien. Not that he'd had any intention of shagging her but that wasn't the issue. He'd proven to Mike that he could do so with ease if it came to it. That ought to be enough to keep him in line because, for reasons that

Julien had never understood, he made no secret of the fact that he adored the woman and was unerringly faithful to her.

In Julien's book, variety was the spice of life. Besides, his devotion made him vulnerable. An easy target, as Julien had just demonstrated. A few more home truths would have to be spelled out, but not yet and not here on board. When they got to Ibiza, they would not be partying because there was someone there who Julien's underlings needed to speak with, did they but know it.

A sound of quiet feet approaching on the teak deck caused Julien to sit up and peer over his glasses. It was Chelsea and her appearance surprised Julien. Still in her bikini, she was bare-footed and had her hair blowing loose, almost down to her waist. It was held back from her face by one of those band thingies that made her look like a schoolgirl. He felt himself stirring at the sight of her.

'Hey,' he said, leaning up on one elbow and smiling at her. 'You've been a while.' He patted the cushions on the bed next to him and she perched on its edge. 'You okay?'

'Never better,' she replied in a subdued manner.

Julien had expected gushing and overt displays of affection as she fought to become the focus of his attention once again. Julien loved to see his dates vying for his affections, which was one of the reasons why he blew hot and cold, just to remind them what they stood to lose if they forgot who paid the bills. He would have put good money on Chelsea being that predictable. Instead, she lay down on the sunbed and closed her eyes without saying another word.

'Take that cover thing off,' he said quietly.

She shrugged, sat up to do as he'd asked, and then lay down again. No comment. No suggestions that they take their party somewhere more private. What the hell was wrong with people today? Julien was paying a fucking fortune so they could enjoy the luxury of his yacht and they all seemed so fucking moody. Chelsea was, he supposed, entitled to feel a bit peeved but even so, she'd made her point and Julien had met her halfway. There was no need to milk it.

'The sunshine makes me randy as hell,' he said when she continued to ignore him. 'Look what you're doing to me, darlin'.'

She opened her eyes, removed her shades and glanced at his groin, where the evidence spoke for itself. Julien was rather pleased with the spectacle, but Chelsea merely raised a brow, returned her glasses to her nose and lay back down again. Now she was being disrespectful and was starting to piss Julien off.

'Come on,' he said curtly, grabbing her hand and pulling her to her feet.

'I only just got here,' she protested, but she went with him anyway. Just as well, or she'd have earned herself a backhander.

Jules was conscious of the gazes of everyone else on the deck boring into his back. They would all know where he was going and what he would soon be doing, and the guys would be full of envy, just the way he wanted them to be.

Eat your hearts out, jackasses!

Julien relieved his frustration quickly, then lay naked on the bed with his hands behind his head, admiring Chelsea's body. Wishing there was a little more flesh on it to accentuate her curves. Images of the new hostess naked in his bed invaded his brain and caused his cock to stir again.

He glanced at Chelsea, wondering if she'd fallen asleep. She usually never stopped talking during sex, urging him on, telling him how good he was. Today, she'd been almost robotic. She wasn't asleep. Her eyes were wide open, and she was staring morosely at the ceiling.

'What is it?' he asked.

'Nothing.'

It drove him crazy when a woman said that.

Nothing was a euphemism; the equivalent of opening a whole can of worms and he wasn't going there. Only his wife got to play the 'nothing' game with him and even she knew better than to pull that stunt too often.

'Did you sleep earlier?' Why was he asking? What did he care?

She shook her head against the pillow. 'Talked.'

'Talked? Who to?' There was no mobile phone signal this far offshore.

'To Freya.'

'Freya.' Julien leaned up on one elbow and looked directly at her. 'The hostess. I thought you didn't like her.'

'I never said that. She came to see if I was okay and we chatted, that's all.'

Julien frowned, not liking where this was going. 'Why wouldn't you be okay?'

'Don't ask me.'

She wasn't looking at Julien, but the implication was clear and, much to his annoyance, he felt a modicum of shame at the way he'd treated her. More to the point, the hired help had witnessed his performance. He tended not to think about the people he employed as... well, people. Not that he ever said anything contentious in front of them but still, showing off, which was what he'd been doing, had backfired, setting Chelsea, his subordinates and now, apparently, his hostess against him.

'Perhaps she was just being kind,' Chelsea remarked casually.

Julien's frown intensified. He was unsure whether or not to be annoyed with Freya and, more to the point, whether she'd done anything that he ought to take exception to. It was her job to look after his guests but not to stick her nose into situations that were none of her fucking business. He was aspiring to become recognised as a man of means, an entrepreneur, friend to the elite. He was some way to achieving that ambition, which was no small feat, given that he'd grown up in social housing and left a failing comprehensive with no qualifications to his name.

Doors were opening up to him now that he was successful, but he knew very well that the upper classes, some of whom he'd leant money to, saw right through him and would never look upon him as a friend, much less an equal. Freya, he sensed, hadn't needed to be taught which knife and fork to use and which side of her plate to reach for her wine glass. So why had she befriended Chelsea, who'd been deliberately rude to her? It made absolutely no sense to Julien, who never forgot a slight and seldom forgave one without a compelling reason.

The possibility of having met Freya before continued to niggle. He'd learned to trust his instincts over the years and didn't like unsolved puzzles. Even so, he reasoned, perhaps Freya was simply being sisterly. She would have seen the way Julien had treated Chelsea at lunch. He'd gotten off on putting her down, which was cheap and unworthy, he now accepted. Even so, if she overstepped the mark again then her days on this tub would be numbered, no matter how good at her job or how decorative he found her.

'Where're you going?' Julien asked, when Chelsea got up and headed for the bathroom.

'To get some more sun,' she responded, returning to the cabin, slipping back into her discarded bikini and leaving without a backward glance.

'What the fuck?'

Julien scratched his head as he watched the door close behind her. *What had that interfering bitch said to her?* he wondered. Chelsea had never shown the slightest inclination for independence before and had always hung on his every word. They all did. He selected them specifically for that reason.

He sat on the edge of the bed, thinking things

through and reluctantly admiring Chelsea's guts. She had just made the game much less predictable and far more challenging.

'Bring it on,' he muttered, pulling on his shorts and heading for his study, where Eddie would be waiting for him. Let Chelsea stew and wonder what he was doing, he decided.

* * *

'Fucking forward port side bilge pump is playing up again,' Derek, the engineer, informed Greg across the table in the crew mess. 'I'll have to take it apart as soon as we dock.'

'That'll keep you amused.'

Greg knew only too well that keeping on top of the maintenance on any vessel was a full-time job. There was always something that needed fixing, even on one as new as the *Perseus*. Greg left the running of the engines entirely up to Derek and his subordinate but the ultimate responsibility was his, which was why Derek had told him of the defect.

'Yeah.' Derek spooned soup morosely into his mouth. 'A laugh a minute.'

'Is it my imagination or is there a tense atmosphere on board?' Gloria asked, sliding into the seat next to Derek.

'Not just above decks,' Derek said, lowering his voice and nodding in the direction of the galley. 'Steer clear of Sandy, is my advice. She's in a right strop. I asked her an innocent question just now and she nearly bit my head off.'

'Surely the guests ought to be enjoying the luxury, and not waste their time squabbling,' Gloria persisted.

'The idle rich make their own rules,' Derek said. 'We up for a party when we hit "the island"?' he asked, grinning.

'Too old,' Greg said.

Derek grinned. 'Yeah, well there is that. Our skipper is past his prime, love,' he added when Freya walked in. 'It'll be cocoa and slippers for him and bed at nine o'clock before we know it.'

Freya smiled as she helped herself to soup and crusty bread and sat at the end of the table. 'He does look a bit past his prime. It has to be said.'

The conversation around the table was light and sporadic as various crew members came and went. Greg wanted to speak with Freya but now wasn't the time or place. He glanced at her as he stood up to leave and she gave a tiny nod, implying that she would come and find him.

Sure enough, twenty minutes later, she tracked him down to the same place on the lower aft deck where they'd held their previous conversation. It was the time of day when the majority of the crew had a few hours to themselves and everything on board was quiet. Sandy, Greg knew, was the exception. She and her galley slave would be busy prepping for dinner. Greg and Freya would never have a better opportunity for a quiet word or two, free from the prospect of eavesdroppers out to make trouble.

'What's wrong with Sandy?' Freya asked. 'She's even grumpier than usual. Derek got that part right.'

'She's territorial.'

'Ah, I see.' Freya nodded and Greg assumed that she very likely did. He was relieved when she asked no further questions on a subject that seemed unimportant to him.

'Be careful what you say around her. I don't trust her,' Greg contented himself with saying, because he felt the need to issue the warning.

'A woman scorned is never to be trusted.' She tutted and shook her head, her expression playful. 'You should take more care when bestowing your favours.'

'Duly noted.' Greg's smile faded. 'There was a lot

of tension at lunch, I couldn't help but notice, even from the wheelhouse bridge.'

'And then some.'

Greg listened, not interrupting as, in a low voice, Freya succinctly outlined what had occurred.

'Chelsea was apoplectic and made a right prat of herself,' she finished by saying. 'And I don't blame her for that. Falcon was cruel.'

'Falcon does so enjoy his little power games but this time, it was more than that.' Greg rubbed his chin. 'Unless I've lost my edge, I'd say he's a worried man and was using Maureen Parker to make a point to her husband.'

'He's losing control, you mean, because of the bitcoin.'

Greg nodded. 'That's my guess.'

'I wouldn't bet against it.' Freya appeared thoughtful. 'Parker looked fit to bust a gut but there was absolutely nothing he could do,' Freya said. 'He clearly adores his wife so I'd have felt sorry for him, but for the fact that he probably saw Falcon with my sister and did nothing to help her. Much as that lot today just ignored Chelsea. I felt sorry for her.'

'You are a good person, Freya Addison.'

Freya shrugged off the compliment. 'I'm not sure about that but I do know Chelsea needs rescuing. She believes Falcon's hype in much the same way that my sister did, and we know how that ended.'

She went on to tell Greg how she'd befriended the girl. Greg smiled, sighed and briefly covered her hand with his own when she ran out of words.

'I understand why you did it and I dare say you were incensed when you compared Chelsea's circumstances to your sister's. Even so, don't get involved, is my advice. She'll listen to you all the time Falcon's ignoring her, which he does with all his women from time to time, by the way. I guess it makes him feel important.'

Freya tutted. 'What a man!'

'The moment Falcon gives Chelsea the attention she craves, which he will, she'll forget what you've said and worse, most likely tell Falcon that you've interfered. And that, trust me, will not go down well. The hired help is supposed to be deaf and dumb, seen but not heard.'

'Yeah, I know.' Freya stared at the deck beneath her feet. 'So, what do we do now? How do we get the proof we need to show Falcon's involvement with the crypto scam? I'd have thought that the best way would be to follow the money.' She giggled. 'Isn't that what they always say in films? But how?' She spread her hands. 'We don't know exactly how much disappeared or where to start looking, unless your tame detective told you stuff that I don't know about.' She glanced up at Greg, whose expression had turned smug. 'He did, didn't he?'

'Well, as it happens, we just might get a handle on that soon. I did wonder why we were going to Ibiza instead of heading straight for Croatia. Falcon has a habit of changing his mind, just because he can, but Ibiza has always been the first stop.'

'To party with Chelsea on his arm and show the clubbing world what a successful creep he is,' Freya said with feeling. 'That's not it, is it? Come on, Greg. We don't have long. Don't hold out on me.'

'Well, it just so happens that a cryptic message came through for him earlier.'

'How? There's no phone signal out here.' She glanced up at the wheelhouse. 'Something to do with all those gizmos up there, I take it.'

'Right. We have a telecommunication system that helps maintain reliable connectivity offshore. I can access data and voice communications when out of range of the coast. Fortunately for us, any messages for the boss have to come through the bridge.'

'And?' Freya wriggled impatiently on her seat. 'What did this particular one have to say?'

'It was from a name I recognise. One Robert Irvine.'

Freya shrugged. 'Who is?'

'An investment banker.'

She nodded as the penny dropped. 'Ah, I see.'

'I happen to know because my friendly detective told me that he and Falcon are as thick as the thieves they undoubtedly are. And, here's the clincher: the message was to confirm Irvine's arrival on Ibiza.'

'Wow! We're onto something.'

'Not really. Don't get your hopes up. There could be a hundred and one legitimate reasons for their meeting and we'll never know the truth unless we get creative.'

'What do you mean?'

Greg smiled. 'I have absolutely no idea. I suppose it all depends where the meeting takes place. If it's in a hotel room then we don't have a hope in hell of listening in without getting caught. If it's in a crowded place, same thing applies. We'll be noticed and recognised.'

'Even so, there has to be a way.' Freya fell momentarily silent. 'Chelsea mentioned something about a casino on Ibiza. Is there one?'

'Of course.'

'Then I'm betting that's where they'll talk. Think

about it, Greg: it's the ideal situation. Everyone there gets caught up with the gambling and concentrates on that, not on their surroundings. And Chelsea will be the ideal window-dressing. If anyone takes any notice of Falcon and Bairstow, they will assume they're there to show off their dates, not for any sinister reasons.'

'Even so, you can't ask Chelsea to spy for you. You can't trust her. She won't have given up on winning over her rich lover.'

'Nope, and I won't ask her. But I'll bet you a fiver that Falcon upsets her again, which will be my cue to step in and offer her a shoulder.'

'Nothing to stop us going to the casino,' Greg said, making no comment about her admittedly rather thin plan. 'We'll have to anchor off and go in by tender but Alex can look after that side of things. How do you fancy a night out, Ms Addison?'

A very good question, Freya thought but did not say. She was almost convinced that his offer was business only. How would she feel if he expected more from her? It was hard to know. He was a formidable guy who wouldn't lack for female company if that was all he wanted. Besides, what choice did she have?

'How will that go down with our feisty cook?' she contented herself by asking.

'I'm not inviting her.'

'Blimey, you're brave.'

Greg smiled. 'Keep telling yourself that,' he said, standing in order to return to his duties. 'Catch you later. Be careful.'

'Aye, aye, skipper,' she replied, offering him a mock salute.

'A little respect at last,' he replied, laughing as he took the stairs to the crew corridor two at a time.

9

Freya watched Greg leave but remained where she was for a while, enjoying the feel of the sea breeze on the side of her face. She had become a little more accustomed to the motion of the boat and could move around it more easily now. Even so, she doubted whether she would ever become a fan of cruising any time soon.

Members of the crew were slowly emerging from their siestas and working away at keeping the salt from the guardrails, ensuring that their efforts couldn't be seen from the sundeck, which most of the guests still occupied. Chelsea and Barb were there but Falcon and Bairstow were conspicuous by their absence.

Seizing the opportunity, Freya made her way up to the sundeck. The conversation being conducted between Parker and Pyke abruptly halted. Pyke's wife had her nose buried in a book and didn't glance up. Maureen Parker looked groggy, her face was a patchy red, presumably because she hadn't applied sufficient sun block. She had trouble focusing on Freya and looked away again, covering her mouth with her hand. Freya recognised a poor sailor who hadn't helped herself by drinking so much with her lunch. Maureen appeared to have just woken and glanced frequently at Chelsea with hostility in her eyes, probably wondering where Falcon was and if she could expect a resumption of his attentions any time soon. Barb sat on a sunbed, filing her nails and looking bored.

Chelsea, either unaware of or indifferent to Maureen's hostility, looked considerably better than when Freya had last seen her. She was the only person who bothered to acknowledge Freya's presence with a little wave and a friendly smile. It was true what Greg had said, it seemed. Even the hangers-on dismissed the presence of paid employees as irrelevant. If that was how things worked on all privately owned yachts, then Freya had no desire to pursue a career in that sphere. Not that she'd ever intended to. She reminded herself that she was here for one reason and one reason only. Glancing at Chelsea, so young, so vulnerable, so trusting, increased her determination to keep her safe from Falcon's ubiquitous clutches.

'Would anyone care for refreshment?' she asked in a neutral voice.

'Some tea would be nice,' Mrs Pyke replied, briefly removing her nose from her book and staring straight through Freya.

'Fuck tea,' her husband said. 'A G&T would hit the spot.'

'Same goes for me,' Parker said.

'Tea for me. Please,' Barb added belatedly.

'Where's our host?' Maureen demanded to know.

'Resting,' Chelsea said sweetly. 'He's just expended a lot of energy, the poor baby,' she added with a giggle.

'I'll just bet his has!' Pyke's raucous chuckle drew a frown from Maureen and more giggling from Chelsea. Freya sent her a brief nod of approval. She was playing it exactly right, displaying a little class and a lot of restraint in a tacky situation.

And clearly enjoying herself.

Freya went off to organise the required drinks and returned quickly with a loaded tray. Tea for Mrs Pyke, Chelsea and Barb. G&Ts for the other three. Freya placed dishes of crisps and salted nuts on the side tables and asked politely if she could get anyone anything else.

'Yeah, darling,' Falcon's voice coming from behind her said, giving her the creeps. 'Gin for me an' all.'

'Me as well,' Bairstow said.

Freya sensed an enhanced tension now that Falcon had returned. Parker and Pyke instinctively moved a little closer, like kids in a school playground sticking together when confronted by the class bully.

'You two ought to get a fucking room,' Falcon said in a joking tone with underlying menace, nodding at Parker and Pyke. 'You've been standing there with your heads together like thwarted lovers for the past two hours.'

The two men drew apart. Neither looked at Falcon. Pyke scowled. A deep flush made its way up Parker's cheeks, but he swallowed and refrained from comment. Freya sensed a simmering resentment slowly coming to the boil and wondered if Falcon had done the right thing in deliberately antagonising a man who could do him so much harm. Not only had he come on to his wife, but he'd also publicly ridiculed him. Parker might have a lot to lose financially if he dissed Falcon, but Freya could see that his pride had taken a severe denting and imagined that the desire to get his revenge must be compelling. She wondered if there was any way to get him alone and sound him out. Would it be worth taking the risk even if there was? If she showed her hand for no good reason, it would give Parker an opportunity to sell her out to Falcon and regain the man's trust.

What to do?

Freya organised drinks for Falcon and Bairstow, sensing Falcon's gaze frequently focused upon her. His attitude was remote, far removed from the friendliness he'd displaced when he'd first come aboard and they'd briefly been alone. Had Chelsea told him about their chat, or had he realised she was Polly's sister? Freya felt nervous, unsure of herself, but tried not to allow her uncertainty to show.

She glanced around the deck, taking in its sumptuous fittings, and then looked at the flushed faces of the people populating it. None of them appeared to be enjoying themselves. They were like actors in a play, working up to the grand finale without knowing what it entailed, she thought.

Falcon had plonked himself down on the same bed as Chelsea, suggestively running his hand up and down her thigh. How Chelsea tolerated it without smacking his hand away, Freya was at a loss to know. Maureen watched them, her eyes narrowing with, presumably, jealousy. Parker watched his wife

watching Falcon and his frown grew increasingly for-
bidding.

Freya wanted to run off and never see any of them
again. She hated Falcon, his ostentatious display of
wealth and obvious controlling tendencies. She hated
even more the manner in which he used people and
then discarded them like old shoes when they'd
served their purpose or if, as in Polly's case, they became loose cannons. It was Falcon's fault that Polly
had become an addict, Freya reminded herself, suppressing a shudder of revulsion when she glanced at
the man. He'd fed her cocaine, well aware how addictive it could be, but had done nothing to help her
overcome her cravings. Instead, he'd set her to work
on her back.

Oh yes, she despised the man and would do whatever it took to prevent him from harming Chelsea, or
anyone else, no matter what the risk to herself. Hopefully, she and Greg would find a way to bring him
down, remote though the possibility seemed.

Chelsea remained impassive as Falcon continued
to maul her in front of the others. Freya wondered if
Chelsea's disinterest would make Falcon suspicious,
or more determined to keep her in her place. The
promise of a modelling career ought to have made
Chelsea eager and attentive: putty in his hands. Just as

Polly had fallen for his hype. At least he didn't appear to have introduced her to drugs yet, which was something. However, the chances were that if she did try to break ranks then Falcon would have the last word.

Drugs or something worse.

She wondered if Polly had seen through him, which would account for her having been forced to whore for him, simply because she'd stopped falling for his empty promises. Now that she'd seen Falcon in action for herself, that vague possibility seemed more plausible. At the beginning, Polly had said she could control her drug usage; it was recreational and helped to curb her hunger. Freya hadn't believed it.

Now she was prepared to give her sister the benefit of the doubt.

Ensuring that everyone had everything they needed, Freya withdrew and made her way to the galley to check that the dinner preparations were on course. She didn't relish the idea of seeing Sandy, who appeared to hold her responsible for Greg's lack of personal interest in her, but wasn't about to shirk her duties because she was afraid of a woman wielding a knife.

Much to her astonishment, Sandy greeted her with a sunny smile. There was a first time for everything.

'Hey,' she said. 'How's the love fest going?'

'Er... Lots of tension.'

'Well, that's Falcon for you. He's never happier than when he's stirring things up. Makes him feel powerful, I guess.'

'You don't like him?'

Sandy shrugged. 'Not much but I do admire the way that he's dragged himself up by the bootstraps and made money which, as we all know, makes the world go round.'

'But he exploits people, don't you think?'

Another shrug. 'Chelsea, you mean? Well, she's an adult so it's up to her. Anyway, she won't last. They never do. I've seen the way he operates. Once he has them, he loses interest. Promises the earth, shows them the highlife for a while, parades them in front of his mates and then moves on. He uses women as status symbols but if they're daft enough to let it happen then they only have themselves to blame.'

Freya wanted to keep Sandy talking. She'd clearly seen a lot and might be able to help her. The problem was, Freya didn't trust her and was pretty sure that this blatant attempt at friendship was a ploy. The moment she said anything indiscreet, Sandy would pounce all over it and could report back to Falcon, so she wasn't about to fall for that one. Of greater concern was the reasons for Sandy's change of tack. She could see the strain in Sandy's smile and the effort it was taking her to behave in a friendly manner. Had Freya somehow roused Sandy's suspicions about her reasons for taking the hostess position? Was Sandy on a fishing expedition? Had she overheard part of her conversations with Greg? Had she met Polly and noticed a resemblance between the sisters?

Questions without answers tumbled through Freya's mind in a swirl of indecisiveness.

'Yeah, I guess you're right,' Freya agreed. 'Anyway, it's none of our business why girls young enough to be his daughter take up with the boss.'

'It's entertaining though.' Sandy couldn't completely hide her disappointment when Freya failed to ask questions. 'Are you a party animal? Ibiza offers all sorts of opportunities if you wanna let your hair down.'

Freya smiled and waved the suggestion aside. 'Too old for all that.'

'You're never too old. Me, I love a bit of club music.'

'Do we get an opportunity to go ashore?'

'Sure. They won't dine onboard. Well, he never has in the past. He likes to book high-end restaurants and be seen.' Sandy rolled her eyes. 'Talking of which,

I'd best get back to it. Dinner's on course, if that's what you came to ask.'

'Okay, great.'

Freya heard voices and the sound of feet on steps as the occupants of the sundeck made their way back to their cabins. There was two hours before drinks and then dinner. Presumably, they would all sleep off the excesses of the day, ready to start again and Freya would have the main body of the boat to herself for a while.

She waited until all was quiet and then went up to the sundeck to clear up. She stopped abruptly when she discovered Daisy Pyke still on her sunbed, discarded book laying open and facedown at her side, sunglasses covering her eyes. Freya thought at first that she must be asleep but as Freya approached, she lifted her glasses, her eyes wide open.

'Sorry if I disturbed you,' Freya said. 'I thought everyone had gone. I'll come back.'

'No, stay.' Daisy's voice was low, conspiratorial. 'I was hoping to catch you alone. Sit down.'

Freya perched on the edge of the adjoining sunbed. 'Is there something I can help you with, Mrs Pyke?'

She squinted up at the sun and replaced her glasses over her eyes. 'Call me Daisy.'

'Okay, Daisy. Is there a problem?'

'I know who you are,' she said in an undertone.

Freya frowned whilst her stomach performed Olympic-standard somersaults. 'Sorry, I'm not with you.'

'I tried to help your sister.'

Freya gasped, unable to temper her surprise. Pretending that she no longer understood wasn't an option. She had to know what Daisy knew and, more to the point, why she'd deliberately caught her alone. 'You knew Polly?' she asked.

'I've watched all his women come and go over the years. He treats them like trophies. They never last for long though. He'll never leave his wife and when they start making demands, he gives them the heave-ho.'

Freya nodded, thinking it wasn't the first time that day she'd heard something similar said.

'But Polly... well, she was different. He was smitten. I've never seen anything like it before. Falcon likes to play the field but never gets emotionally involved with his conquests. Like I say, it's a game to him and he's committed to his marriage, even if he has a funny way of showing it.' Daisy drew in a deep breath, watching a gull as it swept in low over the boat and then soared back into the sky. 'Anyway, nothing was too good for her. Nothing was too much trouble. What Polly wanted, Polly got.'

'Including drugs,' Freya said, more forcibly than had been her intention.

Daisy nodded. 'He never touches them himself but they're available. Polly had an addictive personality, that much was obvious to anyone with eyes in their head, but Falcon didn't try to stop her.' She paused. 'Until she was too far gone, by which point she *couldn't* stop.'

'And then he made her whore for him,' Freya said, an aggressive edge to her voice. 'Presumably because she'd disappointed him.'

'I guess so.' Daisy touched her hand. 'I'm sorry.'

Freya thought it odd that two women on the yacht had offered the hand of friendship in one day. Sandy's motives she suspected, but Daisy... well, if she'd recognised her and not told Falcon who she was, then presumably she had her reasons. For her part, Freya both liked and trusted the lady even if it was clear that she wanted something from Freya. Perhaps they could help one another.

'How did you know me?' she asked.

'I used to chat with Polly and she spoke of her sister a lot. She knew you didn't approve of her relationship with Falcon but was determined to prove you wrong and make you proud of her.' Daisy paused to examine Freya's face. 'You look like her and Freya's not a common name so...' She spread her hands and let her words trail off.

'You haven't told him.'

It wasn't a question and Daisy simply nodded. 'No, but I've seen the way he looks at you. He obviously thinks he knows you. It's only a matter of time before he connects the dots.'

'Why have you warned me?'

'Because I think we can help one another.'

Freya allowed a significant pause. 'Go on,' she said. 'I'm listening.'

'How much do you know about the mess that Julien has gotten my husband and Mike Parker into?'

'Assume I know nothing.'

'Very well.' Daisy cleared her throat. 'Long story short, they fronted a crypto fund for Julien. It went belly up and the majority of the funds disappeared just before the regulators shut it down. My husband and Mike are being investigated and the chances are they'll serve jail time unless they can point to where the funds have been stashed.'

'Which, presumably, Falcon has.'

'You can bet your life on it, even though he says not.'

Freya frowned. 'If he took a back seat, how was he able to move them without anyone knowing?'

Daisy shrugged. 'I guess there are ways.'

'I'm sure there are.'

'Jason advised against going into the crypto game but Julien saw others making fortunes and wanted a part of it. Mike sided with Julien. Not that it would have made any difference if he'd taken Jason's view. Julien wanted in and he'd find a way. My husband and Mike were beholden to him and had no choice but to do as he asked unless they wanted to be cut loose.'

'Why didn't they just walk away then if they knew they were being drawn into dodgy dealings?'

'That ship had well and truly sailed. All Julien's business deals flirt with the letter of the law and Jason and Mike made them all happen, so they were as much to blame. Besides, Julien doesn't have a good reputation in the business world. He's known for cutting corners or getting others to cut them for him.'

'Your husband and Mike Parker.'

Daisy nodded. 'No one would have taken him on. But now, the shit is about to hit the fan, hence our being forced into this cruise from hell.'

'I did notice the tension.'

'And saw Julien's behaviour at lunch.' Daisy wrinkled her nose. 'I saw you watching him. And Maureen was too stupid to realise that she was being used as a pawn in Julien's vile games. He needs an edge if Mike and Jason find the strength to resist him. Mike adores Maureen.'

'Which makes Falcon's strategy high risk, don't you think? I mean, if Parker already has his doubts about keeping Falcon's name out of things when the investigation gets under way, threatening to seduce the wife he adores is hardly likely to make him toe the line. Quite the reverse, I should have thought. Especially since Falcon suspects that he'll be unwilling to act as his fall guy.'

'I agree but Mike has always been under Julien's thumb.' She lifted her sunglasses onto the top of her head and Freya could see the worry etched into her features. 'Julien never wastes an opportunity to remind him that he lifted him up and could as easily crush him again.'

'Has Falcon tried it on with you?' Freya asked. 'You are more sophisticated than Mrs Parker. Younger. More his type.'

Daisy laughed and waved the compliment aside. 'I'd knee him in the balls if he tried it and I suspect he knows it. Julien doesn't take rejection well so never targets an individual who's unlikely to be receptive.'

'You're not convinced that Mike will agree to give evidence against him.'

'It's not that simple.' Daisy waggled a hand from side to side. 'If he and Jason do so then a good defence barrister will tear them to shreds. On paper, the crypto fund was theirs and Julien's name doesn't appear anywhere. The buck stops with them, in other words.'

'I get that but I'm sorry, I don't see how I can help you.'

'You want revenge for your sister. I assume that's why you're here. You must have some sort of plan.'

'I really don't.' Greg did but Freya wasn't about to bring his name into things without his prior consent. She was as sure as she could be that Daisy was on the level but she really needed to think their conversation through and talk to Greg before she did anything about it. 'Even so, I hear what you say. Let me think about it and I'll get back to you.'

'Don't take too long. We'll be in Ibiza tomorrow.'

'What difference does that make?'

Daisy shook her head. 'I don't know. All I can tell you is that some sort of meeting is planned and it's vital.'

Freya knew it was but again, it wasn't her secret to impart. 'Can't you ask your husband?'

'He won't tell me. He doesn't want me implicated and so says that the less I know, the better.'

The boat swayed as Greg made a correction to the course. 'All right. I think we both want to bring Falcon down and the only way we can do that is to find the missing funds. I'll get back to you before we reach Ibiza if I find anything out but don't hold your breath.'

'Thanks.' Daisy collected up her possessions and stood. 'I'd best get back to our cabin before Jason comes looking for me.' She touched Freya's shoulder. 'Stay strong.'

10

Julien smiled at his guests as they reassembled on the deck for sundowners. The new hostess poured their drinks and handed round plates of canapes, moving with a lithe grace that captured his attention. There was just something about her that intrigued him, and which seemed familiar. The hell if he could think what it was. Attractive women came on to him all the time, and yet this one didn't show any personal interest in him whatsoever.

He couldn't complain about that, he reasoned. She had performed her duties faultlessly but managed to make him feel inadequate, which infuriated him. And now Chelsea had gone all moody on him, too. What was it about this fucking cruise that had screwed everyone up? No good deed goes unpunished, Julien decided, trying not to scowl as he watched Chelsea sipping at her drink and studiously ignoring him. She'd lost some of her sparkle and found a quiet sort of dignity, almost as though she was doing *him* a favour by being seen with him. What the fuck was that all about?

Maureen was the only one still hanging on his every word and never wasting an opportunity to touch him. She laughed a little too loud and a little too long if he cracked a joke and was seriously starting to get on Julien's wick. But needs must. She'd served a purpose insofar as Julien's feigned interest in her would be screwing with Mike's head.

'Come on, darlin',' Julien said, snapping his fingers at Freya. 'Another bottle of Krug. We're dying of thirst here.'

A guy he'd done business with along the way, an aristocrat with class, had once told Julien that it wasn't the done thing to snap one's fingers at the hired help, much as he'd told Chelsea the same thing at lunch. The fuck to that! The guy might ooze class, but he didn't have a pot to piss in and was in serious debt to the type of people it wasn't wise to keep waiting, hence the need to ask Julien for a favour. Now Julien owned the guy and could call in his loan at any time of his choosing. He wouldn't be able to pay, Julien had known that when making the loan, but he'd forked out anyway simply because the guy's connections could be useful to him.

That was one of the reasons why he'd invited – make that ordered – the Honourable Adrian Tucker-Smythe to meet them in Ibiza. His poodle hadn't been happy but had no choice but to do as he was told. He'd softened the blow by sending him club class tickets and reservations in a five-star hotel.

Good doggy!

The old bill still hesitated to feel the collars of the upper classes, which was one of the reasons why Julien kept Tucker-Smythe in funds that fed his gambling addiction, which got him even deeper in debt. Julien despised weaknesses in either sex but didn't hesitate to exploit them to further his own ends.

He sensed more than one disapproving glance settling upon him when he snapped his fingers and resented his guests' judgement. He paid a fucking fortune in wages to keep this tub afloat and if he wanted to snap his fingers then he damned well would. Freya glanced at him, her expression impassive, somehow managing to make him feel uncouth as she deftly opened a new bottle and topped up glasses.

'We'll be at Ibiza tomorrow,' he told everyone,

even though they were well aware of that fact. Some were looking forward to it considerably more than others. It would be crunch time for Mike and Jason; their final chance to make up their minds whose side they were actually on and also time for Julien to apply the pressure. Adrian could earn his corn by helping him in that respect.

Freya interrupted Julien's internal dialogue by telling him in a quiet aside that dinner was ready to be served.

'Come on, ladies and gentlemen,' he said, ushering his sheep towards the gangway. 'Time to fill our bellies.'

The boat lurched as it hit a swell. Julien reached out to steady Chelsea and kept hold of her hand.

'Careful, darlin'. Can't have you turning one of those shapely ankles, can we now.'

She didn't show any sign that she'd even heard him, increasing Julien's slight concerns about her attitude. What the hell was wrong with everyone? Why did he feel that his guests were looking down at him? Sneering. Fuck it, he could buy and sell the whole damned lot of them without breaking a sweat. And he'd gotten himself in that position through the application of his wits and admittedly by cutting a few corners. But that's what savvy businessmen the world over did every day. No one remembers who came second.

He thought of his tortured childhood and the manner in which his father had ruled literally with a rod of iron, his caustic comments cutting deeper than the belt that he regularly took to his only son. He could still hear his father taunting him, telling him to get his head out of the clouds because he'd never amount to anything.

The sneer was on the other side of his father's face now – or would have been if he was still breathing. He'd met with an unfortunate accident not long after Julien had made his first million and turned up outside the council house he'd been born and brought up in driving a brand new Porsche.

Happy days.

Julien glanced up at the wheelhouse and noticed Greg Larson standing on the bridge. He didn't acknowledge him, even though their gazes briefly clashed. Julien wasn't in the habit of acknowledging employees for doing the jobs they were paid to do. All that employee of the month bullshit that companies went in for nowadays was meaningless. He'd hired Larson because he had a solid reputation as a skipper and because his conscience, such as it was, occasionally bothered him when he thought about Larson's father's unfortunate end. Not that it had been Julien's fault. Business was business and there was no room for sentiment, weaknesses, or crises of conscience, as Mike and Jason would soon discover if they tried to drop him in it.

* * *

Greg hadn't seen Freya since their discussion on the aft deck earlier. He'd watched her though as dinner was served on the main deck and a forced sense of jollity prevailed. The tension was palpable, but Falcon ignored it. He probably enjoyed being its cause as he played the part of the bountiful host with aplomb. Maureen Parker continued to bat her sparse lashes at him, and Falcon gave her just enough attention to annoy her husband and to keep the silly woman lusting after him. Greg was appalled by behaviour that implied desperation but also heartened by it. Desperate men made mistakes.

'He doesn't know which way they'll jump or how to keep them on the leash,' Greg muttered aloud. But how to make use of that information?

'Dinner's ready,' said Alex, coming up behind him. 'Get yourself down there before those greedy deck-hands scoff the lot. It's my watch.'

'Thanks, buddy.'

Greg entered the crew mess. There was no hope of seeing Freya because she would still be serving Falcon and his guests. He nodded to those present and helped himself to a generous portion of a spicy chicken dish, grabbed a bottle of water and sat at the end of the mess table to consume his meal.

'How long until we get to party island, skipper?' someone asked.

'Should drop anchor about nine in the morning.'

'Just in time to see the clubs turn out.'

'They have morning after clubs now,' Gloria said.

'Always useful,' Greg remarked drolly.

'That's not what they're called or what they're for. I think they're places where you can go to chill, watch the sun come up and stuff.'

'What, people who party all night want to carry on?' someone asked.

'You're past your prime, old man.'

'If having the stamina for one long party qualifies as young and hip then I'm with you, mate,' Greg said, nodding towards the engineer who'd spoken. 'You can have too much of a good thing.'

'Who can?' Sandy asked, walking into the crew mess still in her whites and wiping her hands on a cloth hanging from her back pocket.

'Greg's past it,' the deckhand told her.

Sandy sent Greg a playful smile. 'Tell me something I don't know,' she said.

Greg was a little perplexed by her laidback attitude, especially when she turned away from Greg and fell into conversation with some of the others. Sandy was taciturn at the best of times. This was a side of her he'd never seen before and it bothered him. She hadn't given up on him, he sensed, but had changed tack and was out to make trouble.

'I'd best go and help Freya,' Gloria said, wiping her mouth with her napkin and standing. 'They ought to have finished stuffing their faces by now.'

Freya came through the door minutes before Greg finished his meal.

'They're back on the sundeck having drinks,' she said, flopping into the nearest chair and letting out a long breath. 'Gloria's looking after them.'

'Food's still hot,' Sandy astonished Greg by saying in a friendly manner. It was the first time he'd ever heard Sandy address Freya with anything other than veiled hostility.

'Thanks.'

Freya got up and helped herself to a modest serving of the spicy chicken. Everyone else had returned to their duties and it was just the three of them left in the mess.

'How's it going out there?' Sandy asked.

'A lot of tension,' Freya replied. 'I don't think any-one's enjoying it much. Seems a shame. I mean, all this luxury and no one appreciates it.'

'The ways of the indolent rich will always be a mystery to me,' Sandy replied.

Greg was glad when a couple of deckhands came in, having been relieved by those who'd just eaten. He hadn't wanted to leave Freya alone with Sandy but she couldn't do much harm, verbally or otherwise, if they had company.

'No rest for the wicked,' he said, getting up and leaving the mess.

He retired to the wheelhouse, wondering how soon he'd be able to have another chat with Freya, guessing that she wouldn't be free until Falcon called it a night. And that wouldn't happen until the early hours, he knew. He took the opportunity to get his head down for an hour, aware that he'd have to take a big chunk of the night watch.

He woke and took over at the helm just as the lights were extinguished on the aft deck. It was only just past midnight. Clearly the party had broken up early. That wasn't usual, Falcon liked to party late and hard, but if there was tension in the air, perhaps he'd decided to quit early. Besides, he was presumably thinking ahead to his meeting with the investment banker tomorrow.

'Penny for them.'

Standing on the wheelhouse bridge, Greg turned to smile at Freya. He hadn't heard her approach.

'My thoughts aren't worth that much,' he told her.

She stared up at the crystal-clear sky, the constellations putting on a show for their exclusive benefit.

'It's lovely,' she said. 'I wish I knew which was which though. I'm a bit ignorant in that respect. Anything other than the plough defeats me.'

'I'll give you a potted lesson some time but right now, I guess we have more pressing matters to discuss.' He kept his voice low, aware that not everyone would be asleep and that voices carried over water. Uncomfortably conscious of the fact that there was one member of the crew who might make it her business to eavesdrop. 'Has it been a difficult day?'

'It's been an interesting one.' She went on to tell him about Daisy Pyke's revelations. 'My instinct is to trust her,' she finished by saying. 'Do you think that we can?'

'I'd say so. She has a lot to lose if Falcon forces her husband to take the rap.'

'Should I be worried that she knows I'm Polly's sister? She says she recognised me because we look so alike. I never saw it myself. Polly was way prettier but still, Daisy thinks it can only be a matter of time before Falcon realises who I am.'

'He's got bigger concerns. Everything's building up for Ibiza. I'm absolutely sure the matter will be thrashed out there. We just need to decide what to do about it. Now that we know Daisy's on our side, that ought to make it easier.'

'She wouldn't be included in any business discussions, I imagine, and anything her husband tells her will be hearsay. Besides, she says he seldom tells her anything because he wants to protect her.'

He nodded. 'There must be a way to make use of her. I need to think about it.'

'There's more to think about.' She paused to briefly chew her lower lip. 'It's Sandy. She's had a personality transplant and seems to want to be my bestie, but I absolutely don't trust her. The problem is, I don't know what her game is.'

'Yeah, I noticed that she's changed her attitude.'

'But still wants to get her hands on your body and thinks I'm a threat to her ambitions.'

Greg smiled down at her. 'Would you like to be?'

She punched his arm. 'Behave!'

Greg laughed. 'Can't blame a guy for trying.'

'Seriously though, I think it would be a mistake to underestimate her. I wouldn't put it past her to run to Falcon if she overhears anything to my disadvantage. She has a lot of spite and suppressed anger building up inside her.'

'We'll be careful.'

'And it's always possible that she'll see the resemblance between me and Polly too.' Freya's brow creased. 'I know Polly came on this yacht when she and Falcon first got together. She went on and on about the luxury and about how Falcon often used it to impress business associates. It's one of the reasons why I took this job when I saw it advertised. It seemed like a golden opportunity.'

'If she'd made that connection then she'd have said something by now. Try not to worry.'

'Okay, I won't worry,' She replied, rolling her eyes.

Greg smiled. 'I know it isn't that easy but trust me, if she knew who you are then she wouldn't have kept it to herself. Besides, there's absolutely nothing she can do to make me want her. That ship has well and truly sailed, so to speak.'

Freya suppressed a smile. She was absolutely not here to link up with a member of the opposite sex, but it would be far too easy to lean on Greg. They had a common cause *and* she liked him far more than was perhaps wise. Dangerous territory, she knew, but she would never allow the attraction to get in the way of her reason for being on Falcon's floating gin palace.

'Okay, so tomorrow, what will we do to try and catch Falcon out?'

'I'm not sure. Yet.' He paused. 'Do you fancy a trip to the casino?'

'You think that's where the meeting will happen?'

'Probably but frustratingly it's likely to be in a private room. We'll have no access.'

'Who's Adrian Tucker someone or other? Falcon dropped his name several times over dinner. Said he was looking forward to seeing him in Ibiza.'

'The Honourable Adrian Tucker-Smythe.' Greg scowled. 'Bit of a mouthful of a name for a prat of a man. He's been onboard once or twice. A viscount's son who Falcon latched onto because he has a bit of class.'

'Why would he want anything to do with... Ah, let me guess. He's short of cash and Falcon bailed him out.'

'That's about the size of it. Now he's at Falcon's beck and call and absolutely hates it, even though he likes the lifestyle.'

'Thinks he's better than Falcon, is my guess.'

'I wouldn't bet against it. He's a right self-entitled, chinless wonder but he can be useful to Falcon, which is why he bailed him out, I reckon. He has connections.'

'Connections in the banking world, presumably.'

Greg spread his hands. 'Possibly.'

'Connections that might have helped Falcon hide the money he stole from the bitcoin fund?'

Greg shook his head. 'That will have gone through a series of shell companies that he already had set up.'

'Ah, but who set them up for him?'

Greg stared down at her. 'Darling, you're a genius!'

'Well, with all due modesty...'

'I should have thought about it myself. Company names can be bought off the shelf and there are certain banking territories that look upon the regulations as optional. But you have to know your way around and Tucker-Smythe certainly would. I researched his background when he appeared to be joined at the hip with Falcon and discovered that he had been a stockbroker before he got the push for not hitting his targets.'

'This is getting confusing. If this Adrian guy did all that for Falcon in return for having his debts cleared, or whatever, where does the investment banker, who we think Falcon's meeting tomorrow, fit into things?'

'No idea, but I can tell you one thing for sure.' Greg picked up his night goggles and briefly scanned the dark sea. Satisfied that there were no hazards looming and aware that the navigation system would give him advance warning if there were, he returned his attention to Freya, which was absolutely no hardship. 'Falcon won't have relied upon one person to set up his... set up. Robert Irvine, our friendly investment banker, will either have arranged the shell companies or somehow got involved in moving the money. The thing about our not-so-esteemed boss is that he doesn't absolutely trust anyone and so the left hand is never in tune with the right. With good reason, I reckon.'

'All well and good, but unless we can find that money then we'll never manage to prove Falcon's involvement.'

'Don't look so downhearted.' Greg briefly touched her shoulder. 'It's not tracing the money that ought to be our priority, although it would be the icing on the cake. No, what we need is firm evidence of what's said by whom at that meeting tomorrow.'

'You have something in mind, don't you?' She frowned up at him. 'Come on, Larson, give. What're you thinking?'

'If Daisy really wants to keep her husband out of

clink then we're going to need her help.' He paused. 'My detective friend gave me some listening devices. He wanted me to bug Falcon's study here on board but I never did it.'

'Why not?'

'Because it's a bit hit and miss. Not worth the risk.'

'How does it work?'

'Using a microphone that captures the sound, converts it to digital data and then transmits it over a network to a computer. The chip is tiny, a bit like a small disc but it has to be—'

'So, if Daisy dropped one in her husband's pocket, he'd be none the wiser.' Freya bounced on her toes. 'We have to ask her. I'm sure she'd do it.'

'Okay, but don't get too excited. Falcon hasn't survived this long by being careless. Besides, nothing that's recorded on an illegal bug can be used to trap him.'

'Then why did your detective suggest it?'

Greg grinned. 'Why indeed. Speak to Daisy, darling, but be careful what you say to her.'

A slight sound caused them both to turn round. They shared a worried look when they saw Sandy emerge from the shadows and stroll onto the wheelhouse bridge.

'Well, isn't this romantic,' she said. 'Can anyone join you?'

The friendliness had been replaced with sarcasm.

'Know something about constellations, do you?' Freya asked.

'Did you want something?' Greg asked at the same time.

'Just taking the air. Didn't mean to interrupt.'

'Well, don't mind me,' Freya said, sounding tense. 'It's late so I'll wish you both goodnight.'

Greg frowned and she shrugged an apology. She was right. Sandy was his problem, not hers, and he didn't need her to hold his hand while he dealt with it. Of greater concern was Sandy's propensity for lurking in the shadows. He wondered how long she'd been there, how much of their conversation she'd overheard and what it would cost him to persuade her to keep her mouth shut.

'Night, Freya,' Greg said, returning to the wheelhouse and checking the radar. 'Sleep well.'

Freya waved over her shoulder and left him alone with Sandy, who'd followed him back into the wheelhouse.

'Something I can do for you?' he asked, not looking at her.

She responded with a question of her own. 'What's your game?'

Her acerbic tone guaranteed her his full attention. 'Go to bed, Sandy,' he said with an exasperated sigh. 'And just remember that I'm the skipper on this tub. You don't get to question me or to invent your own rules.'

'But miss fancy pants gets a lesson in the constellations.' Her pinched expression and narrowed eyes said much about the extent of her envy. 'Is that how it works?'

'Jealousy is an ugly trait.' Greg let out a long breath as he spoke. If it was just a case of a woman having the hots for him, he'd have simply avoided her until she got the message. But this situation was more complex than that. It was impossible to be completely sure of privacy on any boat, even one as big as *Perseus*, and he needed to make it clear to Sandy that stalking him wouldn't get her what she wanted. Nor was he willing to put up with her snide comments and innuendo. 'There's nothing to see here. Just let it go.'

He went over his conversation with Freya in his head as she stomped away, trying to decide if she could have heard the substance of their discussion. Had they mentioned Polly by name? On balance, he thought most likely not. They had spoken in undertones standing out on the bridge where their voices would have been covered by the sound of the hull cutting a path through the sea and the rumble of the engines.

He withdrew to his cabin to get a few hours' kip when Alex relieved him. In spite of everything, he was a worried man. Not so much for himself; Falcon knew who he was and it made him feel like a philanthropist to employ the son of a man he'd driven to suicide. But Freya? He wondered if she knew what she'd actually taken on and, more to the point, if she would be strong enough to see it through when the going got tough. Falcon didn't fight fair when the playing field was even. If he was backed into a corner, there was no telling what dirty tricks he'd employ to get himself out of it.

Greg shuddered as he punched his pillows into a more comfortable nest and sought sleep that he knew would be a long time coming. As things stood, he and Freya had taken on an uphill struggle, the chances of success minimal. Add a scorned woman who was intent upon interfering to the mix and they were doomed before they'd begun.

The sensible thing to do would be to let it go, but he suspected that Freya didn't do sensible. They both had compelling reasons to bring Falcon down. Neither would find peace of mind if they let him get away with riding roughshod over people's feelings, ruining lives.

'Okay then,' he said, addressing his comment to the cabin's ceiling. 'Bring it on!'

11

Freya hadn't realised that it was gone two in the morning. Damn! The day had gotten away from her. She was exhausted but would have to be up again by six. She slid between the sheets with a sigh, worried about Sandy's unwanted intrusion but not surprised by it. She really was determined to get her claws into Greg and was too thick-skinned to take no for an answer.

God in heaven, it was like being back in the school playground! Random thoughts continued to tumble through her mind, fighting against the pressing need for sleep.

What seemed like ten minutes later, Freya was woken by sunlight streaming through her portlight.

She glanced at the clock and swore. Ten minutes more and her alarm would go off. Not much point in trying to get back to sleep. She threw back the sheet and headed for the shower, standing beneath the luke-warm jets until her body reluctantly came back to life. A headache threatened, brought about by a combination of stress and a lack of sleep. She threw a couple of painkillers into her mouth, washing them down with a swig of water from the bottle beside her bed.

Dressed in a fresh uniform, she tied her hair up and made for the crew mess. No way on earth was she going to avoid Sandy. If the woman wanted a fight then Freya would deliver. Known for her mercurial temper, most of the crew was scared of Sandy and avoided getting in her face. That's what Freya *should* do; she knew that very well. She had other priorities and didn't need any distractions, but she also despised bullying in all its forms and wouldn't put up with it from a disappointed woman.

Fortunately, there was no sign of the yacht's temperamental chef but the sound of pots being crashed about in the galley made her location clear. Greg wasn't there either, but other bleary-eyed crew members put in appearances, speaking little, all intent upon their duties now that they were getting close to Ibiza.

'Land in sight,' one of the deckhands remarked as he helped himself to a fry up.

Freya's stomach turned at the sight and smell of the fried food. She glanced through the portlight and saw the rocky outcrop of an Ibizan pinnacle way in the distance. Freya had never been to the island that boasted transparent turquoise water, hidden coves and beautiful beaches.

She thought it a shame that its reputation for party central disguised the fact that it had so much else to offer. She understood that the authorities had belatedly woken up to the fact that their haven was being wrecked by mindless party goers who had little or no respect for the natural environment. Under different circumstances, she would have made a point of exploring all the areas that hadn't been invaded by hordes intent upon having a good time. She'd heard about the famous hippy markets and would have loved to have a good old browse.

Freya finished her fruit and yoghurt, drained her coffee mug and smiled across the table at Gloria.

'Ready when you are,' she said.

'The fun never ends,' Gloria agreed, standing also.

Freya went into the salon to ensure that coffee had been laid out for the guests. That was the system apparently, until they were ready to breakfast on the aft deck. She was surprised to find Falcon there on his own, drinking coffee and tutting at something he'd just read on his phone.

'Oh, sorry,' Freya said. 'I didn't think anyone would be about yet. Shall I organise breakfast?'

'No need, love. We'll go ashore for it. I've made a reservation at the Gran Hotel.'

'Okay. I'll let Sandy know.'

Hers was not to reason why and so she turned away, preparing herself for Sandy's tirade. She had some sympathy for her on this occasion. It wouldn't have killed Falcon to have told her the night before that they didn't want breakfast, thereby saving Sandy and her helpers from unnecessary work, to say nothing of the unnecessary waste of good food. She wondered too why he'd mentioned a particular hotel. Presumably, it was exclusive, and he felt the need to name-drop, even to the hired help.

Creep!

'How are you enjoying the job?'

Falcon's voice stopped her in her tracks. She reluctantly turned to face him again. Just the thought of his vile hands doing to Polly what he'd done publicly to Chelsea the day before made her skin crawl. She fought the growing desire to knee him in a place where the sun don't shine and instead schooled her features into an impassive expression, forcing a polite smile.

'It's certainly different.'

Falcon frowned. Presumably, she was supposed to wax lyrical about having such a fabulous opportunity. *Dream on, mate.*

'I'm absolutely convinced that we've met before,' he said after a prolonged pause, subjecting her to a critical look.

Freya shook her head. 'I'd remember. Besides, it's unlikely. It's not as if we mix in the same circles.'

He narrowed his eyes, still conflicted. 'Where do you come from, love?'

'South coast. My family moved about. I've been making my own way for years now, taking live-in jobs, so I don't really have any roots.'

'A free spirit, eh.' He chuckled, seeming to imagine that she'd be enthralled by his charm offensive.

'Can I help you with anything?' she asked, swallowing down her revulsion. Getting up close and personal with him hadn't formed any part of her plan and nor would it. Not ever. It was a concern that he seemed determined to impress her and she wasn't sure how to handle the situation.

'We'll have to have a drink onshore while we're

here, just you and me. You must have time off. I'll show you around.'

It wasn't a request and Freya didn't know how to respond. She could hardly turn him down flat. He'd most likely look upon rejection as a challenge. His considerable wealth ensured that it didn't happen to him often. That being the case, perhaps it would be best to play along. What other choice did she have? 'What about your guests?' she asked, realising how lame that sounded.

'You let me worry about them, darlin'.' He undressed her with his eyes, making her skin crawl. 'It's a date then. I'll let you know when.'

Freya said nothing but her mind went into overdrive as she left the salon. She would need to talk to Greg about it. If Falcon was serious about wining and dining her, it might be an opportunity to get something out of him. She could wear one of Greg's listening devices. Or record their conversation on her phone. She brightened considerably. Now that really was an option.

She felt more than a little shell-shocked by this unexpected development. He *would* make the connection to Polly sooner or later and would hardly accept that her taking a job on his yacht was a coincidence.

Her headache had defied the best efforts of the

painkillers. With a sigh, she returned to the galley and imparted the glad tidings to Sandy, who responded with a shrug.

'Their loss,' she said, not even looking round at Freya. 'Will they want lunch?'

'The boss didn't say otherwise,' Freya replied with equal verbal economy.

She left Sandy to her sulking and wondered what she was supposed to do now. She couldn't help Gloria clean the cabins while the guests were still in occupation but couldn't go in search of Greg either. He would have his hands full, she realised, as she stood on the aft deck, watching Ibiza grow larger as he eased the yacht between a cluster of smaller craft, heading for an anchorage in Cala Talamanca, just east of Ibiza Town and adjacent to the marina in the next bay. Gloria had told her that there were beach clubs and restaurants strung along the cala waterfront.

It was already crowded with other boats but a sixty-metre yacht required deeper water and so remained well clear of the shoreline. The sun was doing its thing already and it still wasn't nine o'clock. Freya withdrew beneath the shade of the overhanging deck, watching the marine activity with fascination and temporarily forgetting her other problems. The deck hands were moving up and down, tying bumpers on the guard rails and dropping them over the sides.

'Why are those bumper jobs necessary if we're going to anchor?' she asked Gloria when she came to join her.

'They're called fenders.'

'I still want to know why they're needed.'

'Whizzing round superyachts on jet skis is a bona fide pastime.' Gloria leaned on the guardrail and gave one of the deckhands a little wave. 'Will you look at all those muscles,' she added with an appreciative sigh.

'The fenders,' Freya prompted, smiling. Gloria was irrepressibly cheerful and never seemed to let anything get her down. Her good humour was infectious. She'd worked on Falcon's yacht for a few months, after Polly's time, and probably knew a lot about his modus operandi. Freya was tempted to pick her brains but resisted. She didn't want to drag Gloria into the quagmire and risk her job, or worse.

'Like I say, the yacht is a target for the curious and envious alike. They find all sorts of ways to approach, from jet skis to paddle boards, or even snorkels. The fenders prevent them from crashing into the hull.' She grinned. 'Mostly.'

The engines slowed to a crawl. She heard the sound of footsteps and voices on the deck above her head. The guests had emerged, presumably to see and be seen as Greg anchored the boat. The yacht turned into the wind and came to a halt. The sound of a rattling chain indicated that the anchor was being lowered. The boat moved backwards a little and then came to rest again when the anchor caught. It was unnaturally quiet when the engines were closed down, but not for long.

'Get us ashore, Larson,' Falcon shouted imperiously.

Freya didn't need to look up to imagine Greg's reaction. A deckhand – the one with the muscles that Gloria so admired – rushed past them with a remote control on a long cable in his hand. He winked at Gloria and she blew him a kiss.

'Way to go, Gerry!' she said.

Occupants of the closest boats, including another smaller superyacht, lined the decks to watch Falcon's arrival and the man was clearly lapping up the attention. Gerry pressed his remote and a large door opened upwards on the bathing platform.

'The garage, full of boys' toys,' Gloria explained.

A tender large enough to take all the guests and a crew member emerged smoothly on a hoist and was deposited in the sea with barely a splash. Gerry tied it to a cleat on the bathing platform, climbed on board, lowered the outboards and started them up. Not one but two, Freya noticed. Clearly size mattered in the world of marine one-upmanship.

A light breeze ruffled Freya's hair as she leaned on the guardrail, watching the activity. She made a mental note to apply copious amounts of sunscreen when she went back inside. She wasn't blessed with a natural ability to tan. Instead, she tended to burn an unbecoming shade of red. Polly, by contrast, had only to look at the sun, and she would turn a delicious golden brown. Freya's heart briefly stalled, just as it always did when thoughts of her feisty sister who'd had so much going for her, so much to live for, crept up on her unawares. She chased those recollections away. Now wasn't the time.

Gerry motored to the starboard beam and manoeuvred the tender close alongside. A deckhand caught the rope that Gerry threw and secured the craft to a cleat. The guests were assembled, some looking happier than others, ready to board the tender. No inelegant clambering down onto the bathing platform for them, obviously.

Falcon ushered the ladies aboard, ignoring the deckhand who stood by to provide that service. Chelsea looked up, saw Freya and gave her a little wave. She was dressed in white shorts that showed off her smooth tan and a bikini top. She looked very pretty and impossibly young. Maureen looked unsteady as she boarded the tender. Only the deckhand's hand shooting out to balance her prevented her from tumbling into the water.

'Whoops!' she giggled, looking at Falcon through devoted eyes.

Freya glanced at Mike Parker; he wore sunglasses so it was impossible to interpret his expression, but his stiff body language did all the talking for him.

'There's going to be trouble in paradise,' Gloria said, coming up beside Freya in time to witness the scene. 'He always plays his guests off against one another. God knows what he gets out of it.' She shrugged. 'Makes him feel like the big man, I guess.'

'You don't like him?'

Gloria shrugged. 'He's no better or worse than the majority of new rich. They all like to flaunt it.'

'How many yachts have you worked on?'

'This is my third. There's nothing to choose between them. We're all paid skivvies at the end of the day. But still, at least we get to see some cool places.' She glanced down at the tender, now being smoothly driven away by Gerry. 'And some decent sights.'

'Yeah well, I guess we'd better earn our keep.'

'I hear you.'

Gloria and Freya worked swiftly and efficiently for the rest of the morning, changing bed linen, dusting, polishing and hoovering. Cleaning bathrooms and leaving everything looking pristine. Glamorous work it most decisively was not.

'What do we do with this lot?' she asked when they'd finished, glancing down at a pile of linen and towels.

'Gerry will take it ashore to the laundry service in the marina. I'd best go with him though, just to make sure that he gets it right.'

Freya laughed. 'How hard can it be?'

'Well, you never know.'

'Knock yourself out.'

'Come on,' she said, linking her arm through Freya's. 'We've earned ourselves a decent lunch. Hopefully, old grumpy guts will be ready to feed us now.'

'You don't like Sandy?'

'Do you?' Gloria sent Freya a look of mild surprise. 'She's made an art form out of antagonising just about everyone on board and we all tend to give her a wide berth when she starts crashing about in the galley. She. Works. With. Knives.'

Freya smiled. 'Chefs are too precious about their knives to actually throw them at a person.'

'Perhaps but I'm not taking any chances.'

'Ah, I thought it was just me that she'd taken against.'

'Sorry to disappoint you, darling, but you're not getting the VIP treatment.'

Freya was pleased to learn that she hadn't been singled out for the cold shoulder. 'Why is she so touchy?' she asked.

'Hell if I know. I suppose she's been disappointed at some point but then, haven't we all. I do know that she has her sights set on Greg.' Gloria sighed dramatically. 'Greg made the mistake of letting her come on to him one night when we were ashore, and we'd all had one too many. Now she's probably looking at wedding dresses, even though it's obvious to anyone with eyes in their head that her feelings aren't reciprocated.'

'Perhaps he shouldn't have led her on, in that case.'

'He didn't. I was there. I saw it. As I say, we'd all over-indulged and were getting silly. Playful. Greg doesn't often let go like that and probably regrets it now. Living on a yacht is a bit like living in a goldfish bowl, but you've probably figured that one out already. There's no real privacy but you learn to roll with the punches and not to read anything more into situations than actually exists. It's us and them,' she added, pointing to the upper decks, 'so we need to pull together as a crew, otherwise it all starts to unravel.'

They reached the door to the crew mess and were greeted with enticing aromas.

'At least she's a decent cook,' Freya said, giggling when her stomach rumbled.

'Be careful that she doesn't spit in yours,' Gloria replied in an undertone.

There was no sign of Greg in the mess. The rest of the crew came and went, eating quickly and then dashing off again.

'Cleaning,' Gloria explained in response to Freya's quizzical look. 'Endless cleaning on boats to fight against the erosion caused by salt water. They'll be hard at it for the rest of the day but then tonight, most of us will get to go ashore. Virtually all of us if they don't dine on board.'

Freya knew that Falcon and his guests would be gambling the night away in the casino.

'Right well, that's me off for a few hours,' Gloria said. 'Get your head down, Freya, is my advice. If they do stay on board then we'll be at their beck and call all night.'

'I hear you,' Freya replied, standing and leaving the mess with Gloria. Sandy hadn't shown her face, but Freya knew that she'd been in the galley all along, most likely listening to their conversation.

* * *

Since anchoring the boat in the crowded bay, Greg had busied himself with his logs, made sure that the crew had the cleaning under way and checked in the engine room to ensure that there had been no calamities. It had been a smooth passage and so he hadn't expected any. Apart from the dodgy bilge pump that he'd already been told about, there were no dramas to report.

Tired after a sleepless night, he got his head down for a couple of hours, then had Alex bring him something to eat. He wasn't ready to face Sandy's hostility and couldn't speak to Freya unless they were alone.

Feeling re-energised mid-way through the afternoon, he was thinking about going in search of her. They really did need to firm up their plans for that evening, such as they were. His phone rang when he was halfway down the companionway. It was Falcon, demanding to be picked up. Greg took the tender himself this time, aware that Falcon liked to have his skipper in all his uniformed glory dancing to his tune. Greg didn't care. Let him play his silly games. Hopefully, his days of lording it over others would soon come to an end.

Greg reached the marina, unsurprised to find Falcon's guests all a little the worse for wear, the ladies more so than the men. Falcon himself appeared to be relatively sober, reinforcing Greg's opinion that the meeting he had planned in the casino that night was of vital importance to him.

He'd never seen Falcon seriously pissed, he realised as he motored them all back to the yacht. He could put the booze away, he'd seen him do it, but obviously had a high tolerance level for the devil drink. A control freak who was never completely out of control and knew when it was important to keep a clear head.

Gerry awaited the tender's return on the starboard side deck. He secured the craft and then helped the passengers to board. As Greg had known would be the case, they tottered off to the cabins to sleep off the excesses of the day.

His duties completed for the time being, Greg wondered if he'd be able to run Freya to ground. She saved him the trouble by joining him in the wheelhouse.

'I saw you come back,' she said by way of explanation. 'We need to talk.'

'We do indeed. You go first.'

He'd expected her to express annoyance about Sandy's interference but instead she surprised him by revealing that Falcon wanted to take her on what amounted to a date.

'You can't go!'

'I don't want to, but don't see that I have much choice.'

'He's your boss but that doesn't give him control of your downtime.'

'He might loosen up a bit if he wants to impress me. Let something slip,' she suggested with a marked lack of conviction.

'I'm betting that you and your sister share more than a passing facial resemblance.'

'What do you mean?'

'Habits.' He watched her as she picked up a strand of hair that had escaped her ponytail and twirled it round her forefinger. 'For instance, did Polly do that twirly thing with her hair?'

Freya abruptly dropped hers. 'Lots of people do.'

'And I'm betting you share phrases that you heard growing up without realising it. Perhaps you both tilt your heads when listening to a person. I've noticed that you do it a lot. It's the little things, Freya, that often strike a chord.'

Freya momentarily froze. Could he be right? Falcon seemed to like her but if he even suspected who she was then he wouldn't hesitate to turf her off his boat and all her carefully laid plans would be for nothing. She knew it but wasn't ready to accept it, much less admit defeat.

'Perhaps,' she said, 'but he's too much up himself to notice.'

'Not if he was as stuck on Polly as Daisy suggested.'

'What other options do we have? Even if we risk asking Daisy to drop a listening device into her husband's pocket, that will be no good to us unless we can get close enough to hear what's being said on your receiver.'

'Yeah, I realise that.' He thumped the control console with his fist. 'It's so damned frustrating.'

'If I have a drink with him, I could leave my phone on record.'

Greg could hear the uncertainty in her tone and was himself having none of it. But he also knew better than to tell her outright not to do it. He didn't have that right but was surprised by the extent of his determination to save her from doing something downright stupid.

'Let's see how tonight pans out first,' he said. 'I

know for a fact that they won't be dining onboard. He mentioned it on the tender ride back. I've had someone inform Sandy.'

'Coward!'

Greg laughed. 'I pick my battles.'

'All well and good but why do I get the impression that Sandy's out to make as much trouble as she can for you and for me, just because you don't want to date her?' She spread her hands. 'None of it is my fault. Can she really be so juvenile? I can't help thinking there must be more to it than that.'

'She's always been moody.'

'So Gloria tells me, but still...' Freya's words trailed off but she still looked deeply concerned.

'Forget about Sandy. The majority of us will be able to go ashore tonight, which is a good thing.'

Freya twitched her nose. 'You can bet your life that Sandy will make sure she comes with us and will cling. That will prevent us from stalking Falcon.'

Greg grinned. 'Have a little faith, woman.'

She opened her mouth to respond, making it clear that she wasn't going to let the matter drop.

'I did a little online sleuthing into our friend, The Honourable Adrian Tucker-Smythe while on watch last night.'

'Did you indeed.' She bit her lower lip. 'I should have thought of that. What did you find out?'

'He got the push from his stockbroker employers for not meeting his targets, but that we already knew. He's the youngest of a viscount's three kids but has been disowned because of his gambling habit. There's a lot of pictures of him leaving casinos in the early hours, always with a different woman on his arm. There're whispers of drug abuse too. Seems he was on the brink of bankruptcy until—'

'Until Falcon bailed him out, I'm guessing.'

'Yep, that's the way it looks.'

'How's he keeping his head above water now?'

Greg shrugged. 'Absolutely no idea but I do know that he's staying at The Gran Hotel.'

'Where Falcon had breakfast this morning.' Freya tapped a finger against her lips. 'Can't be a coincidence.'

'Nor can the fact that the casino is based in that hotel.'

'Blimey! That's akin to letting an alcoholic loose in an off-licence, isn't it?'

Greg shrugged. 'One of Falcon's petty little acts of one-upmanship, I guess. Reminding Tucker-Smythe who the boss is.'

'And convenient for tonight, when his services will be presumably in demand.'

'I'm guessing that Tucker-Smythe thinks he's better than the rest of us, simply because he was born into the aristocracy. He won't like having to dance to Falcon's tune. He'll think of him as being *nouveau riche* and will dislike him even more because he's a self-made man.'

Freya nodded. 'You think he might be the weak link in Falcon's inner circle?'

'The possibility occurred to me.'

'I can see why you'd think so, but I'm guessing that Falcon knows the man looks down on him and so keeps him on the payroll. If Tucker-Smythe rats Falcon out then he won't have anything to live on.'

'We're making assumptions. I'm guessing that he's deep in debt to Falcon but there won't be anything on paper and so if we give him an opportunity to wipe that debt out...' Greg rubbed the back of his neck in frustration. 'Never underestimate the determination of a disgraced man. Anyway, let's see how things play out tonight.'

'Okay.' Freya looked dubious, as well she might. 'I guess.'

'Now go off and make yourself beautiful. Shouldn't take you long. Get a few hours' sleep too.

You won't be needed before then. They'll all be sleeping off the excesses of the day. Anyway, you're allowed some downtime.' He winked at her. 'Meet me on the aft deck at eight.'

'What about Daisy? I need to talk to her.'

'You won't get the chance without arousing suspicions. Just leave it to me.'

'Okay, captain.'

She gave him a mock salute and took herself off. He watched her go, thinking she didn't need to know that he'd let himself into Jason Pyke's cabin that afternoon when the boat had been quiet and slipped a device into the pocket of Pyke's dinner jacket.

12

Freya felt peeved because Greg had taken control, and more peeved still because she was glad that he had. She'd been alone in her quest for too long, floundering beneath a burning sense of injustice that had eaten her up inside, making it difficult to form any sort of coherent plan. It felt good to have a like-minded person along for the ride. It didn't hurt that the person in question was so easy on the eye, so naturally authoritative and self-assured.

'Get your mind out of the gutter,' she told herself as she entered her cabin and closed the door behind her. Her headache had waned, but she felt washed out and in no fit state to pit her wits against a master manipulator of Falcon's ilk. How had she ever imagined she would manage it? And more to the point, why had she taken this job with no clear plan in mind? Greg had taken his position for similar reasons, she reminded herself, and had yet to make any progress. That realisation made her feel a little better as she took his advice and slipped between the sheets, this time falling asleep almost immediately.

She woke again over an hour later feeling refreshed, her self-doubts partially eradicated, ready to take the fight to Falcon. He would never be more vulnerable, she reminded herself as she took her second shower of the day, this time washing her hair and psyching herself up for the battle to come.

'This is for you, Polly,' she muttered, as she dried her hair in front of a small mirror and pinned it up in a scruffy bun. She already knew enough about life at sea to realise it was no respecter of hairstyles and if she left it down then she'd look like a scarecrow on steroids by the time she got ashore.

She opened her wardrobe, trying to figure out what to wear. Not that she had much choice. She suspected that the rich posers who frequented the Gran Hotel were likely to dress to impress. All she had with her was a red bodycon tube that finished just above her knees. The neckline was high but it was tight enough to show off her figure. She didn't feel she had to disguise her shape and so pulled the dress over her head and smoothed it down, twisting in both directions in the hope that she hadn't developed any telling rolls of fat since last wearing it.

'This is as good as it gets,' she told her reflection.

She dabbed on a minimal amount of makeup, sighing when she noticed that her nose had burned. She disguised the evidence with concealer. Glancing at the time, she picked up her red sandals with four-inch heels and carried them to the aft deck, along with her matching red bag.

'You can do this,' she muttered aloud, attempting to calm the horde of butterflies that had taken up residence in her stomach. 'You absolutely can!'

The tender wasn't there, presumably because one of the crew had taken it ashore to deposit either the guests or other members of the crew. Where was Greg? Had he taken them himself and lost track of time? She absolutely didn't want to be seen standing around in her figure-hugging dress like a spare part. She glanced around, nervous and unsure of herself. She looked towards the shore but there was no sign of the tender returning. When it did come back, other crew members would want to go ashore along with her and Greg. Done up to the nines, they would all think she was trying to impress the skipper. Not that it mattered if they got the wrong end of the stick. Better that than the likes of Sandy stumbling upon the truth and ratting her out to Falcon.

'Ah, there you are!' Greg's head appeared over the steps to the bathing platform and Freya felt her anxiety abate. He caught sight of her and let out a low, appreciative whistle that did a lot for Freya's confidence. 'You look amazing. Come on.' He held out a hand to help her down the steps.

'The tender... Oh no, not on your life!' She caught sight of a jet ski, it's engine idling, planted her fisted hands and her hips and shook her head decisively.

Greg laughed. 'It's the only way to ensure our privacy.'

'You could have warned me. I'd have worn trousers.'

His gaze lingered upon her legs for longer than seemed necessary. 'That would have been a travesty.'

She again shook her head but couldn't help laughing. 'You're not going to let this go, are you?'

'Not a chance. I figured you'd be up for a challenge.'

'Just don't get me wet.'

'Trust me, I'm a captain.'

Freya rolled her eyes. 'That's what worries me.'

He was wearing a lightweight, pale-blue, linen

suit, a white shirt and striped pink and blue tie. His hair was tossed by the wind as he stood in front of her, smiling at her hesitation. He looked sensational and despite her reservations about their mode of transport, she *did* trust him.

'Come on then, what're we waiting for?'

He laughed as he swung a leg over the contraption's saddle and settled in the seat. All well and good but how was she supposed to get up behind him, elegantly or otherwise in her tight dress? She sensed him struggling to contain a smile, which made up her mind. She walked about all day long in short shorts. This would be no different, she told herself. Besides, he didn't have eyes in the back of her head the last time she checked and there was no one else to observe her struggle.

Defiantly, she hoisted her dress up round her thighs and, still holding her shoes and bag in one hand, slid as elegantly as she could manage onto the seat behind him. The ski swayed as it dipped beneath her weight, and she almost dropped her shoes.

'Hold tight,' he said, glancing over his shoulder at her.

Unsure whether he meant for her to hold onto him, she decided against it and clasped her spare hand around a grab handle instead. He would be far too easy to hold onto, to depend upon, to cede control to and that wasn't about to happen. Feeling exposed, she glanced over her shoulder as Greg moved the ski off slowly, creating a minimum of spray, and groaned when she observed Sandy leaning on the guard rail on an upper deck, watching their departure.

'Great,' she muttered. 'Just great.'

'You say something?' he asked, his words partially carried away on the wind.

'Not a word.' No point them both worrying.

Pushing thoughts of the yacht's vindictive chef to the back of her mind, Freya made sure that she kept her face sheltered behind Greg's broad back in the vain hope of preserving her hair do. He kept moving far less recklessly than she'd seen drivers of other skis doing as they darted around the bay, sending up spray and enough wake to sway the much larger vessels at anchor. Gradually, she began to relax and enjoy the ride, taking in the scenery as the ski rounded a headland and brought them into Ibiza town marina.

Greg manoeuvred the ski alongside a pontoon as smoothly as he seemed to do just about everything else. His proficiency impressed Freya but also made her feel a tad inadequate.

'Okay?' he asked, killing the engine, stepping ashore and attaching the ski securely to a cleat before locking it in place. 'Can't leave anything unlocked around these parts,' he told her, pocketing the key and then holding out a hand, ready to help her span the gap between the bobbing ski and the pontoon, which suddenly looked like a chasm.

She wasn't about to let that deter her though and had no wish to draw unnecessary attention to herself by hesitating. She threw her bag and shoes onto the dock and then took his hand, allowing him to pull her up, which he did with ease. She trusted to luck that her dress would fall back to where it belonged the moment her feet hit the deck, giving it a helping hand the moment Greg released his hold on her.

'It was different, I'll give you that.'

She slipped her feet into her shoes, sighing as she decided that her hair was probably a lost cause and slinging her bag's strap over her left shoulder. Greg's thick locks were decidedly wayward, but he simply ran a hand through them and they fell obediently into place. It was *so* unfair!

'Okay,' she said. 'Lead on.'

'It's a ten-minute walk, give or take.' He glanced down at her footwear. 'But we can get a cab if you'd prefer.'

'No, I'm good. I want to see the sights.'

'Beware what you wish for,' he replied, wincing as

he nodded towards an overweight woman sunbathing on the foredeck of a small boat even though the sun had almost disappeared over the horizon, wearing nothing but a thong.

There was definitely an eclectic mix of people, Freya soon realised. Most were young, on holiday and out for a good time. Glances were sent their way, presumably because they were so well dressed. Casual was the theme of the day, and even that was being taken to extremes. The bars were already filling up and loud music emanated from them all. Flyers were being handed out at all the restaurants and by others attempting to entice all and sundry into the various clubs, most of which didn't open until ten. Even then, the action didn't start until gone midnight, Freya knew.

'I feel old,' Freya said.

Greg laughed. 'Join the club.'

'Just so long as it's not one of those clubs,' she said, shaking her head when someone attempted to push a flyer for yet another hot night spot into her hand. 'Even so, if we feel our age, I wonder how it makes Falcon feel.'

'Invincible, I expect. Money transcends age barriers and just about every other barrier you can think of. The usual rules of engagement don't generally apply to the super rich and that, I hope, will prove to be our employer's downfall.'

'Because he thinks he's untouchable.' Freya nodded in response to her own observation. 'Problem is, he probably is.'

'Don't be so defeatist, darling. He's in trouble, boxed into a corner, and we're never likely to have a better opportunity to bring him down. Least ways, we have to give it our best shot.'

'I know, and I'm not bailing on you if that's what you're thinking. I want to see him brought down to size, or better yet, behind bars, as much as you do. I haven't come this far to give up now. I was just having a wobble.'

Greg smiled that slow smile of his which easily settled her jangling nerves. 'We all have those from time to time. Anyway, we're here.'

Freya glanced up at a massive hotel, built in a curve that allowed all the rooms to have an unimpeded view of the sparkling bay. Lights were coming on the various boats at anchor as darkness fell, as they entered the grounds to the hotel itself.

'It's enormous and full of tourists,' she said, twitching her nose. 'I thought it would be small and select.'

'Parts of it are,' he replied, 'and that's where we're

going.'

They entered the foyer with its vaulted ceiling, marble floor, elaborate flower arrangements and comfortable clusters of sofas. People were everywhere but the five-star status was now more apparent. There was no raucous behaviour, the clientele was better dressed, and the music piped through invisible speakers bore little resemblance to the sounds that they'd heard in the bars they'd passed. Freya was grateful since she'd never been able to get her head round the monotonous throb of club music.

But for all that, it was still a mainstream hotel.

'Have patience,' Greg said, apparently reading her mind. 'Come on, this way.'

He took her hand. The gesture seemed natural and appropriate. After all, they were playing a part. It would have been churlish to object, she decided, thinking that all the same, there was such a thing as feeling *too* natural.

Don't get used to leaning on him.

Greg led the way to a sweeping staircase, beside which was a bank of elevators which he ignored, instead tripping up the stairs, still holding her hand and seemingly oblivious to the appreciative looks sent his way by more than one female.

'Over there,' he said quietly, nodding towards a

cluster of people around a circular bar.

Freya recognised the person he was pointing out immediately. Tall, with a sweep of thinning, blond hair and an aquiline nose, Adrian Tucker-Smythe was holding court, causing the people surrounding him to snort with laughter at whatever he'd just said to them. Freya had never met him but the resemblance to the pictures that Greg had shown her of the disgraced stockbroker were too similar for there to be any doubt about his identity.

'He isn't acting the part of a bankrupt,' Freya remarked. He was dressed impeccably in black tie, as were the people surrounding him.

'Appearances and all that.'

'Who are they all?' she asked.

'Fellow high-rollers, I expect, heading in due course for the casino. Standards have to be maintained, don't you know.'

'He has a weak chin,' she remarked, thinking that he didn't cut an especially formidable figure. 'I wonder why that lot are so taken with him?'

'Doesn't matter what you look like when you come from his sort of family.' There was a note of contempt in Greg's tone. 'Everyone wants an in. If you think we're now a classless society in England, then you're wrong. The upper classes still protect their boundaries almost as fiercely as they did two hundred years ago.'

As though sensing that he was being talked about, Adrian glanced in their direction. He did a double take when he noticed Greg but quickly turned back to his conversation without acknowledging him.

'He recognised you?'

'I know. That was my intention.'

'Why?' she asked, as Greg led her towards a door protected by a red, velvet rope and a man dressed in evening clothes. 'Come on, Larson, give. What aren't you telling me? You clearly have a plan and if it involves me, the least you can do is keep me in the loop.'

'In here.'

The man nodded to Greg and removed the rope so that they could enter the room beyond it. A windowless casino half full of gamblers. Slot machines were popular, lights flashing and coins rattling into trays. Most of the clientele weren't tarted up but Freya was already getting the picture. The serious gambling would take place away from the prying eyes of the hoi polloi beyond yet another guarded set of double doors that Freya noticed at the far end of the room.

Greg found a couch positioned away from the gaming tables and slot machines that gave them a clear view of the doors to the inner sanctum. He turned to speak to her once they'd settled but she could see that half his attention was still on the comings and goings. A trickle of people made their way towards the high-stakes rooms and Greg watched them without making it obvious. No one in the room appeared to be paying them any attention. They were all too intent upon the turn of a card, the spin of a wheel, the machinations of a slot machine, to care about anything else.

'I slipped a listening device into Pyke's pocket,' he admitted.

'Really?' She offered up a cautious smile, wondering why he was being so reticent. 'Well, that's good, isn't it?'

Greg shrugged. 'Possibly.' He tapped his pocket. 'I have a receiver but unless we can get close enough, then the chances of hearing anything are slim. Falcon is likely to take a private room and we won't be able to get near enough to pick up what's said but I figured it was worth a shot.'

'So what's plan B? Come on, I know you have one.'

'Not really.' He paused. 'Well, kinda...'

'Define kinda.'

'Adrian. We need someone on the inside, right?'

Freya nodded. 'Go on.'

'Adrian is itching to get out from under Falcon's

control.'

'You obviously know him, but why would he throw in his lot with you?'

'I'm not sure that he will. I have nothing more than instinct and an understanding of the resentful nature of a man from a top-notch family being exploited to guide me.' Greg offered up a rueful smile. 'Not very much to go on, I'll grant you.'

Freya glanced at the door when a commotion occurred and shuddered. 'It's Falcon's party,' she said, stiffening.

Greg took her hand and led her away from the door, positioning them at the other side of the room where they were unlikely to be seen, even if Falcon looked their way. His glance did frequently flit around, just to make sure that his arrival was being noticed, Freya assumed. He was loud, his tone full of good humour, like he had a point to prove: an image to project.

He slapped the doorman on the shoulder as he gave them access to the high-stakes room. Chelsea, wearing a sparkly, off-the-shoulder number, looked stunning at his side. Maureen seemed frumpy by comparison. Daisy was elegantly understated as she walked beside her husband. She glanced around the room and her gaze briefly rested upon Freya. She raised a brow and smiled but didn't do anything else to draw attention to Freya's presence.

'She saw us,' Freya pointed out. 'We'll soon know if she's on our side.'

'What can she say? We have every right to be here.' Greg patted her hand. 'Besides, Falcon didn't see us and Daisy didn't let on. Try not to worry.'

They watched Falcon putting on a show as the last of his party entered the high-stakes room.

'Now what?' Freya asked.

* * *

Julien made sure that his entrance was seen, sensing envy as heads turned in his direction. Even fingers were pointed, making him feel like the successful entrepreneur that he deserved to be. That he would have been if only the people clinging to his fucking coat-tails did their work right. Not only had they failed him, but they seemed stumped when it came to ideas to extract him from the mire of their making, or at the very least taking the fall for him. If he hadn't taken the precaution of getting a few high-ranking police officers on his side, bribing them to tip him the wink when his activities came under scrutiny, then he knew that his collar would have been felt long since. As it was, the bitcoin fiasco crossed international borders and so he could no longer control a situation that was fast slipping from his grasp.

He ushered his party into the inner sanctum, wishing he could enjoy the experience more. People looked at successful men and thought they'd had it easy. The fuck they know! Every day was a struggle to keep one step ahead. Always there was someone wanting to shaft him. Never before had he felt that his inner circle was on the point of turning on him though and the hell of it was, he didn't have a fucking clue how to keep them in line.

He glanced at Parker, who looked uncomfortable, as though he'd much rather be somewhere else, and Julien felt rage boiling up inside of him. After all he'd done for the man, that he could even consider turning on him defied belief. Julien knew he shouldn't be surprised. Rats leaving the sinking ship and all that.

Except Julien's particular ship was still afloat and would remain so whilst he still had breath in his body to keep things that way. He might be temporarily down, but he was far from out. He hadn't graduated from the school of hard knocks without having a surprise or two waiting in the wings. If Parker and Pyke wanted a fight then Julien was in the mood to take it to them.

Bring it on!

It had been a mistake to come on to Maureen Parker quite so blatantly; Julien realised that now. He'd antagonised Parker as opposed to making him toe the line and now he couldn't get rid of bloody Maureen, who clung to him like a limpet every chance she got. Chelsea couldn't possibly feel threatened by the old crow, but she was clearly still a bit peeved by the way that he'd treated her and was behaving aloofly, like she was the one with money, for fuck's sake! Had the entire world gone mad?

He turned to take a final look at the wannabes in the casino's public room and caught a glimpse of red in the periphery of his vision, but the ubiquitous lady in red disappeared from view before he could get a better look at her. Julien shrugged the feeling of unease away. At least he had nothing to fear from the women in his life. Well, nothing he couldn't handle.

'Ladies, enjoy yourselves,' Julien said, with an expansive wave of one arm. 'My credit is good here, so knock yourselves out.'

'What are you playing, Julien?' Maureen asked, sidling up to him.

'The ladies are playing blackjack,' he said distractedly, pointing to Chelsea, Barb and Daisy already installed at a table. 'Join them.'

Maureen pouted like a teenager and skulked away.

'Tucker-Smythe's just come in,' Eddie said in Julien's ear.

Julien turned to watch the man as he swanned through the door, accepting the deference shown to him by the employees in a manner that suggested true style. It annoyed Julien that he would never be able to emulate Tucker-Smythe's air of natural superiority. He reminded himself that he owned the man but Tucker-Smythe's arrogance continued to irk.

The two men shook hands and Julien could almost sense Tucker-Smythe salivating as he watched the high-stakes games taking place around him.

'A little poker?' Julien suggested, slapping his shoulder, well aware that it was his game of choice.

'Can't afford to lose,' Tucker-Smythe replied in a casual, upper-class drawl.

'I'll stake you.'

'Thanks but no thanks. I don't want to get in any deeper.'

Julien frowned. He'd heard rumours that Tucker-Smythe had joined Gamblers' Anonymous, but he hadn't believed it. Apparently, his family had insisted but Falcon thought they'd already disowned him so why would they bother?

'We need to talk in private.' He encompassed the

rest of the men in the party with a sweep of his eyes. 'A poker room is the best place to do that. You can watch if you don't want to participate.'

Julien's first priority now was to get Tucker-Smythe gambling again. He would lose, of course, they always did eventually and then his family, if they had agreed to bail him out, would wash their hands of the black sheep. And then he'd be back in Julien's pocket, right where he belonged.

Tucker-Smythe sank his hands into his pockets and shuffled his feet. 'As you wish,' he said.

Julien wondered how the man could make him feel so inadequate, as though he was doing Julien a favour, when it was actually the other way round. He checked to ensure that the ladies were engrossed in their game and then indicated to the men to follow him towards the select area at the back of the room, guarded by another employee who nodded politely at Julien and ushered his party through.

'Thanks, Alberto,' Julien said, slipping the man a fifty-euro note.

'Always a pleasure, Mr Falcon.'

That was more like it: a little respect. Julien walked taller as he followed Alberto to a vacant poker room. A waitress materialised and took orders from them all. A dealer appeared but Julien ushered him away.

'We'll look after ourselves,' he told the man, issuing a further note.

'Where's Irvine?' Julien asked, suddenly realising that his tame investment banker was missing. He snapped his finger at Alberto, who was just about to depart. 'Have someone go to Mr Irvine's room and tell him we await his pleasure,' Julien instructed, a curt edge to his voice.

He could, of course, have simply called the man himself but Irvine was obviously playing mind games so Julien wouldn't give him the satisfaction. Julien accepted the whisky that the waitress delivered to him without looking at her or acknowledging her in any way. He was severely pissed off and in no mood to thank the hired help for doing the jobs they were paid for.

The others were chatting in a desultory manner, clearly aware that Julien was clinging to his patience by a thread. No one wanted to talk him down from the precipice, it seemed. Tucker-Smythe picked up a handful of chips and ran them through his fingers, his expression wistful. He would be *so* easy to bring to heel but right now Julien was more concerned about Irvine's petty act of rebellion. Julien could hang him out to dry and Irvine knew it, which was why he'd always been so keen to do business with Julien. It took a thief to know one. Irvine would never grass him up, Julien repeatedly told himself as he resisted the urge to pace the room, his sixth sense warning him that something was severely wrong. He was aware of the others watching him and knew better than to reveal any signs of weakness.

No, Irvine would keep quiet, Julien decided. He'd been a very naughty boy in the business world and also supported a bastard child that his wife knew nothing about. She'd leave him in a heartbeat if she thought he played away and that would cost him an expensive divorce that he couldn't afford. Anyway, even if he did spill the beans, Irvine wouldn't be able to avoid prosecution because Julien would make sure that his every misdemeanour was brought to the financial regulators' attention.

Julien looked up when the door burst open and Alberto stood there, looking uncharacteristically flummoxed.

'Come at once, Mr Falcon,' he said curtly.

'Come? Who the hell do you think you're talking to?'

'It's Mr Irvine.' Alberto wiped perspiration from his brow. 'He's dead. Murdered.'

13

Greg watched the hotel's duty manager, a man he'd heard addressed as Alberto, fawning over Falcon. That would stoke his ego, Greg thought disdainfully. He liked nothing more than to be the centre of attention, the big man who got shown the respect that he thought he deserved. Bile rose in Greg's throat as he watched Falcon lording it over all and sundry like he didn't have a care in the world.

A commotion at the door to the private rooms caught Greg's attention when he realised that Falcon was at its centre.

'Something isn't right,' he said curtly.

Freya, looking a million dollars in her sexy red

dress, clutched his arm. Her nerves were already shot and Greg's reaction had made matters worse.

'What's happening?' she asked, following the direction of his gaze.

'I don't know.'

Alberto had just rushed back into the private area, reappearing almost immediately with Falcon and Bairstow keeping stride with him.

'There's one way to find out though.' Greg grabbed her hand. 'Come on!'

She went with him willingly and followed close behind Falcon's party. They were talking animatedly but there was too much noise for Greg to hear what they were saying. He could tell that something unexpected had occurred since Falcon didn't look round to make sure he was being seen. For that reason, Greg was pretty sure that he wouldn't look back and see him and Freya following in their wake. Freya appeared to understand the urgency, shared Greg's curiosity and asked no questions.

Greg cursed when Falcon's party got in a lift.

'What do we do now?' Freya asked.

'They're going up to the hotel rooms.'

'Irvine's staying here, isn't he? Do you think something's happened to him?'

Greg's concentration was focused on the lift,

watching the lights flashing as it ascended through the floors.

'It's a possibility. Tenth,' he said when the lift came to a stop, pushing the call button and getting into the next car when the doors opened. He pressed the button for the tenth floor. Mercifully, no one else got on and he was able to close the doors straight away.

'If no one else called their lift on the tenth, which seems unlikely since it was going up, that's where the action must be.' Greg tapped a toe impatiently as he waited for the lift to reach their floor. 'Okay,' he said when the doors swished open. They stepped onto thick, patterned carpet that disappeared into infinity. 'Let's see what we have.' He slid an arm around Freya's waist. 'If anyone asks, we're looking for a little privacy,' he added, winking at her.

Freya shook her head and said nothing. Greg looked in both directions and was just in time to see someone disappearing into a room on his left.

'This way.' He again took Freya's hand and was just passing the stairwell when a sound of muted crying caught his attention. Without conscious thought, he pushed open the door to the stairs and stopped dead in his tracks.

'What the fuck...' He glanced down at a familiar

figure curled into a foetal position without quite be-
lieving what he saw.

Freya was less circumspect. She freed her hand
from Greg's, sank onto her knees and pulled Sandy
into her embrace.

'It's okay,' she said, soothing the chef as though
she was a distressed child.

At that precise moment, that was exactly the impression she gave. She was in shock, Greg realised,
and clearly not in any state to talk to them. A dozen
questions tumbled through Greg's mind but at the
sound of heavy footsteps, audible despite the thick
carpeting, he knew now was neither the time nor the
place to ask them.

'Let's get out of here,' he said, taking control and
pulling Sandy gently to her feet.

'No!' she cried when Greg made to open the door
to the corridor.

Despite her distress, Greg was impressed by her
quick thinking. Left to his own devices, he would have
led them directly into what appeared to be a police
presence, leaving them to face a ton of questions he'd
much prefer not to answer.

He turned back to the stairs and led Sandy to the
floor below with Freya bringing up the rear, constantly glancing over her shoulder. On the ninth floor,

he summoned the lift and after what seemed like an eternal wait, during the course of which none of them uttered a word, it eventually arrived. Once again it was empty, and they reached the lobby without anyone on the lower floors halting their progress. There was a busy bar in the foyer. Greg headed for it and found a vacant booth.

'Look after her,' he said to Freya once the two ladies had slid onto the soft, leather seat.

Freya nodded and Greg briefly left them to go to the bar. He ordered drinks, including brandy for Sandy, who looked like she could use it. He didn't have time to wait for table service, nor did he need any interruptions from persistent waiters. What he did urgently need to know was what had happened upstairs and why Sandy was in such a state about it. It could prove to be the vital link in his quest to bring Falcon down.

'Here,' he said, forcing the glass into Sandy's hand.

'Take a sip,' Freya said gently. 'It will help.'

Obediently, Sandy raised the glass to her lips with a shaking hand. She took too large a gulp and subsided into a fit of splutters. Once she recovered from it, she took another, more moderate sip. A little colour returned to her pale cheeks, and she seemed to regain a modicum of self-control.

'Can you tell us what happened?' Greg asked, watching the activity centred around one lift that had drawn curious glances from more than just him. Fingers were being pointed and, as always, mobile phones were recording the kerfuffle, even though no one could possibly know what was going on.

'It's Robert,' she said, shuddering.

'Robert Irvine?' Greg asked for clarification.

Sandy nodded. 'He's dead. Murdered.'

Her shoulders shook and she began sobbing again. Freya passed her a tissue from the box of napkins on the table and waited for the storm to abate. When it did so, she wiped her eyes, blew her nose and squared her shoulders. The defiant Sandy he was more accustomed to dealing with was re-emerging and Greg was willing to guess that there would be no more tears.

At least not in public.

'You weren't trying to get Greg's attention for romantic reasons, Sandy, were you?' Freya suggested.

Greg quirked a brow. 'She wasn't?'

Freya waved his response aside. 'Not everything's about you, Larson. I notice things. Sandy doesn't look at you in that way.'

Sandy raised a watery smile. 'Truth to tell, you're more my type than he is,' she said to Freya.

'Blimey, I never saw that one coming,' Greg said, scratching his head.

'Like I say, I had an inkling,' Freya said, 'but there was nothing obvious. Anyway, we need to know what your relationship with Irvine was all about.'

'Agreed,' Greg said assertively. 'How did you know the guy and what was he to you?' he asked. 'More to the point, why didn't you raise the alarm when you found him dead, which is presumably what happened?'

'I did find him,' Sandy confirmed, nodding. 'I'd arranged to meet him in his room before he met with Falcon but I was delayed. The tender didn't come back from dropping Falcon's party off for ages. I think Alex must have stopped for a drink or six.'

'I saw you when we left on the jet ski,' Freya said. 'You were watching us, and I thought you were mad because Greg hadn't asked you to join us.'

'Yeah, I figured. I rang Robert and told him I was held up. But we needed to talk before he saw Falcon and he said he'd wait in his room.' She swallowed. 'When I finally got here, I came up and his door was ajar. I thought... well, I don't really know what I thought. I just pushed it open and called his name. He didn't respond so I walked into the room and there he was, sprawled over the bed, a knife sticking out of his chest.' A sob did escape her now. 'There was blood everywhere. I didn't know what to do, who to trust or what the hell was happening. And so I just hid. My legs were like jelly and the stairwell was close by. I was going to run down them once my legs stopped shaking but you found me first.'

'It's okay.' Freya squeezed her hand.

'But it's not, is it, and won't be ever again. Robert was my only hope of getting justice and now that will never happen.'

Freya gaped at her. 'Now I get it. You want to bring Falcon down?'

'I thought Greg did too and that we could join forces, but I had to be careful, which is why I came on to him when we'd all had too many that night.' Her mouth kicked up on one side. 'I have to be wasted before I can put out for any man, no offence.'

'Oh, none taken,' Greg replied, fighting a smile despite the gravity of the situation.

'I figured that if we became friends then I could sound you out, Greg,' she explained. 'I knew that Falcon had shafted your father and driven him to suicide, but I couldn't be sure if you cared or not.' She held up a hand when Greg scowled. 'Sorry, that came out wrong. My point is, I didn't know if you'd taken his thirty pieces of silver, to coin a phrase, or whether you'd taken the skipper's position for the same reason that I cook his fucking meals.' She glowered at Greg through eyes shiny with unshed tears. 'Retribution.'

'You could have just said,' Greg remarked gently.

'I tried... well, kinda. But you obviously thought that I wanted your body and didn't give me the chance.'

Greg nodded. 'Okay,' he said.

'Falcon's ruthless, in case you didn't already know it,' Sandy said. 'He knows who you are but had no idea that I had an axe to grind. But how could he think you didn't? Unless you were on his payroll for reasons that have nothing to do with driving his gin palace.'

'So you came on to Greg, hoping to get a better idea of his reasons for being on Falcon's boat,' Freya said.

Sandy nodded. 'That's about the size of it but every time I tried to talk to him after our drunken fumble, he pushed me away.'

'Sorry,' Greg said meekly.

'Don't worry, Sandy. His poor, damaged, male ego will recover eventually.'

'Okay,' Greg said, 'leaving aside my dented pride, start from the beginning. Tell me what happened, why you were in league with Irvine and what you hoped to gain from that contact.'

Sandy glanced at Freya and hesitated, clearly unsure about whether to reveal more.

'If it helps, my sister, Polly, was once just like Chelsea,' Freya explained. 'Falcon got her hooked on drugs and she died from an overdose and it's all Falcon's fault. I hate him with a passion!'

There could be no doubting the sincerity behind Freya's words, which appeared to convince Sandy to open up.

'Join the club, sister.' This time, it was Sandy who patted Freya's hand. 'I've heard mention of Polly. Some of the older hands reckon that Falcon was really keen on her.'

'Then he had a despicable way of showing it,' Freya replied bitterly.

'Irvine,' Greg prompted, glancing uneasily over his shoulder at the increased activity, wanting to know what was going on without being drawn into it.

'His young sister and I were an item. She was the love of my life.' A tear trickled down Sandy's face. 'We met when I ran a cooking class and she wanted to improve her skills.' A smile broke through. 'She never would have managed it. She was a terrible cook but there *was* a red-hot connection between us. We'd made plans for our future, but they were cut short and...'

'She died?' Greg asked gently when Sandy appeared incapable of completing her sentence.

'She disappeared so no one knows for sure, but I haven't given up hope of finding her or at the very least finding out what happened to her and making Falcon pay. I mean, what do we have in life if we give up hope?' She seemed momentarily lost in a reverie but spoke again quite quickly. 'The thing is, Robert adored his little sister. His mistake was letting it show. It was a weakness that Falcon exploited, and I think we all three of us know that's what he does the best. He doesn't threaten a person directly but targets whatever happens to matter to that person the most.'

'He certainly does that,' Freya said with a decisive nod.

'Robert had been bending the rules for Falcon, I now know, but was under investigation and so told Falcon that he couldn't help him any more. He wasn't about to risk his career because he'd done what he'd thought was favour for a friend, albeit a favour that he accepted payment for, which was his biggest mistake. Falcon owned him after that and could have dropped him in it at any time.'

'Sorry, Sandy, but breaking the banking rules is

more than a favour,' Greg said. 'It could carry a custo-
dial sentence and he must have known it.'

'Yeah, but he told Beth that Falcon had sucked
him in. He's good at that and when he asked for just
one tiny favour, something about a stock dividend an-
nouncement, Robert saw no harm in it. Of course, he
realises... realised how stupid he'd been and tried to
get out from under but...' She waved a hand about
and let her words trail off.

'When Falcon realised that he was losing control
over his tame banker, he targeted Beth to make Irvine
continue dancing to his tune.' Greg shook his head,
wondering why he felt so surprised. 'You're hoping
she's still alive.'

Sandy shot him a pragmatic look. 'If she is,
where's he keeping her? Of course I want her to be
alive but it's been months and I've had all that time to
think about it. You can't just keep a person prisoner
for that long. Someone would notice, wouldn't they?'

'So you arranged to meet Irvine here for a reason?'
Freya asked.

'Yep. Some sort of flap about a bitcoin venture that
backfired on Falcon. Robert says he's backed into a
corner and at his most vulnerable. He needed
Robert's help. Something about moving funds.'

'Hang on,' Greg said, holding up a hand. 'We

know about the failed bitcoin venture and that the funds are missing. We assumed that Falcon had moved them before the shit hit the proverbial. Are you saying that he didn't?'

'I don't think he would be too worried if he had because no one would be able to prove it. You know how lax the regulations are applied in some jurisdictions and if the funds are squirrelled away in one of those places, they would be untraceable.'

Greg nodded. He did know. 'You think Falcon wanted to talk to Irvine not about moving the funds but to ask him where he'd moved them to? Release my sister and I'll give you your money back. That sort of thing.'

'Yeah, I think it's probable. He hinted at it but said it would be better if I didn't know the ins and outs. That way, if our friendship came to light, the worse that could happen would be that I'd get the push from a job that I hate.' She glowered at a hapless stranger as he sauntered past their booth. 'Can you imagine what it's been like, working for a man I despise and suspect of having abducted my partner? Or worse.'

'I can imagine all too well,' Freya said softly.

'Did Irvine suggest that you take the chef's job on the *Perseus*? To be his eyes and ears,' Greg asked.

'Yeah, and I jumped at the opportunity. I had a

decent job in a top restaurant and took a significant drop in pay in order to work on Falcon's tub but I'll be honest, I was starting to lose patience. All the time that Beth's missing, I just can't help thinking there's more I could be doing to find her. Every time he comes on board, I listen when I can, hoping he'll drop a clue or two that will point me in the right direction. He always behaves as though the crew don't have eyes or ears, so I prayed he'd give himself away in front of me. He never did.' She let out a long breath. 'Then Robert messaged me to say he'd been summoned to a meeting here. We both knew it would be about the missing money and that Falcon would expect Robert to have traced it for him. Either that or admit to having it in safe keeping.'

Greg fixed her with a penetrating look. 'And you don't know if he actually had moved it himself?'

'No, but he said he'd see me in his room before he went to the meeting and tell me everything, just in case he didn't come out again, which implies that he knew something.' She appeared exhausted. 'You know the rest.'

'I'm so sorry,' Freya said, giving Sandy's shoulders a squeeze.

'So will Falcon be once I find Beth.' Sandy sat a

little straighter. 'I have to believe that she's still alive.' She shook her head. 'I simply have to.'

'There is one thing that we can be sure about,' Greg said, suspecting that Sandy would prefer practical suggestions rather than sympathy. 'If Falcon's funds are still missing and he thought Irvine knew where they were then he wouldn't have had him killed.'

'But probably wouldn't have hesitated once he got his hands on them,' Freya pointed out. 'We all know that he has zero tolerance for disloyalty. But we also know from your telephone conversation with him that neither Falcon nor anyone connected with him had spoken to your friend before he was killed. It was a very tight timeline. We saw Falcon and his party arrive here at the hotel so there just wasn't time for any of them to have got to Robert.'

'Let's assume that Irvine didn't move the funds himself,' Greg said, 'but he knew where they were. Who would kill him to prevent him from spilling the beans?'

'Anthony Tucker-Smythe?' Freya suggested. 'Or Parker and Pyke. One or both of them. Bairstow even. None of them are trustworthy and only Bairstow has shown abiding loyalty to Falcon.'

'I'll never find out what happened to Beth now,' Sandy said, her expression morose.

'If she's still alive then Falcon will have no further reason to hold her,' Greg pointed out.

'He'll have no reason to keep her alive either, especially if she can point the finger his way,' Sandy replied.

'He seldom does his own dirty work,' Greg said in a reassuring tone. 'So the chances are good that she wouldn't be able to make the connection.'

'So...' Sandy stretched her arms above her head. 'What do we do now?'

A very good question, Greg thought. 'Falcon will be severely rattled by what's happened, especially if he had nothing to do with it,' he said. 'He'll be thrown off balance because there will be something in Irvine's room to prove that he'd come here to meet Falcon.'

'Leaving aside the fact that the casino employee brought Falcon up here before the police arrived,' Freya pointed out. 'All the money in the world won't keep him from being questioned.'

'Right.' Greg nodded his agreement. 'A foreign national being murdered on Spanish soil is a big deal and the Spanish will want to be seen to be proactive.'

'A bad image that will discourage tourism,' Freya suggested with a wry smile.

'What about Tucker-Smythe?' Sandy asked. 'He's been on board once or twice and his contempt for Falcon was palpable on each occasion. He knows his way around the banking system. He might have been in cahoots with Robert and killed him to cover his own back.'

'It's possible,' Greg conceded. 'What precisely did Irvine say to you when you spoke earlier?'

'Only that he'd wait in his room for me and that it would suit his purpose to keep Falcon waiting.'

'What time was that?' Greg asked.

'About two hours ago.'

'Well then, Tucker-Smythe's in the clear at least insofar as he didn't do the deed himself. We arrived at the hotel just before that and he was holding court in the bar.'

'Very visibly,' Freya pointed out.

'True, but even so...'

'He could have arranged it.' Sandy sounded desperate as she made the suggestion and Greg could understand why. She'd set all her stock by Irvine finding Falcon's money and then releasing Beth. Greg didn't want to tell her that the chances of the woman still being alive were slight. She must already be aware in her heart of hearts that was most likely the case.

'He couldn't pay for it,' Freya remarked. 'He has an

expensive gambling habit to feed and is perpetually in debt apparently.'

'But if he knows where the funds are?' Sandy set her chin in a stubborn line of determination.

'If he did then he could have gotten himself out from under Falcon's control. He was sacked by the stockbrokers who employed him, probably because they suspected him of insider trading, so Falcon threatening to expose his wrongdoings would have had no effect,' Greg replied. 'If Falcon had gone to his ex-employers and told them what they already knew, they would have thought of their reputation and swept the accusations under the rug.' Greg shook his head. 'Unless I'm missing something, he didn't need to kill anyone.'

'It's hopeless, isn't it?' Sandy looked glum, devastated and momentarily defeated. Greg suspected that she would rally. Finding Beth was all that mattered to her, and if she gave up looking, she would lose her purpose.

'Not even nearly.' Greg hastened to reassure. 'Falcon has never been more vulnerable. We will never have a better opportunity to bring him down.'

'How?' Sandy spoke the one word with a challenging edge to her tone.

How indeed, Greg wondered, thinking there had to be a way.

'Now that we know we're all on the same side,' Freya said, encompassing the three of them with a sweep on one arm, 'then we have a much better chance of outsmarting him. God alone knows, we all have pressing motives.'

'Amen to that,' Greg replied softly.

14

Julien felt the sweat trickling down the back of his neck as he stared with bald disbelief at Irvine's dead body.

'What the fuck?' He turned to Eddie, who merely shrugged.

Julien felt no sympathy for the banker. His was beyond anyone's help anyway and his only concern was for himself. Who the hell was doing this to him? And why? Irvine was going to tell Julien where his fucking money was but clearly someone else got that information out of him first and had then done away with him.

But who?

Julien wasn't often lost for words, or scared, but

right now he could lay claim to both of those weaknesses. Someone was stitching him up and doing a right royal job of it. Who disliked him enough to shaft him quite so comprehensively? Very few people knew of his connection to Irvine and the precise services he provided for Julien. Of more immediate concern, why had Alberto brought him up here? He needed to be a mile away, heading for Croatia.

'Have the police been called?' he asked, affecting a concerned expression as he glanced down at the murdered man, careful not to touch anything and feeling absolutely nothing other than irritation.

'They are on their way.' Alberto shuffled awkwardly. 'This is most unfortunate and naturally, my manager is keen to keep the matter quiet.'

Julien could well believe it. The same could be said for him, so his thoughts again returned to Alberto's reasons for bringing him to the scene. Was he being made a scapegoat, someone convenient for the police to focus their attention on, thereby absolving the hotel of responsibility?

More than likely. Julien, who'd always hidden behind layers of protection, felt more exposed than he ever had in his entire life. And he didn't care for the experience one little bit, especially now that the hotel's management was attempting to set him up.

Should he slip the guy another bung to keep his name out of things? He wanted to ask Eddie but couldn't do so in front of the man himself. It would look like bribery and imply that he had something to hide. Besides, things had gone beyond that point. The police would go through Irvine's possessions and find a connection to Julien, if only on his phone. It was obvious that the corpse was fresh and so Julien couldn't possibly have been involved.

Even so, he didn't like it. He didn't like it one little bit.

'Right,' he said, turning away. 'I'll go back to my party and let the authorities do their work.'

'I am sorry about your friend,' Alberto said.

'Thanks, but he wasn't a friend. Merely a business acquaintance.'

Julien and Eddie walked away, not speaking until they'd put some distance between themselves and the murdered man's room.

'What the hell is going on, Eddie?' Julien clenched his fists and felt his blood pressure spike, angry enough to commit a few murders of his own. 'Who the fuck is screwing me over and where the fuck is my money?'

'Try and calm down, boss.' Eddie spoke quietly. 'I don't have any answers for you. Yet. But you can count on my finding some before we get much older. It's my neck on the line too, don't forget, if the old bill come snooping around. But at least they can't pin this murder on us. We've been in plain view of other people all day.'

'I know that, you moron, but the old bill won't care! It'll give them an opportunity to haul me in and suggest that I had someone top him for me.'

'They'll have to let you go again. They have nothing on you. You agreed to meet Irvine here in a social situation, and they can't prove otherwise.'

'Yeah, you're right.' Julien let out a long breath and felt his heartbeat return to a more regular rate. 'Even so, if I don't get my hands on that dosh pretty damned quick then I'm well and truly in the mire.'

Eddie didn't look concerned. 'You'll find a way out. You always do.'

'You just don't get it. I'm overextended. All this shit don't come cheap.' He waved a hand vaguely in the direction of his yacht. 'Then there's the houses, the cars, the private flights, a wife with expensive tastes, kids who never stop wanting, and all the other crap that goes with keeping up appearances. That bit-coin venture was supposed to be my get out of jail card but instead it looks like it might see me bankrupt.'

Eddie remained stoic. 'Tucker-Smythe should be able to trace the funds for you,' he said.

'That tosser.' Julien threw back his head and roared, causing a couple walking towards them to give him a wide berth and a tut of disapproval. 'He looks down his aristocratic nose at me every chance he gets and wouldn't cross the road to piss on me if I was on fire. He'll be loving this. Wouldn't be surprised if he was behind it.'

'He doesn't have the balls.'

Julien grunted. 'Anyway, Irvine moved the money somewhere safe and unless someone extracted that information from him before doing him then we'll never get to know where he stashed it. It's probably been moved on already.'

'I thought you didn't invest everything in the bitcoin venture.'

'Don't you dare tell me you advised against it!' Julien stopped walking and poked a finger aggressively in Eddie's chest. 'What do you know? I was up shit creek. I had to do something to stop the rot, everyone was jumping on the crypto bandwagon, and it seemed like a winner.'

'Well, if the worst comes to the worst, you'll just have to liquidate a few assets.'

'And lose face. Get real!' Besides, Julien thought

but didn't say, the majority of his assets had been used as collateral against various loans. He trusted Eddie but some things were just too personal to be shared.

Eddie shrugged. 'You're the boss.'

The two men returned to the private poker room, interrupting a muted conversation.

'Everything all right?' Pyke asked.

'No it fucking isn't!' Julien reached for his discarded drink and downed it in one swallow. 'Some bastard's topped Irvine.'

'What!' Parker's mouth fell open. 'He's been murdered? And we're being dragged into the investigation?'

It took all of Julien's self-restraint, what was left of it, to stop himself from hitting the bastard. 'Not unless you killed him,' he said curtly.

Parker, hands sunk in his pockets, shook his head as he paced the length of the room. He had the sense not to say anything else.

'What does it mean?' Tucker-Smythe asked in the upper-class accent that grated on Julien's nerves at the best of times. And these most definitely weren't the best of times. He wanted to tell the man that he could throw him under the bus whenever he felt like it but refrained, mainly because he was unsure if that was still the case. Everything was unravelling and the hell if he knew how to stop the rot.

'It means that someone close to me knows where he stashed the funds from the crypto fiasco and has fucking stolen them from under my nose!' Julien roared.

'Speaking personally, old chap, I was unaware that you had the funds,' Tucker-Smythe remarked casually, 'and I certainly don't know where they are now.'

'The same goes for us,' Pyke said, scowling. 'In fact, you made it clear to us that you didn't know where the money had disappeared to either.'

'Seems I didn't,' Julien grunted, aware that he'd let his temper get the better of him and had shown his hand for no good reason.

He turned away and took a moment to reason the matter through; something that he should have done before opening his trap. He had Irvine's sister as a long-term house guest, tucked away safely where she'd never be found, and Irvine wouldn't risk her security by shafting him. Who had he spoken to or confided in when moving the money? Someone in this room? There was no way for Julien to know, not for sure. They all looked concerned for their own skins and they'd all been within his sights all night, with the exception of Tucker-Smythe. Eddie was right about him though. Desperate he might be, but violence simply wasn't his style.

Before Julien could say anything more, a tap at the door preceded Alberto putting his head round it.

'There's an inspector here from the *Policia Nacional* who would like a word with you,' he said, his tone apologetic.

'Wonderful!' Julien rolled his eyes and followed Alberto from the room, thinking they hadn't wasted much time calling out the big guns.

'I was asked why I'd gone to Mr Irvine's room and found the body,' Alberto explained as they made their way to the hotel manager's office. 'I had to tell the inspector that you'd asked me to rouse Mr Irvine since he was here to join your party. When I got no response from the phone in his room, I went up to knock and found the door open.'

'Don't worry, Alberto.' Julien patted the man's shoulder. 'None of this is your fault.'

Alberto looked relieved as he opened the door to the office and ushered Julien through it. At a nod from the officious-looking man standing behind the desk, Alberto swiftly withdrew and closed the door behind him.

'I am Inspector Sanchez,' the man said, extending his hand, which Julien took in a firm grasp. He didn't bother to introduce the man in uniform or the other man in the room, presumably a lower-ranked detective, both of whom eyed Julien with open suspicion, making him feel decidedly uncomfortable. 'Thank you for joining me, Mr Falcon. I am sorry about your friend. Please take a seat.'

Julien did so, regretting it when Sanchez remained standing, looming over Julien in a clear attempt to intimidate. And succeeding far better than he could possibly know. 'Thank you,' he replied, sitting sideways on the uncomfortable chair and crossing his legs in a casual manner. 'But Irvine and I were not well acquainted.'

'Oh!' Sanchez, who was middle-aged, with thinning, salt-and-pepper hair and a paunch, raised a brow in an exaggerated gesture of surprise. 'Forgive me, but I understood he had come to Ibiza at your specific invitation.'

Julien cursed a slip of the tongue that he wouldn't ordinarily have made. Then again, he wouldn't ordinarily have been interviewed by police without his brief there to protect his interests.

'That's true. I have... had business dealings with Mr Irvine and this jaunt was by way of a reward. A gesture of appreciation for all the helpful advice that he's given me.'

'What sort of advice?'

Julien wasn't about to repeat his earlier mistake and stood his ground. 'I don't see how that's relevant to his death,' he said mildly.

'And I shall not know if it is or not until you enlighten me.' Sanchez's voice had developed a hard edge. His English was perfect, and Julien knew better than to underestimate him. He didn't like the prospect of spending a night or more in a Spanish jail cell, aware that the British Embassy would drag their heels getting him released.

'Mr Irvine looked after some of my business bank accounts and recommended profitable investment opportunities.' Don't over-explain, he told himself. It was a sure sign of guilt, even though he didn't have anything to feel guilty about, at least not insofar as Irvine's death was concerned.

'I see.' Sanchez remained standing and fixed Julien with a probing look.

'I understand that a hotel employee invited you up to Irvine's room after he discovered the body.'

'He did, and it was one hell of a shock.'

'Why did he do that, I wonder.'

Julien shook his head. 'I have no idea. That's a question you will have to ask him.'

'You can be sure that we shall.' He paused. 'Can you account for your whereabouts this evening?'

On firmer ground now, Julien assured the man that he could.

'My party arrived at this hotel about half an hour before I received the devastating news. We dined at Can Mussonet prior to that. Irvine was to join us here. My understanding is that his flight from England was delayed and he got here too late for dinner.'

Julien knew that the hotel's CCTV would show his arrival and prove that he couldn't have slipped away to kill Irvine. The inspector clearly knew it too.

'I understand your yacht is anchored in the harbour.'

Julien confirmed that it was.

'Then I must ask you to remain here for a day or two whilst we further our investigations.'

Julien had known that was coming and nodded, even though he'd prefer to tell Larson to weigh anchor and get the fuck away from the place.

'Of course.'

He stood, attempting to take control of matters despite being aware that he didn't stand an earthly. He was on foreign soil, at the mercy of local law enforcement who would undoubtedly ask Scotland Yard if Julien was known to them. And wouldn't they just love that back home, he thought, forcing himself to keep his expression bland. He hadn't committed any crimes, at least none that could be proven, and he most definitely hadn't knocked off his private banker.

'But now, if there's nothing else, I should return to my guests.'

'Thank you for your cooperation. If you will give your contact details to this officer before you leave.'

Julien did so, boiling with anger when he finally escaped the confines of the office, aware that he was Sanchez's prime suspect. Once he'd heard from the UK about the number of times he'd been interviewed under caution, Sanchez's suspicions would gain legs. The bugger of it all was that Julien couldn't scarper. His yacht wasn't exactly low key and would be spotted and turned back if he defied Sanchez's orders to stay put. Besides, it would make him look as guilty as hell. He couldn't get a flight home either. His passport would have been flagged.

He hoped that Sanchez's investigation wouldn't focus solely on him and that it would be thorough enough to reveal the murderer's identity. All Julien needed was a name. He'd take it from there himself.

Putting on the sombre expression of a man who'd just seen a colleague murdered, Julien returned to the poker room.

'Right,' he said, closing the door to ensure abso-
lute privacy, his stance hard, uncompromising.
'Enough pissing about. The Spanish cops think I
arranged Irvine's killing and one of you lot knows
something about it.' Eddie stood at Julien's shoulder
and cracked his knuckles. 'Now's the time to enlighten
me.'

The men all stared back at him, showing a defiance that they would never have dared to display
under normal circumstances. But these circumstances
were far from normal and none of them would shed
too many tears, Julien realised, if he did finish up as a
guest of the Spanish prison authorities. He felt like he
was wading through treacle. His entire house was
crumbling around him and no one other than Eddie
gave a shit.

Maureen burst through the door, her timing lousy.
'What's happening?' she asked, clutching at
Julien's arm. 'There's all sorts of rumours circulating
in the casino. Something about a murder. Someone
you know, Julien. It's just awful.'

'Maureen,' Parker said mildly.

Maureen removed her hand from Julien's arm and
sent her husband a reproachful look. 'What?' she
asked.

'Take this back to the boat, boss,' Eddie said quietly, nodding towards the camera discreetly situated in the corner of the ceiling so that card counters or outright cheats could be caught by the casino's pit bosses from the comfort of the control booth. Bent croupiers were caught by similar means.

'Right. Call up and have the tender sent over. The night's over,' Julien said. 'Let's collect the rest of the ladies and get the hell out of here.'

15

Freya, Greg and Sandy loitered by the back wall in the main part of the casino, watching the door to the private rooms as Falcon returned, looking thoughtful and subdued. For once, he didn't glance around to make sure that he'd been seen.

'What do we do now?' Freya asked. 'Presumably, he was just interviewed by the police, and he doesn't look happy about it.'

'Will they arrest him, do you think?' Sandy asked. 'Hopefully not. He's our only hope of finding Beth.'

'Ladies, I have absolutely no idea,' Greg said, holding up his hands as though warding off a further barrage of unanswerable questions. 'But I do think we'd be best advised to return to the yacht. I'm betting that Falcon and his party will head for its sanctuary and I don't want to be seen here. Besides, we can't be sure that you weren't seen going into that hotel room, Sandy, and I dare say you'd prefer not to be quizzed by the local cops.'

'You've got that right.' She shuddered. 'I'm pretty sure that I wasn't seen though. No one passed me in the corridor, that I know for a fact.'

'There might be cameras though,' Freya said. 'There are in the lifts. I noticed.'

'Probably not in the hotel corridors though,' Greg added. 'Something to do with privacy laws, I think.'

'Right.'

Sandy looked dejected and Freya felt an over-whelming urge to comfort her. But now was neither the time nor the place. It was odd, but a few hours ago, she'd been dangerously close to actively disliking the woman. Now she knew what drove her, she felt nothing but the utmost sympathy for her situation. To have her lover snatched from her by Falcon and not know if she was alive or dead must be a living hell. At least Freya knew without a doubt that Polly was dead and could grieve for a life that had been cut short by a man who had all but murdered her.

'How will we all get back?' Freya asked, thinking of the mode of transportation that had brought them to shore. When Greg exchanged a look with Sandy, Freya threw up her hands. 'Oh no!' she said. 'Three up is one too many.'

'It's done all the time,' Greg said, laughing at her dismay. 'And I'm a careful driver, honest.'

Freya had seen people riding three to a ski but none of them had been kitted out in bodycon dresses. Even so, a moment's thought about the current circumstances was sufficient for her to know that she had no choice. What price modesty in the face of murder, or worse? Sandy was still in shock and couldn't be left on her own and Freya sure as hell didn't want to hang about waiting for Greg to return and pick her up.

'Okay,' she said with a resigned sigh. 'Let's get it over with.'

Greg winked at her as he led the way from the hotel, merging with the crowds populating the grounds now that it was fully dark. It seemed that this island only came alive after the witching hour, Freya thought absently as she struggled in her tight dress to keep pace with Greg and Sandy.

The jet ski remained where Greg had secured it. He unlocked it, lowered himself onto the seat and fired up the engine.

'All aboard,' he said, grinning.

'You go in the middle,' Sandy said. 'I'm more used to these things than you are.'

'Right. Here goes nothing.'

She took off her shoes, hitched up her dress and grasped Greg's outstretched arm with her spare hand, landing inelegantly on the ski's seat.

'Cuddle up nice and close,' Greg advised. 'Leave space for Sandy.'

'You're enjoying this, aren't you?' she cried accusingly as she closed her knees around his thighs and pretended an annoyance that she didn't actually feel.

'A guy has to get his kicks.'

He was still laughing as Sandy, without any help, clambered onto the back. The craft dipped low in the water but Greg moved it gently away from the dock without giving any of them a ducking. There was a headlight, a bit like a scooter, but Freya still wondered how he could see where he was going, and how he managed to avoid some of the smaller boats that were anchored up without lights. There was a compass on the ski's console, so she assumed that helped. She was woefully ignorant about such matters and felt no pressing need to educate herself. As soon as they'd orchestrated Falcon's downfall, she had no intention of stepping foot on another boat, luxurious or otherwise, for a very long time.

Greg pulled the ski alongside the *Perseus*'s bathing platform. Freya waited for Sandy to alight, then slid backwards on the seat and took her outstretched hand as she made the small jump up onto the deck. She wouldn't admit it under torture, but despite her reservations, she'd rather enjoyed the ride, to say nothing about getting up close and intimately acquainted with Greg's rippling muscles.

Wordlessly, the three of them made their way up to the wheelhouse, where Alex was on watch.

'Hey, skipper,' he said, 'back already? The night is still young.'

'Whereas I'm getting old. Take yourself ashore if you like.'

'I wish. I've just had a call from the boss. His party want picking up in half an hour. Seems they're getting old an' all.'

'It does seem that way. Make the pickup please. You can have tomorrow night off. I think we'll be hanging out here for a while.'

'Aye, aye, skipper!'

Rob gave a salute, grinned at the ladies and tripped lightly down the steps.

'Okay,' Freya said, perching on the edge of a bench. 'So, what do we make of what we just saw?'

'I think Falcon has been well and truly shafted,' Sandy said, a bitter edge to her voice.

'Couldn't happen to a nicer guy,' Freya replied sarcastically.

'Don't get your hopes up,' Sandy advised. 'He'll wiggle his way out of things and we won't get our retribution. Worse, we still won't know where Beth is or what's happened to her and without her brother being alive, I don't suppose we ever will.'

'He hasn't got an expensive brief on speed dial in this country,' Greg said, tapping his fingers thoughtfully against the control console. 'So if someone were to suggest to the Spanish police, anonymously of course, that he detached himself from his friends while they were at dinner...' He turned to look at Sandy. 'Do you know where they went?'

'Yes, he asked me for a recommendation and I suggested Can Mussonet. It's a pretentious place on the beach. They charge the earth for indifferent food because they have the views. So all the show offs go there to see and be seen. Right up his street.'

'Is it usually crowded?' Greg asked.

'Yep. I made the booking for him. Had to drop the name of the yacht in order to get him in.' She rolled her eyes. 'He would have loved that.'

'I think I've been to the bar. That's separate from

the restaurant and the world and his wife hangs out there,' Greg said. 'If they can afford the price of the drinks, that is.'

Freya grinned at Greg, belatedly catching on. 'Falcon was seen talking to a shady character is, I think, what your anonymous informer will have to tell.' Freya paused. 'All well and good implicating him but to the best of our knowledge, he had no reason to want Irvine killed. Quite the opposite, in fact.'

Greg grinned at her. 'We know that but he can hardly reveal the reason why he wanted him kept alive without dropping himself further into the mire.'

'The charges will never stick, not unless he really did talk to someone at the bar and was seen by a credible witness,' Freya pointed out.

'We won't get the satisfaction of him knowing it was us who orchestrated his downfall,' Sandy said. 'And, for fear of repeating myself, we'll be no nearer to finding Beth if Falcon's banged up.'

'If she is still alive, I bet Eddie Bairstow knows where she is,' Freya replied. 'It seems to me that Falcon can't even sneeze without Bairstow passing him a tissue.'

Sandy grimaced. 'Could Irvine have been killed to stop him speaking out about Beth's abduction?'

Greg smiled at her. 'Anything's possible but if so, it does beg the question why.'

'Perhaps he'd grown tired of being Falcon's poodle and threatened to blow the whistle unless he released Beth,' Freya said gently.

'And Falcon couldn't release her because she was already dead.' Sandy nodded. 'Yeah, I know I'm clutching at straws, but still...'

'I take it Irvine never got to speak to his sister once she disappeared,' Greg said.

'No, never.'

'And he never reported her missing?'

'He couldn't. We spoke about it and decided not to take the risk. We know what would happen if we involved them.'

Greg frowned. 'But you weren't even sure that he had her.'

'Who else would have taken her? Besides, Falcon told Irvine that he had her safe. How would he even know she was missing if he didn't?'

'This is getting us nowhere,' Freya said, aware that their speculations were causing Sandy considerable distress without leaving them with a viable next step. 'There is one way forward that we haven't stopped to consider.'

'Daisy,' Greg said, giving Freya a nod of approval.

'You can't trust her!' Sandy said sharply.

'I'm pretty sure that we can.' Freya briefly explained the conversation that she'd had with Daisy. 'She's desperate to get her husband out from under Falcon. Now that they'll all come under suspicion of murder, I think that will firm up her determination; and her husband's too.'

'It won't hurt to sound her out,' Greg said, 'but be careful. Walls have ears.'

'Here they come.' Sandy nodded towards the approaching tender. Freya could see that she was grinding her teeth and felt a fresh wave of sympathy for her. Her situation must be beyond frustrating and there was little that Freya could say or do to ease her burden. But still, now that she had teamed up with her and Greg, it would make her feel less isolated and give her a fresh sense of purpose, which was something.

Freya and Greg stepped out onto the wheelhouse bridge and watched Falcon and his party alight from the tender. Subdued and unnaturally quiet, a pall of suspicion hung over their heads like a dark cloud trying to decide who to rain down on. Tucker-Smythe was amongst their number.

Falcon glanced up at the wheelhouse and stopped

dead in his tracks for a protracted moment before following Chelsea into the salon.

'We have another guest,' Sandy said, stating the obvious.

'Falcon won't want to let him out of his sight,' Greg replied. 'Go down and see if they want drinks,' he added, addressing Freya, 'but be careful.'

'I'm not supposed to be on duty,' Freya replied, glancing down at her dress. 'Won't he think it odd?'

'They aren't supposed to be back so early. As a good hostess, naturally you'll want to know if they need anything. Falcon's too preoccupied to think anything of it. He expects his underlings to dance to his tune. Anyway, you keep them occupied whilst I pay a little visit to Falcon's study.' He reached into his pocket and extracted a tiny disc that Freya suspected must be a bug.

'I thought you didn't want to chance it.'

'The goal posts have moved and it's now a risk worth taking,' he replied winking at her.

Freya rolled her eyes. 'Aye, aye,' she said, removing her shoes, handing them to Greg with a sweet smile and tripping lightly down the stairs.

'I'm sorry you had to... oh, it's you.' Falcon broke off from whatever he'd been saying to his morose guests and subjected Freya's person to a protracted once over.

'I heard you come back and wondered if there's anything you need,' Freya said politely.

'I thought I gave the crew the night off.'

'You did but we came back early. Partying is a young person's game.'

'Right, well, organise a cabin for Mr Tucker-Smythe. He'll be staying with us for a while, and we'll be remaining here at anchor for the foreseeable.'

'As you wish.' She turned to smile at Tucker-Smythe. 'Welcome aboard, sir.'

Chelsea yawned. 'I'm off to bed,' she said.

'Me too.' Daisy smiled. 'If it's not too much trouble, could you bring me a warm drink to my cabin please, Freya?'

'It's no trouble at all.' She looked at Falcon. 'Anything for you, gentlemen?'

'Look after the ladies, darlin'. We'll fend for ourselves. Make sure we're not interrupted.'

'Of course.'

'You get off as well,' Parker said to Maureen, who'd looked set to remain with the men.

She pouted and left the salon with a heavy tread. Of Bairstow's squeeze there was no sign. Presumably, she'd already had enough drama and taken to her bed.

Freya ran back up to the wheelhouse. Sandy was still there with Greg, deep in conversation.

'Did you plant it?' she asked breathlessly.

Greg nodded. 'All done. What's happening down below?'

'The women have all gone to their cabins,' Freya said breathlessly, 'so your listening device might come into its own after all. And Daisy's asked for a hot drink. Clearly she wants to talk to me, which saves me the trouble of engineering a meeting.'

'I'll make the drink for her myself,' Sandy said, heading for the steps.

Greg ushered Freya in front of him and followed her down the companionway. 'Be careful,' he said. 'I don't want anything happening to you.'

'Too much paperwork for the captain if a member of the crew goes AWOL, I'm guessing,' Freya quipped in an effort to hide her nerves.

'You have *no* idea,' he replied, rolling his eyes.

Her nerves jangling with the expectancy of a development, she grinned at Greg, watching him position himself in the crew corridor immediately behind the salon. The walls were lined with beautifully polished walnut but were far thinner than the brick built walls in a house, for obvious reasons. It would, she realised, be a perfect place to pick up anything that was said in the salon. If anyone left that room then they wouldn't do so via the crew corridor. The majority of them probably didn't even know that it existed.

Freya ran to the galley and collected the steaming mug of hot chocolate that Sandy had prepared for Daisy. She'd placed it on a small serving tray together with a tempting array of petit fours that probably wouldn't have the power to actually tempt a woman whose husband was now involved in a murder enquiry.

'Good luck!' Sandy said as she passed the tray to Freya.

'We're onto something,' she replied with more confidence than she actually felt. 'I've never seen Falcon so rattled before.'

'Yeah, but he's a survivor who doesn't fight fair. Never lose sight of that fact.'

'I hear you.'

Freya carried the tray to Daisy's cabin and tapped at the door.

'Hey,' she said, poking her head round it when Daisy invited her to enter.

Daisy had taken her makeup off and was sitting on a stool in front of a mirror, brushing out her hair.

'Hey,' Daisy replied. 'I saw you in the casino with Greg.'

Freya placed her tray down and perched on the edge of the bed. 'You hid it well. Did any of the others notice us? Did Falcon? Not that it matters. We had the night off and were free to do as we pleased, but still...'

'I don't think he saw you.' Daisy blew air through her lips. 'He was too busy posing for an indifferent audience.'

'Right. Yeah, he certainly flaunted himself.'

Daisy turned towards Freya. Without her makeup, she looked older and Freya could see the worry lines etched into her face. 'You know what happened?' she asked.

'Yep. How's Falcon taking it?'

'He's a very worried man. He feels vulnerable and wants to get the hell out of Dodge but the inspector dealing with the case has said the yacht can't sail until he gives permission.'

Freya nodded. 'I figured that would be the case.'

Daisy shuffled on her stool and leaned towards Freya. 'Falcon's been boxed into a corner, which makes him even more dangerous. He no longer trusts anyone except Eddie. He'll be grilling Jason and Mike as we speak, demanding to know what they know about Irvine's death.'

'They couldn't have done it.'

'No one on board could have, at least not personally,' Daisy agreed nodding, 'but any one of them could have arranged it.'

'But why?'

'To drop Falcon in it, or that's what he'll be thinking anyway.'

'I can see why a paranoid man might reach that conclusion, but your husband and Mike Parker aren't stupid enough to take the risk, or to kill an innocent man for that matter. They know that the UK authorities will be salivating at the thought of finally getting their hands on Falcon. And if that happens, he won't think twice about dropping all his cohorts in the mire, so they have absolutely no reason that I can think of.'

Daisy nodded. 'Falcon won't trust anyone until he gets answers, no matter how unlikely their reasons might be for killing off the golden goose, so to speak. We're in for an uncomfortable few days.'

Freya hesitated before responding, wondering whether to trust Daisy and reveal everything she knew. Greg and Sandy had told her to exercise caution but she would prefer to use her own judgement. She was as convinced as she could be that she and Daisy were on the same side and so took the plunge. If she ratted her out to Falcon, what was the worst he could do?

'Besides anything else,' she eventually said, realising that she'd been quiet for too long and that Daisy was sending her quizzical looks, 'Falcon had a compelling reason to keep Irvine alive.'

Daisy blinked. 'He did? Do share.'

'Falcon really doesn't know where the funds from the crypto fiasco disappeared to and was depending upon Irvine to find them for him.'

'Wow! You haven't let the grass grow, have you. How do you know all this?'

'This is where I'm going to have to trust you.'

Daisy grasped Freya's hand. 'You know that you can. My husband and Mike aren't criminals but got dragged into dodgy dealings with Falcon without stopping to think about the consequences.' She rolled her eyes. 'There's men for you. Anyway, now there's no way out for them.'

'Okay, I get that, and I will tell you what I know but it can't go any further than your husband. If Mike tells Maureen then she'll run to Falcon. She's obviously smitten.'

'There's no cure for the delusional,' Daisy said with a derisive snort. 'But you know my back's against the wall. Jason and I stand to lose everything we have, including his freedom. I know he's brought that on himself and don't expect your sympathy, but I do want to at least try and get him out from under. He will tell everything he knows, so long as Falcon's under lock and key and can't retaliate. That would be gold dust to the UK authorities.'

'Falcon's trodden on an awful lot of toes on the way up.' Freya took a deep breath. 'He's now going to regret his cavalier attitude.'

She went on to succinctly tell Daisy about Greg and Sandy.

'Blimey!' Daisy pulled at the ends of her hair. 'Half the crew has an agenda.'

Freya smiled. 'It seems that way.'

'I had no idea about Irvine's sister. I didn't even know that he had one. I've only met him a couple of times, briefly in social situations, but I liked him and felt that he'd been sucked into Falcon's web of deceit in much the same way that Jason and Mike have.' She shook her head. 'Poor Sandy. The girl's dead, isn't she?'

'Probably but unsurprisingly, Sandy needs to know for sure.'

'I'm surprised she hasn't poisoned Falcon's food.'

'I expect she's been tempted.' Freya flashed the

suggestion of a smile. 'Anyway, Greg dropped a recording device into your husband's jacket pocket and—'

'He could have given it to me. I'd have put it in place.'

'We didn't want to show our hand.'

Daisy nodded. 'I understand completely. It won't do much good though: the bug, that is. What you really need to hear is anything said in private between Falcon and Eddie Bairstow.'

Freya grinned. 'Which is why I just persuaded Greg to put another bug in Falcon's study. Greg was reluctant before, worried he'd be caught. Falcon has been known to sweep his private rooms with a detector apparently, but the time has come to throw caution to the wind.'

'So, what's the plan? Do you have one?'

'Not really. I suppose the same old mantra applies. Follow the money but we can't because no one appears to know where it is. If Irvine had known then he would have told Falcon in return for his sister's release.'

'Tucker-Smythe,' Daisy said pensively. 'He's the only other one who could have moved it.'

'I agree, but Falcon must have drawn the same conclusion. And anyway, if he had access to it, why would he have responded to Falcon's summons and come to Ibiza? He'd have enough money to live in luxury for the rest of his life, expensive gambling habits notwithstanding.'

'Not everyone wants to live in exile, no matter how luxuriously, and leave everything familiar behind them.'

Freya, unconvinced, waggled a hand from side to side. 'True, but still...'

'Tucker-Smythe is flamboyant and enjoys his status as a member of the aristocracy. He wouldn't want to leave that behind. Besides, he probably thinks he's smarter than Falcon and can get one over on him. He clearly resents him so it wouldn't surprise me.'

'So you think he's bluffing it out?'

'If I had to guess. But still, he's stuck on board with the rest of us now so perhaps you, in your capacity as a member of the crew, can find out more.'

'That's a bit tenuous.' Freya paused to reason the matter through. 'I know desperate people do desperate things but even if you're right and he's moved the funds, why would he kill Irvine?'

'Well, that's kinda obvious. If Irvine knew or suspected that Tucker-Smythe had the funds... perhaps they were in it together. Whatever. Anyway, if he appealed to him to give it up in order to save his sister and Tucker-Smythe refused then our aristocratic friend would have had to cover his own back.'

'It's all getting a bit James Bond.' Freya stood up. 'I'd best get out of here, just in case anyone notices that I'm missing. I'll talk to Greg and Sandy and get back to you tomorrow.'

'Take my mobile number.'

'Best not. We don't want to leave a trail.'

Daisy offered up a strained smile. 'Now who's being all James Bond?' Her expression sobered as she stood and gave Freya a brief hug. 'Don't take any un-necessary risks.'

'That ship has already sailed,' Freya replied, with her hand on the doorlatch. 'Pun intended.'

16

Julien waited impatiently until Maureen could be persuaded to leave them alone, her tenacity an irritating reminder of Julien's stupidity in coming on to her in the first place. That's what came of being such an arrogant sod, he told himself. He blamed his error of judgement on desperation, and a growing fear that his complex business affairs were running out of his control. His behaviour had further antagonised Parker rather than persuading him to toe the line and left him to fend off the unwanted attentions of a woman who overestimated her own attractiveness.

Way to go, Falcon!

As soon as the door closed behind her, Julien headed for the brandy decanter and poured healthy measures for them all. As things stood, he still had a reputation as a philanthropic millionaire to live up to. God alone knew how much longer that situation would endure. Chances were, he'd need these men on his side if they were to escape Ibiza without being detained indefinitely and right now they were all looking at him with varying degrees of suspicion.

What happened to loyalty, he wondered, suppressing his annoyance with difficulty. There was Eddie, of course, solid and reliable, who always had his back. Maybe he should thank him more often for loyalty which, he had good reason to know, was hard to find when the chips were down. He glanced at Parker and Pyke, both looking uneasy but neither of them having any qualms about swigging his expensive brandy. Rats and sinking ships seemed like an appropriate analogy, given the current circumstances, he thought with a disdainful shudder.

'Okay,' Parker said. 'So what's the story, Jules?'

'The story is that someone stabbed Irvine through the heart with a sodding great knife, the local plod has my name in the frame, and I have no fucking idea where my money's at.' He glowered at Parker for asking such a stupid question before remembering that he'd decided to play nice. For now. 'That,' he said in a more moderate tone, 'is about the size of it.'

'Leaving aside the question of money just for a moment,' Tucker-Smythe said in that languid drawl of his that made Julien want to rip his throat out, 'why on earth would they think you murdered the man? Apart from anything else, you haven't been alone all evening. Am I right?'

'Don't let the truth get in the way of a swift conviction,' Julien replied. All the men in the room would be aware of his reputation for violence. He'd demonstrated his willingness to crack heads, or worse, on the way up but now left that to others, allowing his reputation as a hard man to speak for him.

The Spanish police wouldn't know of the reputation in question quite yet but they sure as hell would do once their enquiries were answered by Scotland Yard. Julien had no doubt that England's finest would break all records in enlightening them. If they also found out that he'd been suspected of killing a rival by identical means as the fate suffered by Irvine then he didn't care to think about the grilling he'd be in for.

'The standards of evidence don't seem to be as strict as they are back in Blighty,' Julien went on to say, his voice intruding upon the uneasy silence in the salon, broken only by the sound of water lapping against the hull and an occasional bout of laughter from other boats anchored nearby. 'They could lock me up and wait for Scotland Yard or the cross-border crypto squad to come and apply the thumbscrews.'

'Hardly.' Tucker-Smythe sounded amused rather than concerned for Julien's dilemma, exacerbating Julien's growing desire to throttle the fucking man.

'We need to give our law enforcement friends a helping hand by pointing them in the right direction,' Julien said, ignoring the interruption. 'Who do we know who would want to bump Irvine off?'

'Don't be shy,' Eddie growled, when Julien's question was met with another deafening silence.

No one seemed capable of holding Julien's gaze. Parker covered his mouth as he coughed and glanced out the window. It wasn't actually a window, it was a portlight or some such stupid thing, but as far as Julien was concerned, a window was a window and that was the end of it. Pyke fiddled with the lapel of the jacket he still wore, the generated air conditioning that wafted through the vents in the study keeping the temperature low enough to make jacket-wearing comfortable. All the fucking luxuries these men had grown accustomed to at Julien's expense, and not one of them appeared to have any helpful suggestions to make. Julien felt his temper rising and took a swig of his drink in a futile effort to remain in control. Losing his temper would achieve nothing other than to antagonise men who he needed in his corner. Besides, he'd learned in the early days of his climb up the slippery ladder of success that angry men seldom made rational decisions.

'Anyone would think that the lot of you had something to hide,' he remarked, 'which makes me suspicious.'

Justin Pyke spread his hands. 'The same goes for all of us as it does for you, Jules. We've none of us been on our own for long enough to murder anyone. Besides, we had no idea that Irvine was staying at the Gran. Speaking personally, I had absolutely no reason to bump him off even if I had known he was there.'

The others nodded in unison.

'If you're saying, and I think you are, that Irvine moved the funds that you claimed to know nothing about from the crypto fund before the authorities moved in,' Mike said in a mordent tone, 'then presumably whoever killed him did so *after* finding out where he'd stashed them.'

'Okay.' Julien held up a hand. 'You've made your point. I told you I had no idea where the funds had gone, which I didn't, but I did know who'd moved them and he did so because I told him to. I knew we'd never see any of them if the regulators got their thieving hands on them. I didn't tell you guys this side

of the investigation because I didn't want you to per-
jure yourselves. You'd have got your share once the
dust settled.' He could see that Mike and Justin didn't
believe him. He couldn't altogether blame them because he was spouting a load of old bollocks. He'd
never had any intention of cutting them in. 'All I can
think of is that someone with a knowledge of both the
banking system and the best places to hide stolen
dosh was on to him.'

All heads turned in Tucker-Smythe's direction.

'Don't look at me, gents.' He sat with one foot elegantly crossed over his opposite thigh, the epitome of
unruffled calm. He held his brandy balloon between
two fingers, swirling its contents around as though
trying to decide if they met with his approval. Over
three hundred quid a bottle and this wanker was
questioning its provenance. Julien felt his anger on
the rise again, belatedly realising when Tucker-
Smythe lifted the glass in an ironic salute that he'd
been winding him up. 'Everyone knows I don't have a
pot to piss in and whenever I am in funds, I tend to
gamble them away. A terrible habit, but what can one
do?' He lifted a shoulder in a negligent gesture. 'If I
had millions sloshing about, you wouldn't see me for
dust.'

Julien grunted, unable to fault his logic but still suspecting him.

'Does Irvine have family?' Justin asked. 'Someone he might have confided in?'

'He has a sister but she's out of the picture,' Eddie replied.

'Well then, the murder must be unconnected with you, Jules,' Mike said. 'He was an investment banker so it stands to reason that he probably severely pissed someone else off.'

The others all muttered their agreement to a weak argument that Jules didn't know how to refute. Spanish plod were unlikely to imagine that Irvine had come to Ibiza and been murdered by anyone other than the person he'd come to meet. What's more, Julien would undoubtedly be quizzed on the need to meet him here and had no idea how he'd respond.

'My suggestion, for what it's worth,' Tucker-Smythe said into the ensuing silence, 'is to phone your brief in the UK. I dare say he will know of someone decent who can represent your interests in this fine part of the world. It will make it harder to pin anything on you if someone who speaks the lingo has your back.'

'Sound advice,' Eddie said, nodding emphatically.

Julien nodded too, unwilling to admit that the very

real possibility of having his collar felt by the Spanish plod scared him shitless. It was ironic, but for once he might be hauled in for something that he *hadn't* actually done.

He glanced at Eddie, who shook his head. They were both out of questions but could sense the unease, the growing discordancy between the group. There was absolutely no point in alienating them further. Julien's world was unravelling, and it was now a case of survival. His chances of finding the missing funds were at present minimal; whoever killed Irvine had undoubtedly got his grubby hands on them. Julien suspected Tucker-Smythe and would not allow him to get away with it. He had friends in low places who would systematically remove vital body parts until he gave it up.

But first things first: he must avoid being arrested.

'Okay. The police will want to talk to us all.' Julien fixed each of them in turn with a hard look. 'You know what to say. And more to the point, what not to.'

'Of course we do,' Justin Pyke said aggressively. 'We're not fucking morons. But have you thought what you're going to say if the financial authorities come asking questions about the missing funds? This murder has conveniently opened the door for them and they won't knock first before barging through it.'

'Nothing to do with me.' Julien regretted his abrupt response the moment the words left his lips. 'With any of us,' he added hastily, 'and if they could prove otherwise, they would have been all over us long since.'

'Perhaps some upstanding member of the constabulary arranged Irvine's murder so that there was an excuse to detain us all somewhere outside of our comfort zone,' Mike said in a speculative voice.

Julien waved the suggestion aside despite the fact that anything was possible. He'd trodden on a few toes in his time and knew just how desperate certain authority figures were to get their hands on him. Be that as it may, some of the plod whom he paid handsomely to give him a heads up couldn't afford not to tip him off if that was the case. One thing was for sure, if he went down, he'd take his poodles in the Met with him, and they knew it.

'Think about it, gentlemen,' he said, draining his glass and putting it aside. 'We'll talk in the morning, by which time one of you will hopefully have come up with an inspired suggestion, otherwise I'll have to start looking closer to home.' He fixed each of them with a hard stare before walking towards the door. Eddie opened it and followed him through it. 'Help yourselves to more brandy. There will be sod all else to do for the next few days other than to come up with inspired ways of getting us all out of this fucking mess.'

Julien walked into the salon, followed closely by Eddie.

'Well, what did you make of all that?' he asked, throwing himself into a chair and indicating to Eddie to pour him a fresh drink.

'You sure?'

'What are you, my mother?' Christ, even Eddie was on his case. 'Of course I'm fucking sure.'

Eddie shrugged and poured Julien a large brandy. He didn't take one for himself and Julien knew that he should have refrained too. He also shouldn't have snapped at Eddie, aware that his faithful sidekick was attempting to prevent Julien from getting wasted. A hangover when he needed to be at his sharpest would not be in his best interests.

Eddie, taking a chair and stretching his long legs out in front of him, addressed Julien's original question. 'I can't think of any reason why anyone on this tub would have killed Irvine or had the opportunity to plan the deed. We didn't tell any of them he was expected until they came on board yesterday.'

'Yeah, but Irvine might have mentioned it to one of them. Specifically to the one who helped him to move the money.' Julien took a swig of a drink he no longer wanted and then pursed his lips. 'All roads lead back to Tucker-Smythe in that case.'

'Possibly, but if so, why murder his partner in crime and set himself up as a suspect?'

'The fuck if I know.' Julien threw up his hands, sloshing ruinously expensive Napoleon brandy into his lap. 'Anyway,' he added, letting out a protracted sigh, 'I'm betting we'll all be hauled into the local nick to make statements tomorrow. Get a message through to Rushton for me,' he said, referring to his English solicitor. 'I need to speak to him now. Tonight.'

Eddie glanced at his watch, causing Julien to tut.

'I know it's one in the morning but I pay the wanker a fucking fortune to protect my legal interests. Tucker-Smythe was right to suggest that I need someone on this tinpot island to look out for me.'

'Okay.'

Eddie used his mobile to put the call through.

'Voicemail,' he said. 'I'll leave a message.'

Julien rolled his eyes, holding onto his temper by the sheer force of his will. 'Keep fucking calling until he picks up. I need to hear from him the moment he opens his eyes.'

'I know this isn't what you wanna hear,' Eddie said, having left a message for Rushton, the lazy, overpaid bastard, 'but you might have to give up on the missing funds and concentrate on consolidating your position. You've got that massive building project going on in Essex. That'll pay a small fortune once it's complete.'

Yeah, it would, if Julien had the funds to see it through, but Eddie didn't need to know that he'd come up short. It had run way over budget and he'd overreached himself in expectation of receiving huge profits from the bitcoin venture.

It had cost him a fortune in bribes to get planning permission for the site and all the environmentalists were still up in arms about it, creating delays that had cost Julien a fortune. Wankers! People had to have somewhere to live. How the fuck was he supposed to have known that interest rates would rise, causing a mini collapse of the British housing market? People were now staying put or moderating their expectations, he'd been told. He'd expected to sell all fifty houses off plan but only a handful had been reserved.

It was a fucking disaster.

'Sales are slow,' he contented himself with saying.

'The market will pick up. It always does.'

Easy for him to say. 'Not soon enough.'

'Boss, you've got tons of dosh squirrelled away offshore. You'll just have to dip into it until this all blows over.'

'How the fuck do you think I've been keeping the building project going, along with everything else? That well has almost run dry and what's left is my rainy-day fund. If I have to leave England in a hurry, if the wankers seize all my assets, I need something to keep me afloat.'

'Ah, I didn't realise things were that tight.'

'They wouldn't have been if Irvine had moved those funds for me like I asked him to. How hard can it be?' Julien downed his drink in one swallow and banged the empty glass down on his desk. 'Cards on the table, mate. I'm up shit street.'

'Sell the yacht. It's a fucking millstone anyway, a status symbol that's turned into a liability, and you own it free and clear.'

'Actually, I don't.'

Julien hated admitting to any weaknesses and wouldn't tell anyone other than Eddie under any circumstances other than the ones he found himself faced with that he'd dug a hole for himself that he might actually not be able to climb out of. Eddie *did* sometimes come up with useful suggestions and right now, Julien was desperate enough to listen to anyone he could trust. Unfortunately, the nature of his business affairs meant that he'd had to play hard ball along the way, alienating most – make that all the guys he'd been tight with back in the day. There was no room for sentimentality in business, which was why Eddie remained his only staunch ally.

'I used the yacht as collateral to get a loan to finish the building project.'

'Geez!' Eddie scrubbed his hands down his face. 'So, how do we get you out of this hole?'

'We find my fucking money! Get yer finger out and start doing something to earn yer keep.'

Eddie stared straight back at Julien, making him feel vaguely uncomfortable. 'Seems to me that unless we find out who killed Irvine, we'll never find the dosh. And we can hardly start asking questions while the plod are on the scene.'

Julien grunted, aware that Eddie was right. 'Those papers,' he said, to fill the heavy silence.

'The ones I told you not to keep in the first place,' Eddie replied, the suggestion of an edge to his voice.

'I keep telling you, computers can be hacked. Happens all the time and mine would be a prime target for my rivals, to say nothing of the filth. I'm old fashioned and like to keep sensitive stuff where only I can get at it.' Julien rubbed the side of his forefinger against his lips. 'If the Spanish plod come on board, can they search the place? Do they need a warrant?'

Eddie shrugged his massive shoulders. 'Hell if I know. Seems to me they can do what the fuck they like.'

'Fuck!' Julien paused for a moment. 'Okay, here's what we're gonna do. At first light, take those papers out of the safe, go ashore alone, hire a safety deposit box and stash them. Make sure you ain't seen.'

'I'm on it.'

17

Greg waited until he heard the door close behind Falcon and the two men went to their cabins. He then returned to the wheelhouse and found Freya and Sandy on the bridge, chatting like old friends. What a difference twenty-four hours made, he thought with a wry smile. Sandy being gay had come as a shock. He never would have expected it, perhaps because she'd come on to him so blatantly a few nights previously. He chuckled, wondering why she couldn't just have talked to him about her dilemma.

But then again, perhaps he understood why. A lot of things were now more obvious to him, including Sandy's permanently sour mood. Greg found it hard enough to work for the man who was indirectly responsible for his father's suicide. How much harder must it be for Sandy, given her circumstances? He hoped she felt the relief of a burden shared and less isolated now that she had partners in retribution.

'Hey.' Freya turned and smiled at him as he approached them. 'How did the sleuthing go?'

'Perfectly. I heard every word.'

'Something we can work with, I hope,' Sandy replied.

'Possibly.'

Greg proceeded to relate everything that had been said.

'I'm not surprised that they suspect Tucker-Smythe,' Sandy said, 'but I still don't get what his motive would have been. I can imagine them having joined forces to take Falcon's money though. Presumably, they intended to do so and to lay a trail that led to Falcon. That way, Tucker-Smythe could have remained in the UK without having to worry about Falcon gunning for him.'

'Yeah, but obviously they didn't get that far. Not that you would know it from Tucker-Smythe's languid attitude.'

'It's all an act,' Freya said, biting her lip.

'Then he deserves an Oscar,' Greg replied. 'He must be aware that he's suspect *numero uno*.'

Sandy nodded. 'Probably. But he's also safe enough all the time the local police are sniffing around. Falcon doesn't have a death wish. Besides, if he thinks that Tucker-Smythe killed Irvine for... I don't know, so he can keep all the funds for himself? then Falcon won't bump him off until he knows where they are.'

'Falcon's desperate to get his hands on the funds. Not because he thinks they're his necessarily but because he's broke,' Freya said. 'All of this,' she added, waving a hand towards the wheelhouse, 'is an expensive façade. A house of cards on the point of collapse.'

'He is very worried indeed about being questioned by the Spanish police,' Greg said. 'He doesn't understand the lingo or the customs and has no expensive brief to hide behind. At least not yet.'

'I don't blame him for being scared. Let him see how it feels to be on the receiving end for a change,' Sandy said aggressively. 'Do you think he'll try and scarper?'

'Nah.' Greg shook his head. 'He can't, not if he wants to return to the UK, complete his building project *and* try and get his hands on the missing funds. He'll have to front it out. He has no choice. Besides, he wouldn't willingly walk away from his comfortable home life.'

'Do you think they'll be taken ashore to be questioned?' Sandy asked. 'Or will someone come to the boat?'

'I reckon someone will come here, at least to talk to the others,' Greg said. 'It would save a lot of time. Falcon though might be asked to accompany them ashore, so to speak. He's trying to get hold of his UK brief. He wants someone over here to represent him but I'm guessing that won't be possible to arrange in time if the interviews take place first thing.' He grinned. 'Such a shame.'

Freya grinned back at him. 'My heart bleeds.'

'I don't suppose any mention was made of Beth.' Sandy sounded touchingly hopeful as she voiced the question that must have been uppermost in her mind ever since Greg joined her.

'Sorry.' Greg smiled apologetically.

'Ah well, I didn't imagine anything would have been said in front of the others but I did hope that Falcon and Bairstow on their own might have...' Sandy's expression brightened. 'Those papers Falcon's so keen to move but not destroy. They must be the key. If we could get our hands on them before Bairstow moves them tomorrow. There might be mention of Beth's whereabouts.'

Freya smiled at Sandy's naked optimism. 'Unlikely

that he'd need to write something like that down,' she said.

Sandy's face fell. 'There might be something,' she insisted.

'Sandy's right about one thing,' Greg said. 'We need to get our hands on those papers before Bairstow makes off with them.'

'But if we break into the safe then Falcon will know that someone on board is responsible.' Freya slapped a hand against her thigh. 'We're so damned close to bringing him down and yet we can't hammer in the final nail.'

'Might have to leave that to the police,' Greg said, an apologetic edge to his voice.

'How will Bairstow get ashore?' Freya asked speculatively.

'One of us will have to take him.' A slow smile spread across his face. 'He's never shown any interest in the toys, at any rate.'

Freya quirked a brow. 'He's never driven one of the jet skis?'

'Can't recall him ever doing so, but it's not that hard. Just twist and press the accelerator lever on the right and go. A bit like a road scooter. Any idiot can do it.'

'Well then, captain,' Freya said, sharing a collusive

smile with Sandy, 'it sounds to me as though you're the one to take him.'

'And what? Mug him for the papers?' Greg replied.

'Ah, I hadn't thought about that.'

'So we just do nothing? Admit defeat?' Sandy scowled. 'That is *not* what I want to hear.'

'If you think about it, leaving aside Beth's where-abouts, current events have done our work for us,' Freya said pensively. 'We know that Falcon is definitely facing bankruptcy and possibly also a murder charge. He'll have a tough time recovering, no matter what happens. I can't see him coming back from this fiasco.'

'It's not enough!' Sandy cried. 'I want to see him squirm. Not to mention, telling us where Beth is.'

'You're suggesting that we just walk away?' Greg asked, addressing the question to Freya.

'No way!' Sandy cried.

'I'm being pragmatic,' Freya said, holding up her hands to ward off Sandy's protest. 'I want to squash the bastard like the cockroach that he is but despite what we now know about him, we're no nearer achieving that ambition, are we? Nor can I think of any way to get our hands on those papers.'

'Those clubs that he runs back in England, the brothels,' Sandy said. 'They'll still operate and girls will be forced to work in them, a bit like your sister was, Freya.'

'I don't like it any more than you do but we can't right all the world's wrongs,' Freya said with a sigh. 'I think I'm right in saying that a person suspected of fraud can have his assets frozen.'

Greg nodded. 'Falcon knows it too. He's scared shitless. But I doubt if his name is on the deeds to those clubs so...'

'From what you tell us, Greg, it seems that all the guys on board are anxious to distance themselves from Falcon and the murder enquiry,' Sandy said. 'But none of them know enough about Falcon's myriad activities to be of help to us. There's only one person who does.'

'Eddie,' Freya said softly.

'Right. I wonder if he's ready to leave the sinking ship too, so to speak.'

Greg shook his head. 'It's too risky to approach him. Those two are solid. They go way back.'

Sandy grunted. 'Falcon must pay him well, is all I can say, because he uses Eddie as his whipping boy, puts him down all the time in front of others, and Eddie just shrugs it off.'

'Well, anyway,' Freya said, hiding a yawn behind her hand. 'What's our plan? Do we actually have one?'

'Not as such,' Greg said. 'I think we'll have to bide our time for now and see how things develop. If Falcon is arrested then the Spanish will have done our work for us.'

'Apart from finding Beth,' Sandy pointed out.

'I haven't lost sight of that fact,' Greg said softly. 'But if Falcon is taken then that would be the time to approach Bairstow, always assuming he's not locked up too. He'll know where she is and will hopefully be persuaded to see sense.'

Sandy looked unhappy but nodded. 'Right,' she said. 'Beth and I were going to open our own restaurant; we'd laid plans. She'll make a stunning front of house hostess, guaranteed to drag the punters in. My food will guarantee their return.' She sighed. 'I have to believe that will still happen, otherwise what's the point?'

'We'll find her,' Freya said softly.

Greg wished she wouldn't make promises that they were in no position to keep, even though he knew she'd only said it to try and comfort Sandy.

'I'm going to ring my tame detective back in the UK and let him know what's happened, in case he hasn't already heard,' he said. 'Hopefully he'll know what the Spanish police have found, or suspect, and that might point us in the right direction.'

'What can they know that we don't?' Sandy asked.

'Plenty. They will probably have Irvine's phone, unless the killer took it, and can see who he's been calling and who's in his address book. Significantly, they'll also be able to check the hotel's CCTV. We know there's none that were obvious in the corridors but there still might be something, somewhere.' Greg spread his hands. 'Sorry guys, that's all I can suggest for now but tomorrow will be interesting, that's for sure.'

Freya nodded. 'Falcon's at breaking point and we can use that to our advantage. Somehow. My brain's too addled to think straight right now but there has to be a way. I'll wish you both good night and we'll come at this fresh in the morning... make that later this morning. I guess it all depends what the police do.'

'Right,' Greg agreed, patting his shoulder. 'Night. Sleep well.'

Sandy took herself off too and Greg was left alone to enjoy the stillness of the night – well, stillness by Ibiza standards – as he stared at the lights twinkling on other boats anchored in the bay and listened to the sound of the water lapping against the hull. He could understand the ladies' frustration. It was all so tenuous, and they both needed some sort of definitive closure, not to mention answers and the opportunity to

remind Falcon of how many lives he's carelessly destroyed. Allowing the authorities to bring him down
and destroy his empire would be satisfying.

But not nearly satisfying enough.

Especially for Sandy, who still clung tenaciously
to the belief that her lover was alive and being held
against her will.

Sighing, he returned to his cabin behind the
wheelhouse and dialled Ray Milton's private number.
It would be gone two in the morning now in the UK
but the detective sergeant never seemed to sleep. That
belief was vindicated when the man answered on the
second ring, not sounding as though the phone had
roused him from a deep sleep.

'Hey, Greg, what you got for me?'

'You haven't heard?'

'Heard what? Sorry, mate, not with you.'

Greg succinctly outlined the events that had occurred at the Gran and went on to tell the detective
what he'd overheard on board. Milton didn't interrupt
once. Greg wondered if he was scribbling notes or
recording the conversation.

'Well, well,' he said, when Greg ran out of words.
'So the mighty are finally getting their comeuppance.'

'Hopefully. But, Ray, there's one other thing you
should know.' Greg explained about Beth's abduction.

'I'm assuming her disappearance hasn't been reported.'

'I'll check it out.'

'Will you be able to find out what the Spanish have on Falcon and let me know, just in case I can help to orchestrate his downfall?'

'Stitch him up, you mean?'

'You said it, not me,' Greg replied, a smile in his voice.

'It'll be better than a wet dream for my bosses. Falcon's been laughing at them for years. They've never been able to get anywhere near him. He's too well protected by his fancy lawyers. Add the international aspect of the fraud into the mix and it's all way above my paygrade but let me see what I can find out for you.'

'Okay, Ray, get back to me as soon as you can.'

* * *

Julien returned to his cabin, aware that he wouldn't be able to sleep. The lights at floor level surrounding the bed illuminated the tempting image of Chelsea as she sat, pushed the hair from her eyes and smiled sleepily at him.

'Hey, baby,' she said. 'You've been a while. Everything okay?'

Julien knew, to his considerable distress, that he'd be no good to her that night. He'd been experiencing increasing difficulties in that department, even though he'd never make that admission to anyone, resorting to the little blue pill for the most part.

'Everything's good,' he replied. 'Go back to sleep.'

Despite everything, Julien was glad that she was showing a little consideration again. She appeared to have put the episode with Maureen behind her and recalled which side her bread was buttered. Make the most of it, darling, he thought but didn't say, unaware how much longer he'd be able to keep her in the lap of luxury. Wondering too how to keep her name out of things if this business got out of hand and was reported in the UK press. His wife pretended not to know about his other women, happy to lead her own life just so long as he behaved with discretion. Having pictures of him and Chelsea plastered all over the tabloids would cause merry hell with his domestic arrangements.

But that, he knew, was currently the least of his problems.

She muttered something, turned on her side, curled her legs up to her chest and seemed to fall straight back to sleep. Julien watched her for a while, then attended to his ablutions and climbed in beside her. This, he knew, could well be his last night of freedom for a while. Wherever he laid his head the following night, it sure as hell wouldn't be nearly as luxurious.

Make the most of it.

He ran a hand over the curve of Chelsea's hip, but she didn't wake. His mind whirled with ever more unlikely scenarios as he tried to figure out who had his money and more pressingly, who'd knocked Irvine off. Whichever way he came at it, it made absolutely no sense. The only conclusion he could reach was that Irvine had an accomplice: someone Julien knew nothing about. And he'd killed Irvine off so he could keep all the dosh. But if that was the case, why wait until Irvine was in Ibiza and had a meeting planned with Julien?

Because, Julien concluded, seething with anger, someone had set him up to take the fall. And had done a fucking good job of it as well.

If there was a mystery person involved, Julien would never find him. At least not immediately. First, there was the small matter of a murder charge to get out of. And he would get out of it because there was no way in this world that he could be placed in Irvine's room. He hadn't been there. Had no idea which room he'd been in and could prove where he'd been every second of the vital time. But, of course, the Spanish plod would probably insist that he'd paid someone else to do his dirty work. They couldn't prove that he had, but that thought didn't offer him much comfort.

He'd probably have to swallow his pride and flog the building project off to the competitor who he'd beaten by means of bribery and a strong-arm tactics into winning the contract. He'd get a fraction of what it was worth and would lose face but at least he'd re-alise enough capital to regroup.

And then, God help whoever it was who'd ripped him off and then set him up. He was now convinced that's what this was: one humungous stitch up and someone had gone to a lot of trouble to pull it off. Who had he pissed off sufficiently to make them bother? Ha, he thought, that would be a long list but it had to be someone on the inside who had the ability to get to the bitcoin funds and move them about. That narrowed the field of candidates down considerably.

It narrowed it down to the people sleeping on his boat.

He thumped his pillows, pulled Chelsea close so that her back rested against his chest and inhaled the fragrance of her youth. She didn't stir. Her breathing was light and even – the sleep of the innocent –

something he'd not been able to lay claim to for years, if ever. Perhaps it wouldn't be such a bad thing if he was taken in and grilled, he thought, now that his anger and fear had subsided and he was able to think more rationally. That way, he'd be able to tell from the nature of the questions thrown at him, how much the local plod knew, and what they suspected. Even so, it would be a humiliation too far and someone would have to pay.

And they would. Eventually.

Julien had a long memory and an even longer reach. He was akin to a wounded animal, boxed into a corner and ready to fight for his life.

He might be down, but he most definitely wasn't out.

18

Freya was up again at six, having managed four hours' sleep, if that. She'd stared at the ceiling of her cabin as she attempted to process the day's developments, wondering how she and Greg could use them to their advantage. She felt elated that Falcon had been boxed into such a tight corner, but it was a hollow victory because she couldn't claim the credit for putting him there.

'It really doesn't matter, just so long as he's brought down and can't manipulate any other young, impressionable females,' she muttered, as she dressed and tied her hair back.

She made her way to the salon, feeling tired yet

full of expectancy, and walked straight into Falcon, who was sprawled across one of the sofas.

'Oh, sorry,' she said. 'I didn't think anyone would be up and about yet.'

She turned to walk away but his voice stopped her in her tracks. 'Don't go.'

'Is there something I can get you?' she asked politely.

Falcon looked terrible. He clearly hadn't slept at all. His features were drawn, his complexion sallow, and lines were etched deep into his forehead. He looked every day of his age, and then some.

'Nah, I'm good. Stay and talk to me.'

Freya dutifully perched her backside on the arm of another sofa. 'You look as though you have the weight of the world on your shoulders,' she said, striving to force sympathy into her tone when inside she was rejoicing at the sight of his desperation.

'Yeah, you could say that.' He let out a long sigh. 'A friend of mine was murdered last night.'

Freya gasped. 'That's awful. I'm so sorry. Where, back in the UK?'

'Nah, here in Ibiza. He was here to meet me, but someone knocked him off before we could get together.'

'Why?' Freya shook her head. 'I don't understand.'

'Join the club, love. The thing is, the reason why I'm telling you this is that the local plod will want to talk to all my guests, and to me. I don't know whether they'll come to the boat or if we'll have to go ashore. Either way, we'll be stuck here for a few days. I thought you should know so you can make the rest of the crew aware.'

'Okay.' Freya stood. 'Well, I hope they find out who did it.'

'You and me both, love. You and me both.' He paused, regarding her quizzically. 'You know, I'm sure we've met before. There's something familiar about the way you tilt your head in a particular way, but I just can't put my finger on it.'

Freya felt his astute gaze boring into her profile and momentarily froze. 'We've never met before,' she managed to say in a neutral tone that she hoped didn't betray the fact that being in the same room as the man responsible for her sister's death made her skin crawl. 'I would remember if we had.'

'Ah well, it don't matter. It'll come to me.'

Freya left the salon, her mind twisting between Falcon's growing awareness of her and Bairstow's need to get hold of those papers. There *had* to be a way to get sight of them. Despite Greg's insistence that it would be too risky, she wasn't about to back down now that they were so close to nailing the bastard. No murder charge would stick if Falcon could prove he'd not been alone the previous evening, which presumably he could, so he would walk away from this fiasco and continue to exploit the vulnerable. Unless, of course, it could be proven that he'd paid someone else to do the deed. But it all came back to motive, which even Freya could see that he didn't have.

She pottered about, watching the guests emerge from their cabins far earlier than she'd expected them to. They were edgy around one another and spoke little as Freya and Gloria attended to their breakfast requirements. Of Bairstow there was no sign, but Freya knew that Greg would be keeping an eye out for him. There was no way he could go ashore without asking Greg either for the keys to a jet ski or having him act as ferryman. Even so, the wait was playing havoc with her nerves.

'Hello, we've got company,' Falcon said with a heavy sigh as a *Guardia Civil* launch approached the *Perseus*.

Freya manoeuvred herself around the deck until she was in a position to look down at the bathing platform. A man and woman and two uniformed officers stepped off the launch. The driver cut the engine and secured the craft to a cleat.

'Looks like Sanchez and his sidekick,' Falcon said with a heavy sigh. 'They haven't wasted any time.' He glanced at the mobile in his hand. 'Where the fuck is Rushton?' he muttered. Freya assumed he was referring to the call back from his lawyer he was expecting which probably accounted for his being out of bed so early. 'Ah well. Inspector,' he said, hand outstretched as Sanchez climbed the steps to the aft deck. 'Have you come to tell me that you've discovered who killed Irvine? And why.'

'We are efficient, Senor, but not *that* efficient.' He nodded towards the guests gathered round the table. 'We need to talk to you all individually. My colleagues will take your statements whilst Senor Falcon and I have a friendly chat.'

'Always a pleasure to be of service to law enforcement,' Falcon replied amicably. 'Would you like some coffee, gentlemen? And lady.'

'We would prefer to get down to business.' Sanchez was polite yet distant. 'Is there somewhere that we can conduct the interviews?'

'Feel free to use the salon to speak with my guests.' Falcon indicated the space in question with a wave of one arm. 'You and I can chat on the forward deck, Inspector.'

Bairstow still hadn't put in an appearance. Since

Falcon had deliberately not invited the inspector to join him in his study, it could only mean that Bairstow was busy concealing the papers that Falcon didn't want Sanchez to know anything about. There would be no opportunity for him to take them ashore now but surely there must be dozens of hiding places on a boat where they would never be found.

Freya's heartrate quickened as she and Gloria cleared away the breakfast plates. If Greg had the presence of mind to keep Bairstow in his sights then perhaps they would finally get their hands on something to use against Falcon without taking any risks. Bairstow could hardly fight back when there were four members of Spain's finest on board.

'Life is never dull,' Gloria muttered to Freya as she sent one of the uniformed cops a flirtatious look.

Freya smiled and shook her head, wishing that her life could be as uncomplicated as Gloria's.

As soon as breakfast had been cleared away, Freya sprang into action. She ran up to the wheelhouse but there was no sign of Greg. Alex grinned at her and said he had no idea where the skipper had got to, suggesting mischievously that she might like to check his personal cabin. Freya laughed but didn't bother to follow his advice. She knew Greg wouldn't be in it.

She found out why when she ran back along the

companionway and heard his voice coming from the deck outside the galley's door. She cursed when she leaned over the guardrail and realised he was in conversation with the female detective who appeared to be spending a little too long flicking her hair over her shoulder and not nearly long enough making notes.

Freya's mind went into overdrive. If Greg wasn't keeping tabs on Bairstow then Freya would have to do the job herself. Thinking quickly, she entered the main deck by a side door and slipped along the passageway to Falcon's study. The door was closed, and she couldn't hear any sounds coming from within.

'Here goes nothing!'

Without giving her nerves an opportunity to get the better of her, she turned the handle and walked straight in, an excuse on the tip of her tongue if Bairstow was in there and challenged her.

The room was empty.

'Now what?'

Freya expelled a long breath as she stood with her hands fisted on her hips, her gaze roving round the richly appointed room. The walls were bursting with books on an array of subjects. All for show, no doubt. She thought it highly unlikely that Falcon would have actually read any of them.

Ignoring the lure of the reading material, Freya

wondered what she was supposed to do now. The chances were that the papers were long gone. Bairstow would have removed them sometime during the night. And even if she could locate the safe, there wasn't a hope in hell of her getting into it.

Even so, a combination of determination and desperation compelled her to look for it. She opened lockers and looked behind pictures, with no success. Then she recalled that the crew cabins all had storage beneath the floor. She looked around, moved a rug from behind Falcon's desk chair and there it was. The handle to a hatch. She gave a cry of triumph as she wrenched it open and was confronted by a safe.

A safe protected by a numeric keypad.

'Fuck!' she muttered, sitting back on her haunches. A part of her had hoped that it might have had an old-fashioned key. She'd had a crash course in lockpicking once in her previous job where she'd work in an old country house and someone had locked themselves in a toilet. The locksmith had shown her how to open the door without a key and she remembered most of what she'd been taught. A fat lot of good that embryonic skill would be to her now, she thought with a sardonic smile.

'Now what?' she muttered for a second time.

'The code's 74615.'

Freya's heart thumped and she almost toppled over from her crouched position. Slowly, pulse racing, she stood up and faced Bairstow. 'I was... that is, I'm trying to...'

Her excuse, such as it was, stuttered to a halt. There was no excusing what she'd been caught doing. She was glad that the yacht was currently swarming with law enforcement, and that she had Greg and Sandy on her side, otherwise she didn't want to think what might have happened to her then and there. Bairstow was a hard man who hurt people. She'd always known it. Now she was about to gain first-hand knowledge of just how ruthless he could actually be.

'I know what you're looking for.' He leaned against the closed door and folded massive arms across his torso. 'I've always known.'

Freya swallowed, thinking that there still being several feet of daylight between them could only be a good thing. 'Known what?'

'Who you are and why you're on this tub.'

'You do?' Freya suspected that she sounded like a moron, repeating everything he said, but at that precise moment her brain was ticking over on idle and she seemed incapable of coherent thought.

'I liked Polly, as it happens.'

'You *do* know me then,' she said, struggling to

emerge from a mental mire of uncertainty and accepting there was no point in denying it. He hadn't hurt her yet and didn't give the impression that he intended to. She'd settle for that and, just possibly, a few answers. 'But you didn't tell Falcon.'

'He didn't ask.' Bairstow chuckled. 'Well, he did say he thought he knew you and that there was something familiar about you, and so I did some digging. When I saw you befriending Chelsea and overheard you trying to convince her that he was a master manipulator of young women, the penny dropped.'

'I didn't know you were watching us.'

'That's what comes of being part of the woodwork. No one notices me. Good old Eddie, solid and reliable. It's quite liberating in some respects. Anyway, where were we? Yeah, like I say, I got curious and it wasn't hard to find out about your relationship to Polly. I'm sorry about what happened to her. She was a good kid: too good for him. He promised her the earth, just like he promises them all but when they start to press, as they all inevitably do, he drops them like hot bricks.'

'I already figured that much out.'

'Polly was special and got under his skin. But when she got hooked on the drugs, she became a liability so...' Bairstow spread his hands. 'You know the rest.'

'You must have realised that I'd taken this job in the hope of getting back at him. Yet you didn't warn him.' She canted her head. 'I can't help wondering why.'

'You still don't get it yet, do you?'

Freya had an inkling, impossible though it seemed, but needed to hear him say it. 'Get what? You're Falcon's righthand man. His go-to person. The keeper of his secrets. He doesn't sneeze without you knowing about it.'

'Darlin', we've been in each other's pockets since our school days, or more to the point, I've been Falcon's bag carrier all that time, grateful for the crumbs from his table and doing whatever it took to keep him out of jail.'

'Having your advice ignored and being his whipping boy,' Freya added softly. 'I've heard the way he talks to you. The way he puts you down in front of people. I couldn't understand why you'd let him humiliate you that way.'

A slow, malicious smile spread across Bairstow's face, which is when all the pieces fell into place and Freya realised that she'd royally underestimated him.

'It was you,' she said. 'You stole Falcon's money from the bitcoin fiasco.'

* * *

Greg cursed the amount of time that the cute detective spent asking him inane and unnecessary questions. By the time she ran out of excuses to detain him, Greg knew that he'd lost the advantage and would never run Bairstow to ground now without his actions being questioned.

'Bugger!' he muttered, wondering where Freya had got to.

He returned to his cabin, thinking about his next move, when his phone rang.

'Hey, Ray,' he said, taking the call when the detective's name flashed up on the screen. 'What's happening?'

'The fraud squad are wetting themselves with anticipation at finally getting something on Falcon.' Ray chuckled. 'The phone lines between London and Spain must be red hot.'

'We have some of Spain's finest on board as we speak.' Greg gave him the gist of the conversation they'd overheard between Falcon and Bairstow the previous night.

'Did you tell the Spanish?'

'They didn't ask. Thought you'd prefer to be the purveyor of glad tidings.'

'Those papers are obviously the Holy Grail,' Ray said. 'Thanks, I'll pass that on.'

'Have you got an update on Irvine's murder?'

'He checked in alone but there were signs of a woman's presence in the room.'

'A hooker?'

'Unlikely. There were a few women's clothes and toiletries in the room but nothing to identify her. There's CCTV in the lobby but Irvine checked in alone.'

'And let me guess, that lobby's so busy that any lady joining Irvine would go unnoticed.'

'That about sums it up. We did manage to get pictures of lone women going up in the lift to his floor from the time he checked in until just after the time of his murder. It's a long shot but we're running them through face recognition now. If any of them are known to us then it will be somewhere to start.'

'You're thinking a lover's tiff gone wrong.' Greg paused to consider the possibility. 'Were there any defensive wounds on the victim?'

'No, and their absence would support your theory.'

'Any sign of the murder weapon?'

'Nope.'

'Then that implies premeditation, taking a knife to a tryst, I mean.'

'Yeah. Can't trust anyone nowadays.'

'But Irvine clearly trusted the woman, if we're right about her being the killer. Send me over the pictures you have. I'll see if I can help with identification.' Not that he was sure he could but there was an outside possibility that the woman had been on board with Irvine at some point.

'Will do. Most are too blurred, or backs of heads or what have you. But one or two are clear enough.'

'Okay, great.'

'Let me know how the grilling goes.'

'Sure.'

'Oh, and one other thing, Greg. Someone's been telling you porkies. Your missing woman, Irvine's sister.'

'You have news?'

'Not the sort of news you were hoping for.' Ray paused. 'Greg, Irvine was an only child. He doesn't have a sister.'

'Shit!'

'I'll leave you to ponder on that one. Someone, somewhere has either screwed up or been deliberately misled. I have bigger fish to fry right now so I can't delve. I have no real reason to anyway. Your intelligence has earned me a ton of brownie points and my star is currently in the ascendency, so I need to focus all my efforts on bringing Falcon down.'

In other words, Ray had earned himself a seat at the table of a major investigation that would do his career no harm, especially if Falcon was finally convicted.

'Glad to hear it. Let me know if there are developments your end and I'll do the same.'

Greg ended the call and wandered onto the bridge with his phone still in his hand, wondering why Beth had posed as Irvine's sister. He pulled up the pictures when they came in and scrolled through them, thinking it would be a wild goose chase. Ray had been right to say that the majority of them could have been... well, anyone of any age. All they had in common was that they were alone and female. In some cases even their sex was debateable but it wasn't Greg's problem. The Met had sophisticated means of identifying faces and all these lucky ladies would be blissfully unaware that they were currently being put through that system.

'What have you got?'

Greg instinctively shut down his phone, not having heard Sandy approach.

'Hey,' he said. 'Have you been interviewed yet?'

'Nope. I think they're more interested in what Falcon's guests have to say.'

'I got grilled.'

Sandy chuckled. 'By the pretty female detective. I noticed her giving you the third degree.'

Greg knew he had to break the news about Beth and was a firm believer in ripping the plaster off in one go. 'I've heard from my detective friend,' he said. 'Seems Irvine had female company.'

Sandy widened her eyes. 'She killed him?'

'That's what they're thinking. I was just looking at some possible candidates caught on camera in the lift.'

'Let's have a gander. You never know.'

'There's something you need to know first.' Greg cleared his throat. 'The thing is...'

'Come on, Greg, spit it out. You're making me nervous. It's not like you to dither.'

'Okay.' Greg took a deep breath. 'It seems that Irvine was an only child. He didn't have a sister.'

'No.' Sandy smiled and shook her head. 'Someone's got their wires crossed.'

'I doubt it. The Met aren't infallible, but they don't make those sorts of mistakes.'

'But... but, that makes no sort of sense.' Sandy plonked her backside down on a locker. 'Why would Beth have lied about something like that?'

'That I couldn't say.'

She looked shell-shocked.

'I'm sorry, Sandy. I know it's not what you wanted to hear.'

'I detest anyone who lives a lie, but I can't and never will accept that Beth deliberately deceived me.' Sandy tossed her head, as though defying Greg to argue. He didn't and remained silent as she tried to justify in her own mind a situation that had left her baffled and disappointed. 'There has to be another explanation and once we find her, it will all be cleared up.'

'I'm sure you're right,' Greg said, not feeling particularly sure of any such thing.

'Let's look at the mystery women on your phone then,' she said, standing again and clearly making a huge effort to pull herself together. 'Two heads are better than one.'

'Here we go.'

Greg accessed the file and scrolled through the images.

'You're right. They're not clear.' She gasped. 'Hang on, go back to that last one. Make it larger.'

Mystified when Sandy's body went rigid, he did as she asked and watched as the colour slowly drained from her face.

'That's Beth,' she said, pointing a shaking finger at Greg's phone.

19

Freya probably looked as shell-shocked as she felt. 'I never would have suspected you,' she said, shaking her head in bald admiration.

'Don't beat yourself up over it,' Bairstow replied easily. 'Everyone underestimates me, which is why it was so easy for me to get away with it.'

'A benefit of being invisible, I suppose. You were able to hide your activities in plain sight, so to speak.'

'Clever girl. Like I say, I knew who you were almost from day one. I know Greg Larson has it in for Falcon as well. I advised Jules not to take him on, like the caring right hand I'm supposed to be. Well, I had to warn him, but Jules sometimes fancies himself as a bit of a philanthropist. Anyway, you and he played into my hands by joining forces. I reckoned that if you made a nuisance of yourselves then it would distract Jules and create a further layer of protection for me. All the time you two were stirring the pot, he'd be even less likely to suspect me.'

'Yes, I can quite see that.'

'I knew you'd bugged this room, of course. I sweep it as a matter of course on a daily basis.'

Freya thought it interesting that he didn't mention the listening device that Greg had placed in Pyke's pocket which had enabled them to hear the conversation in the salon. Presumably, even Bairstow, who seemed remarkably well informed, knew nothing about that and Freya felt no pressing need to enlighten him. He was in the mood to boast about his achievements and had every reason in the world not to muddy the water by harming Freya, but even so, it wouldn't be sensible to poke the bear.

'You obviously didn't mention the fact to Falcon.'

'Course not. Jules is a suspicious bugger, with just reason it seems, and doesn't feel safe from prying ears even on this tub. That's how I knew that one of you would fetch up here today looking for those papers. I didn't have the slightest intention of hiding them for him, of course. I'm done watching his back.'

'What's in them?'

'Financial dealings that he would prefer his accountant, not to mention the plod, to know nothing about. Details of loans he's made, interest rates charged, that sort of stuff. Plus details of various agreements he's made off the record including, significantly, with Parker and Pyke over the bitcoin fiasco.'

'Isn't that a bit careless, to keep records of anything that sensitive, even if it's not computerised?'

'That's what I've consistently told him but unless his back's against the wall and he seriously needs me to crack a few heads, he tends to do the opposite of whatever I suggest, just to prove that he's the big man. He's got a serious inferiority complex, in case you hadn't already figured that much out, and will never admit that I'm the brains of the operation. It would have gone under, and he'd have had his collar felt long since if it weren't for me.' Bairstow gave a mirthless chuckle. 'Anyway, his grandiose affection made him that much easier to manipulate.'

'I dare say.' Freya fixed him with a penetrating look, no longer afraid of him but still innately curious. 'However, the missing funds. I assume you have them.'

'Perhaps I know where they are.'

She swallowed. 'Did you kill Irvine?'

'No.' He shook his head, looking mildly irritated.

'That wasn't supposed to happen but,' he added with a resigned sigh, 'he got greedy and tried to renege on our agreement.'

'You and he worked alone?'

'No, it was nothing to do with me. Irvine wasn't aware that I was the brains and that he was being used. Like I've said several times already, people tend to underestimate me, which is just the way that I intend for it to remain.'

'So who...'

'Let's just say that my lady friend inveigled her way into Irvine's affections and the rest, to coin a phrase, is history.'

'She killed him?'

Bairstow shrugged. 'Possibly. Probably. She was going to see him in his room before he faced Jules. The shit hit the fan when Irvine was found dead, and I haven't had a chance to speak to Beth yet.'

'Beth?' Freya froze. 'Irvine's sister Beth?'

* * *

Greg stared at Sandy. He absolutely hadn't seen that one coming. 'Pointless asking you if you're sure.'

Sandy nodded, clearly dazed. 'It's her. No question. Look.' Sandy held up her forearm and showed a tattoo of entwined hearts just above the inside of her wrist. With the picture on Greg's phone enlarged and the woman she insisted was Beth holding her hand up to partially cover her face, the identical tattoo was in clear focus. 'We had them done at the same time, and now I don't even know who she is.' A tear trickled down Sandy's cheek and she brushed it impatiently aside. 'I feel like I've been used.'

'That I doubt. Assuming she's involved in the theft of the money, there's nothing you could have told her about it. Did she ever ask questions about Falcon?'

'No, but I ranted about him often enough. Said I should never have taken... fuck!' She clasped a hand over her mouth.

'What is it?'

'It was Beth who pointed out the advert for a chef on a luxury yacht in the trade press. Said it might be a useful outlet for my talents and that I'd get to see the world. I was at a crossroads at the time. I was fighting all the time with my co-owner of the restaurant we started together, which meant we were getting nowhere. That's why I did those cookery courses. It was something different. Something that was mine alone and that I could control.'

'And that's where you met Beth.'

'Yeah, and we hit it off at once. There was an immediate spark between us, chemistry off the scale, and I knew, or thought I knew at once that I'd met my soul mate. Just goes to show what a lousy judge of character I actually am. I believed it because I wanted it to be true. She made me feel happy. She was the missing element in my life that I'd been looking for all that time, blah-de-blah. Ha! What a mug.'

'She played you, but I'm at a loss to know why, so perhaps it really was personal for her too as opposed to your being a business asset. I mean, if she wanted to find out Falcon's movements, there are easier ways to go about it. You could only tell her when he was on board this tub and I can't see what use that information would have been to her anyway.'

Sandy's expression briefly lightened. 'And yet she never asked.'

'Well, there you are then. Her feelings for you must have been genuine.'

'I wish I could believe that. But I can't because she lied to me. If you love someone, you don't lie.' Sandy rubbed her eyes with the heel of her hand. 'If she stole Falcon's money then I can live with that. I mean, it wasn't actually his in the first place. She kept asking me what I'd do if money was no object. I used to wax lyrical about the sort of restaurant I'd like to open, and she told me that sometimes dreams do come true.

Perhaps now I understand why she sounded so convincing.'

'Seems to me that she was planning a future with you but didn't want you involved in her criminal activities. She was protecting you.'

'But if she killed someone.' Sandy threw back her head and growled. 'I can't get my mind round it. Not that I believe she's capable of murder but then I obviously didn't know her nearly as well as I thought I did.' She looked dazed. 'Besides, why kill her partner in crime? More to the point, why did Irvine pretend she'd been abducted when obviously she'd hadn't been?'

'Probably her idea. She wanted to distance you from what she was doing. Stop you from probing.'

Sandy grunted. 'Perhaps, but I'm not sure I buy that. We were apart a lot of the time anyway, given the nature of my job.'

'Come on.' Greg took Sandy's hand and led her down the steps to the companionway, taking a route that would avoid the salon and the foredeck, where Falcon was still being grilled. 'Freya needs to hear about this.'

They looked for her in the crew quarters but there was no sign of her and no one they asked had seen her for a while. Growingly concerned, Greg paused to think.

'Those papers,' Sandy said. 'Would she have tried to get to them?'

'Not unless she's an expert safe-cracker with a death wish.' Greg rolled his eyes. 'But yeah, she might have.'

They headed for Falcon's study. Greg paused with his hand on the door latch, hearing low voices coming from within. Too low for him to identify the speakers. Aware that Falcon was still on the foredeck, he shared a worried glance with Sandy, who gave a decisive nod.

Greg pushed the door open with considerable force and the voices abruptly stopped. The door hit an obstacle that produced a litany of profanities when it crashed into a person standing directly in front of it.

'Greg, there you are!' Freya's voice was bright, tinged with a modicum of relief.

'You nearly broke my fucking shins!' Bairstow complained, hopping from foot to foot as he rubbed his injuries, real or imagined. 'Ain't you ever heard of knocking?' Bairstow frowned when his gaze fell upon Sandy. 'What the fuck's she doing here?'

'What's going on?' Greg asked. 'You okay, Freya?'

'Yeah, I'm good. Eddie here has just admitted that

he and Irvine joined forces to help themselves to the funds from the bitcoin fund.'

Greg nodded as he closed the door and stepped into the room. 'With help, I gather,' he said, placing a hand on Sandy's shoulder.

Freya quirked a brow. 'You know about Beth?'

'My detective friend sent me pictures of lone females caught on the cameras in the lift closest to Irvine's room. Sandy recognised her.'

'I'm not keeping up here,' Bairstow said, scratching his head. 'How do you know my girlfriend?'

Sandy glowered at him. '*Your* girlfriend?'

'They're old friends,' Freya said.

Greg placed a hand on Sandy's arm to prevent her from blurting out the truth. It was already obvious to him that Beth used her sexuality to get what she wanted. But she had no reason to befriend Sandy, he reasoned, not unless her feelings were genuine. She had Bairstow to keep her appraised of Falcon's every move. Part of Greg hoped that Beth hadn't fallen for Sandy. How could she ever be truly content with a woman who deceived at best, and who was looking increasingly like a cold-blooded murderer?

'Eddie's given me the combination of the safe. There's enough documentation in there apparently to put Falcon behind bars for decades. That's the good news. The not so good news is that he has no idea who knocked Irvine off and no clue as to where the funds and Beth have disappeared to.'

Sandy let out a cry that caused Bairstow to look sharply at her.

'So,' Freya said, spreading her hands. 'What do we do?'

'Well,' Greg replied, 'we're not the police and for my part, I don't much care where the money is or who killed Irvine. I don't have a death wish myself and as we're obviously dealing with ruthless people, I have no desire to put myself in the firing line.'

Freya nodded her agreement. 'All I care about is bringing Falcon down and getting some sort of justice for my sister. That was the only reason why I took this job. But I would like to look him in the eye when his world finally crumbles, tell him who I am and make him aware that I'm partly responsible for his downfall.'

'We're agreed then,' Greg said. 'So, how do we play it?'

Freya turned towards Bairstow. 'I take it you'll be staying on board for a bit longer, Eddie, and continuing to play your part.'

'Yep. That was my intention anyway. If I scarpered

at the same time as the money went missing then even Falcon would eventually smell a rat. Anyway, now that the money and my girlfriend have gone AWOL, I have no choice but to stick it out, at least while the police are all over us.' He cracked his knuckles. 'But I will find the money, and her. I'm guessing they'll both be in the same place, and then I'll get what's due to me, as will she. No one does me over and gets away with it.'

'Do you think she killed Irvine?' Greg asked. 'There were woman's possessions in his room.'

'They would have been hers. She was posing as his sister, but I'm guessing you already know that.'

Everyone nodded.

'She was posing as a hell of a lot of things,' Sandy muttered.

'I'd arranged to meet her and Irvine here in Ibiza. He was going to split the proceeds. I already had accounts set up to receive my share. Anyway, do I think she killed him?' Bairstow shook his head emphatically. 'Not unless he did something to severely piss her off, like trying to do us out of our share, and probably not even then. She'd have let me know and I'd have dealt with him. She's creative, not aggressive.'

'My understanding is that there was no sign of a struggle,' Greg said. 'So here's my problem. Would

Irvine have let a stranger into the room and calmly stood there while they stabbed him in the chest?' Greg shook his head. 'It's hardly likely, is it, so the police will be thinking that he let the killer in because he knew and trusted them.'

'Is there any way in this world that Falcon could have gotten away from you all for long enough to do it?' Sandy asked.

'It's vaguely possible, I suppose,' Bairstow said pensively. 'We had a long dinner under the stars walking distance away from the hotel. He got up from the table several times to take calls. And to make them. He said he had to call his wife who was flapping over yet another crisis with his waste of space son. She leaves Falcon to his own devices, unless there's a drama with one of the kids. If... no, when that happens, Falcon moves heaven and earth to resolve it. That way, he keeps her sweet and off his case.'

'How long was he gone for?' Freya asked.

Bairstow shrugged. 'About half an hour, I guess.'

'Surely the others would have noticed his absence and remarked upon it to the police,' Greg said, sharing a *what-the-hell* look with Freya.

'Not necessarily. The meal was over, but Falcon suggested having champagne in the gardens before going to the casino. He said it was too early to be fashionably seen there,' he added, rolling his eyes. 'We were all milling around the gardens and his guests took the opportunity to mix with others and escape his toxic presence for a while, so it's unlikely that he would have been missed. And even if he was, unless someone was keeping deliberate tabs on him, they'd have no clear idea how long he'd been gone for. Like I say, the place was heaving.' Bairstow scratched his ear. 'That aside, I still don't get why he'd want to kill Irvine.'

'Could he have got to the hotel, killed the guy and got back to you in that space of time?' Greg asked.

Bairstow waggled a hand from side to side. 'Just about, but it would have been tight.'

'It's possible that Beth might have been in the room when he got there. Is there any way that he could have linked her to you, Eddie?' Freya asked. 'And then lost it.'

'None that I'm aware of. We've been paranoid about keeping our connection on a need-to-know basis. Besides, as you know, Jules and I had a long heart-to-heart in this room last night. I know him too well for him to be able to hide his moods from me. If he even suspected that I'd gone rogue, I'd have recognised the signs. He's not known for subtlety and would have gone straight for the jugular.'

'Will you tell the police about Falcon's absence after dinner when they interview you?' Sandy asked.

Bairstow emphatically shook his head. 'In the world we come from, we settle our differences in house. We don't ever grass one another up.'

'You just stick the knife in,' Sandy said in a sardonic tone.

'We resolve our own issues, sure. But no one can say that they don't know what they're getting themselves into.'

'Okay,' Greg said. 'What's the combination of the safe?'

Bairstow told him. Greg keyed it in and lifted the lid. There was a heavy wedge of papers inside, along with bundles of cash in various currencies. He left the cash where it was and removed the papers.

'I'll hide these in the wheelhouse amongst the navigational documents. Even if the police search, they're unlikely to find them there.'

'You're not going to just hand them over?' Sandy asked.

'Not yet,' Greg replied. 'I might have done so but that would drop Bairstow here in it. There's only one person who could have given me the safe's combination.'

'Right.' Sandy nodded but she still looked un-
certain.

'Besides, he was supposed to have removed them
all last night and if Falcon wiggles out of these charges
then he'll have Bairstow in his sights.'

'Appreciate it,' Bairstow said with a nod of thanks.

'Besides, we now have Falcon banged to rights, as
they say, for money laundering, loan sharking, prosti-
tution rackets and what have you.' He tapped the
heavy wedge of papers under his arm for emphasis.
'I'm guessing there's all the evidence we need for
forensic scientists to put a case together against him.'

'That's what comes of being too clever,' Freya said.
'Of not trusting computers.'

'Couldn't have happened to a nicer guy,' Bairstow
said with a snort. 'I told him more times than enough
that a paper trail would lead to his downfall one day. I
might just have forgotten to mention that I'd make
sure it did.'

'We'd better get out of here,' Freya said, glancing
at her watch. 'They won't keep Falcon much longer.
This is the first place he'll come once they're done
with him and if he finds us all together...'

'If you're convinced that Beth didn't kill Irvine,'
Greg said.

'She didn't,' Sandy said with conviction.

Bairstow frowned, fixing her with a probing look, clearly not buying the "old friend" explanation and wanting to know what her connection to Beth actually was. Greg hurriedly spoke again before he could ask questions.

'Okay, so she likely witnessed the murder and is running scared. In which case she'll contact you, Bairstow. How would she do that?'

'We have burners.' He pulled a mobile from his pocket and waved it in the air.

'Right well, if you hear from her, let me know. We can help her, but we all need to pull together.'

20

Julien thought the questions would never end. Sanchez was a wily bugger, who kept changing tack, attempting to wrongfoot him. Like that was gonna happen! Even so, the man was nobody's fool and Julien would need to keep his concentration: stay on top of his game. He glanced at his mobile for the tenth time in half an hour. Fuck it, had they been asking questions for that long? Time flies when you're having fun, he thought, wiping perspiration from his brow that was not, he knew, contributable to the warm weather.

'Are you expecting a call, Mr Falcon?' Sanchez asked. 'Something more important than helping me to discover who killed your friend?'

'All my calls are important. I'm a businessman and keep my finger on the pulse even when I'm away from my desk.'

He'd over-explained, he realised and abruptly shut his trap. He wasn't about to tell Sanchez that he still hadn't had a call back from his brief and was becoming increasingly concerned by his silence. He paid a fucking fortune to have Rushton on speed dial but was he there when he needed him the most? Was he fuck!

As though engineered by the sheer force of his will, his phone chirped into life and Rushton's name flashed up on the screen.

'Excuse me, I have to take this,' Julien said, accepting the call and walking to the far end of the deck.

'You called,' Rushton said curtly.

'Where the fuck have you been?'

'How can I help?'

Julien realised that losing his rag with a man whose help he needed rather badly would serve no purpose. He took a deep breath and in a muted tone explained the situation. Even if Sanchez overheard, he hadn't said anything to incriminate himself.

'Oh dear, you are in a bit of a pickle, aren't you?'

'Is that what I pay you for?' In spite of his best efforts to remain calm, Falcon felt his blood pressure spike as the man's languid drawl echoed over the air-waves. 'Stating the bleeding obvious.'

'I'll make some calls. See if I can find someone suitable to have your back. In the meantime, you don't need me to tell you to say nothing.'

'There's nothing to tell. I didn't do the bastard.'

'Well then, you have nothing to worry about.'

'The plod are here now, on the boat, grilling us all. I get the impression that they're not looking for anyone else, so get me some help pronto.'

Julien cut the call without saying goodbye and returned to Sanchez.

'You feel the need for legal representation, Mr Falcon?'

'Too right I do. Never talk to law enforcement without it.'

'Ah, so you are accustomed to speaking with my colleagues in England.' He paused. 'Interesting.'

Fuck! He'd just proved to himself, if any proof was necessary, the futility of losing his rag. He absolutely needed someone beside him to protect his interests. He was so used to having Eddie do the heavy lifting, and to hold him back when he got a bit lairy, that he'd forgotten how to play the game solo.

'We've been talking for a while now, Inspector,' Julien said with a significant glance at his Rolex day-date, all sixty grand's worth, weighing his wrist down as he strove to take control of a situation that had never been his to control. It was an alien feeling and he didn't like it one little bit. 'I've told you all I know. Is there anything else I can help you with?'

'You're absolutely sure that no one left your party for any significant amount of time during your dinner?' He fixed Julien with a searching look as he spoke, as though he already knew that Julien himself had done so. But that was impossible, Julien tried to convince himself. None of his guests would have noticed or said anything even if they'd lost sight of him. They'd all been too busy swigging champagne at his expense at the time to care about where he was. They still clung to Julien's coat-tails for their livelihoods and wouldn't grass him up anyway.

'Inspector, how many more times?' Julien gave an impatient huff as he attempted to cross one foot over his opposite thigh. The fact that he was wearing shorts didn't imbue the gesture with the satirical elegance he'd been hoping for. 'No one other than myself and Mr Bairstow knew that Irvine was expected. And neither of us knew that he'd checked in, or what room he was in.'

'I'm still at a loss to understand what business it was that you hoped to transact with him and why it was necessary for him to come here in order to carry out your instructions.'

'Mr Irvine handled my personal financial affairs, or some of them.' Julien sat a little straighter. 'Men in my position have their bankers come to them,' he couldn't resist adding, knowing at once when Sanchez met his gaze and held it without speaking that it had been an error of judgement to boast. 'Anyway,' he added, standing, 'if there's nothing else, I'll let you get on. You're a busy man, I'm sure. I know I am.'

Sanchez stood too and nodded. 'Thank you for your time. I am sure we will speak again. In the meantime, please remain here on your yacht until we have a clearer idea of what happened to Mr Irvine.'

'I'm always at your disposal, Inspector.'

Julien led the way to the aft deck, where the rest of Sanchez's officers awaited his arrival. Presumably, they had conducted their interviews. If anything of interest had come of them, it was evident that they weren't about to discuss matters in front of Julien, not even in Spanish. They could have done because he wouldn't have understood a word, so hopefully there was nothing of significance to report and Julien would soon be given leave to... well, leave Ibiza.

Julien watched his unwelcome visitors climb back into their launch. The driver lowered powerful twin outboards into the water, turned the boat in a tight circle and headed for shore. Julien glanced into the salon, inside of which all his guests were gathered.

'Sorry about that,' he said, joining them. 'We have to stay here for a while longer but feel free to go ashore at any time. Just ask one of the crew to take you.'

Chelsea was curled up in a chair that swamped her slender form, looking as though she'd like to be somewhere else. The same could be said for all his guests, at least insofar as they all appeared disgruntled. Being interviewed by the plod could have that effect, Julien knew, even when a person was innocent.

None of the men in that salon could lay claim to innocence. They'd all been willing to flirt with the letter of the banking laws when it gave them a good payday but now that the chips were down, they looked ready to abandon ship.

Quite literally.

He turned when he sensed a presence in the doorway.

'Can I get anyone anything?' the hostess asked politely.

'Hot chocolate?' Chelsea asked, looking up.

'In this heat?' Julien asked.

'Of course.' Freya smiled at the girl. 'My sister's

favourite.'

The others gave their orders and Freya walked away to fetch their drinks. But Julien's gaze remained focused on Freya's retreating figure. Something she'd just said had registered with him and things clicked into place. Polly had loved hot chocolate even when the temperature was in the nineties. Julien had teased her about her obsession. Freya had a look of Polly about her and now that he thought about it, Polly had often mentioned her big sister with affection.

'What the fuck?' he muttered, recalling too the woman in the red dress who'd caught his attention in the casino the night before.

Where the fuck was Eddie? Why hadn't he found out who she was, like he'd asked him to? He headed for his study and slammed the door behind him. Not that it was possible to slam doors on boats – they had magnetic catchy things to prevent it from happening – but he gave it his best shot, aware that Freya being on board and Julien having the filth all over him couldn't be a coincidence. What did Freya know about his dealings with Irvine? What had he let slip in front of Polly that she might have passed on? Freya presumably had an axe to grind and wouldn't think twice about dropping Julien in it in the misguided assumption that he was responsible for Polly's death.

Damn it, he'd loved the girl but wasn't responsible for her addiction. How was he supposed to have known that she wouldn't be able to control her needs? She was an adult and Julien didn't subscribe to the blameless society. Why the hell did the whole world hold him personally responsible for all its problems?

He wanted to ask Eddie what to do about Freya. He would come up with sound advice, even if Julien pretended not to take it more often than not, but something held him back. He didn't believe that Eddie hadn't discovered who Freya was and the fact that he hadn't told Julien meant that the trust was gone. Who would have thought it? Julien's one solid, trustworthy subordinate. A childhood friend who'd protected Julien from the playground bully and who Julien would trust with his life. A man whom he *had* trusted with more than just that.

'Why, Eddie?' he asked, shouting the words to the ceiling.

Eddie would have to wait. Julien would give him the benefit of the doubt and an opportunity to explain himself. They'd been together for too long to jump to conclusions.

In the meantime, he'd deal with Freya alone.

He put his head round his study's door and was saved the trouble of sending for her when she walked towards him with a trayful of drinks for the guests in the salon.

'Deliver those and spare me a moment,' he said amicably.

* * *

Greg sat in the wheelhouse, watching the anchorage come to life as people on other boats woke up at the crack of midday after a hard night's partying and took to the water on jet skis, kayaks and paddle boards. The police had just left, and he wondered how Falcon would react to such a tough grilling. He'd been with the inspector, apparently, for more than half an hour. That wouldn't have gone down well. Falcon didn't like losing face, not even in front of his mates.

He would have to make Ray Milton aware of developments, most particularly about the documents now burning a hole in the chart locker directly across from Greg in the wheelhouse. He should probably make him aware of Falcon's absence from the dinner the night before as well. It would be enough to see him arrested, or would be but for the fact that he had no obvious motive for wanting rid of Irvine. Somehow, Greg suspected that wouldn't prevent Sanchez from feeling his collar. Murders were bad for tourism, and he'd be under pressure to solve this one. Once Falcon was safely in custody and Ray had possession of the documents, it would be enough to see Falcon kept under lock and key for the duration.

But what of Beth? Sandy was disillusioned but now that she'd recovered from the initial shock, she was also adamant that the woman she loved wouldn't be capable of killing anyone. And especially by means of something as brutal as a stabbing, unless she was defending herself. And there had been no evidence of a struggle in the room where Irvine died. Tellingly, Bairstow, who was also in a relationship with Beth, agreed with that assessment. Be that as it may, he ought to tell Ray what he knew about her. But he wouldn't. Not quite yet.

If Beth had found Irvine dead then it stood to reason that she'd have scarpered and was probably afraid that she'd been seen. She *had* been. Why hadn't she contacted Bairstow if she needed somewhere to hide? Perhaps she had but Greg's instincts told him otherwise. He threw his arms in the air and his head back, unsure what to do.

Sandy burst into the wheelhouse like a whirlwind while he was still in mid-stretch.

'Beth just called me! She needs help.'

'Slow down!' Greg placed a hand on her shoulder.

'Start at the beginning.'

'She's hiding out in a backstreet backpackers hotel. She found Irvine dead, swears she had nothing to do with it and that she'll tell me everything. But I need to go to her.' Sandy jumped from foot to foot. 'Will you take me?'

'Yes, on the condition that I meet Beth with you.'

'But—'

'No buts, Sandy. We have absolutely no idea what happened with Irvine, or why she called you rather than Bairstow.'

'Okay.' She bounced on her toes like a child on a sugar rush. 'Can we go now?'

'Sure.'

Greg wanted to tell Freya about this latest development but decided against it. She would want to come ashore too but would be missed if she left now. The guests, with nothing better to do to fill their time, would doubtless be demanding. Better to fill her in after the event. And Bairstow too, but only if Greg deemed it necessary for him to know. Beth could have been running, not from the scene of a murder, but from Bairstow. If Falcon had slipped away from dinner the previous night for half an hour and not been missed, what's to say that Bairstow couldn't have done the same?

Greg made sure that Alex was around to keep anchor watch and then went to the bathing platform and fired up one of the jet skis. Sandy jumped up behind him and Greg moved the ski away from the yacht, turning it in a smooth circle that didn't threaten the no-wake rule. A rule that was widely ignored by other ski users, but that was beside the point. Greg didn't want to draw attention to their departure and was as sure as it was possible to be that they weren't being watched by anyone on board.

Once ashore, they followed directions on the map on Sandy's phone and wound their way through increasingly narrow back streets.

'This is it,' Sandy said tersely, stopping outside a rundown building that had definitely seen better days. 'She's on the second floor. Room eighteen at the back.'

The stairs were as crumbling as the rest of the building which, despite its dilapidated state, appeared to be full. There was no substitute for cheap and cheerful when you were a backpacker on a limited budget and not too fussy about where you laid your head, Greg assumed.

Sandy ran up the stairs, mindless of the hazard to life that they represented and only paused when she reached the door to room eighteen. Greg could sense her tension: a tension that warred with blossoming hope. Hope that she'd somehow gotten it wrong and that Beth wasn't a thief, a potential murder suspect and, probably more relevant to Sandy, not in a relationship with Bairstow. She looked up at Greg, moistened her lips and tapped at the door.

It was thrown open a crack.

'Who is it?'

'Me,' Sandy replied.

The door opened wider and the attractive young woman whose image Greg had seen several times that day stood there, looking nothing like her picture. Dishevelled didn't come close to describing her appearance. Scared shitless, alone and vulnerable might better fit the bill. Her clothes looked as though they'd been slept in, and her hair hung in tangled rats' tails round a face that was blotchy, presumably because she'd been crying. It wasn't the face of a criminal mastermind, and she certainly didn't look like a person with an illegal agenda that she hadn't shared with her significant other. Sandy clearly felt the same way and fell into the woman's arms.

Greg followed them into the room and closed the door behind him, shutting out the possibility of prying eyes. He watched the two women hugging and Beth sobbing on Sandy's shoulder.

'Come on, sit down and tell us what happened,' Sandy said gently. 'I've been going out of my mind.'

'Us?' Beth glanced up, appeared to see Greg for the first time, and looked like a rabbit caught in the headlights. 'Who's this?'

Sandy made the introduction. 'You can trust him,' she said.

'You can,' Greg told her, taking the only chair in the room once the ladies had perched themselves on the edge of the sagging single bed, still holding hands. 'We know Irvine wasn't your brother and that you were in league with Bairstow in order to get your hands on the bitcoin funds. What we don't know is who killed Irvine and why and, more to the point, why you lied about so many things to Sandy. Perhaps you'd care to enlighten us.'

Beth turned sideways to look at Sandy, completely ignoring Greg. She now had both of Sandy's hands in hers. 'I originally set out to bring Falcon down,' she said without hesitation. 'My father invested in his bitcoin fund. He knew he was gambling and was prepared to take that risk. I warned him against putting too much in and he promised me that he hadn't.' She swallowed. 'I didn't realise until the fund went belly up that he'd put everything he had in and lost the lot. I thought he would get enough back to keep him from bankruptcy and to perhaps teach him not to be so greedy and he would have, eventually. But... well, you know what happened.'

'How did you meet Bairstow?' Greg asked, getting in before Sandy could bombard the woman with a barrage of more personal questions.

'I joined an online group of people who'd been conned by the fund, and I'll admit that I was quite vocal when expressing my opinion of Falcon. Bairstow sent me a private message, saying he thought he could help me. I was sceptical at first, but also curious so I agreed to meet him in a crowded public place in broad daylight and listen to what he had to say. He bared his soul, and by the time he ran out of words, I was convinced he'd told me the truth. He'd been fetching and carrying for Falcon for years, ever since their childhood in fact, and never got the recognition he deserved. He'd had enough and *had* decided to take those funds for himself. He knew Irvine hated being at Falcon's beck and call, was in urgent need of cash, and would probably be easily persuaded to help himself.'

'But Bairstow didn't trust him not to keep it all,' Greg suggested when Beth paused. 'No such thing as honour amongst thieves nowadays.'

'Right. He needed someone to shadow Irvine and

he knew from some of the things I'd said on the on-line forum that I had a background in banking, as well as carrying a massive grudge and overwhelming desire for retribution. So, he introduced me to Irvine and suggested we pose as brother and sister, aware that Irvine could easily move the money out of Falcon's reach if I wasn't looking over his shoulder. My job was to gather information about his procedures that Bairstow could use to run Irvine to ground if he decided to do us over.'

'How was he going to explain its disappearance when he met Falcon here?' Greg asked.

'He wasn't. He was going to give him details of accounts where it had been moved to, then give us our share and we'd all go our separate ways.'

'The funds would be in those accounts when Irvine opened them up for him but gone again the moment he left Irvine's room,' Greg said.

Beth nodded. 'Something like that.'

'So why the affair with Bairstow?' Sandy asked, unable to keep the hurt out of her voice.

'He wasn't sure about Irvine, and I wasn't sure I could completely trust Eddie. I could see that he liked me and so I played on that, thinking that if we were an item, he'd be less likely to shaft me.' She squeezed Sandy's hand. 'It was business, babe. It meant nothing to me. I was thinking only of our future.'

Sandy twitched her nose. 'You didn't tell him about me?'

'I wanted to protect you. I'll admit that I suggested you take the job on Falcon's yacht when it came up, just to keep an eye on him, but that was before I met Eddie and had a clear plan in mind. Once I was involved with Irvine, I soon realised that it would be better if you knew nothing about my real purpose. That's why I "disappeared". I just wanted to keep you safe so I asked Irvine to tell you that I was on the missing list. I knew that if Falcon had a shadow of a doubt about you... well, it doesn't bear thinking about.' Beth sighed elaborately. 'I wasn't prepared to risk you getting hurt. Or worse.'

Sandy leaned the side of her face on Beth's shoulder, tears slipping down her cheeks.

'Do you know if Irvine showed Falcon those accounts?' Greg asked. 'Were you there when he turned up? Does he know you're involved?'

Beth shook her head. 'He wasn't expecting to see him, but he turned up unannounced. Fortunately, I was in the bathroom at the time. I heard voices and my sixth sense told me to stay there. They argued. Falcon was yelling. He said he knew that Irvine intended to shaft him. That he hadn't come down in the last shower. Irvine opened up the accounts, I think. Leastwise, I heard the sound of fingers on keys and then he swore, presumably because the accounts had been stripped. I know because Irvine had it all on his tablet. I grabbed it when I ran.' She picked it up from the bed and waved it in the air. 'I knew the details and checked when I got here.'

'Let me get this straight,' Greg said, frowning. 'Irvine had already taken the funds. In that case, why *did* he come to Ibiza to meet Falcon? Did he have a death wish?'

Beth spread her hands. 'I don't know why he did it. He was under pressure, being a known associate of Falcon's with banking expertise, to rat him out. Perhaps he did? I don't know.'

'Okay, so we're assuming that Irvine had decided to turn Falcon in,' Greg said, 'but Falcon somehow got wind of his plans, so surprised him in his hotel room and demanded to see proof that the funds were where they were supposed to be. When they weren't, he lost it and stabbed him through the heart.'

Beth nodded. 'That's the only conclusion I've been able to reach. I came out of the shower the moment Falcon left and tried to save Irvine, but he was already dead. There was nothing I could do.'

Sandy squeezed Beth's trembling hands. 'None of this is your fault.'

'I never should have got involved. People have died and I could have prevented it.'

'Nonsense!' Sandy said. 'I'm just so relieved to have you back.'

'So, what now?' Beth asked.

'Now we find you somewhere better to live,' Greg replied. 'This will be resolved soon, if you're willing to tell the truth.'

Beth nodded. 'I think it's beyond time. I haven't actually done anything illegal. Plotting a fraud is not the same thing as carrying it out.'

Greg nodded, feeling surplus to requirements. 'Right.'

'I can't move anywhere else,' Beth protested. 'They'll want to see my passport and until I know that Falcon's under lock and key and that Eddie won't try to get to me, I can't risk that. Places like this aren't too fussy about identification. Cash is king.'

'I have my passport with me.' Sandy patted her bum bag. 'We'll get a room under my name. No one suspects me of anything.'

'Come along then, ladies.' Greg stood and ushered them towards the door. 'Let's get it done.'

21

Freya took her time delivering the drinks and making sure everyone had everything they needed before slowly walking back to Falcon's study. She sent Greg a quick text telling him that she had been summoned into the lion's den.

Come and get me if I'm not out again in five minutes!

A reply came back immediately.

On shore. Beth found. She was in bathroom when Falcon murdered Irvine. Be careful. I'll be back in fifteen.

Taking a deep breath, Freya paused outside the door to Falcon's lair, squared her shoulders and then tapped at it. There was no way she could defer this interview given that she was Falcon's employee and he'd summoned her. Besides, if she played her cards right, she might actually get him to condemn himself with his own words.

'Come in, Freya.'

She did so. 'Something you need?' she asked.

'The truth will do to start with.' Falcon stood with his hands clasped behind his back, his expression an icy shade of grey. The concentrated fury that she sensed him attempting to control played havoc with her strung-out emotions and caused Freya to momentarily doubt the wisdom of confronting him alone. 'Why didn't you tell me that you're Polly's sister?'

Freya simply stared at him, finally making no attempt to keep the hatred out of her expression.

'So you could drug me too?' she eventually responded, her tone scathing, accusatory.

'Polly did that to herself. I warned her to go easy.'

'You started her on hard drugs. You made it sound sophisticated,' she shot back at him. 'She never would have done it otherwise, but she thought you walked on water, that you were her ticket to fame and fortune.' She shook her head in disgust. 'And not content with turning her into a junkie, you then made her whore for you. You disgust me, you worthless excuse for a human being.' Freya was getting worked up. She knew it was dangerous to lose control and to goad such a dangerous and unpredictable man, but she was beyond listening to the voice of reason. And hell, did it feel good to give him a piece of her mind! 'What right do you have to destroy lives?'

'Cut the crap, Freya. I don't have time for feminine histrionics. Polly did what Polly wanted to do. No one forced her into it. But, for what it's worth, she was special. One in a million. I wish I'd kept a closer watch on her drug usage and that's on me.'

A look of genuine loss briefly broke through his aggressive posturing, but it was gone again before it could grow roots. Falcon didn't do emotion, Freya knew. He had developed feelings for Polly but when she proved to have feet of clay, he threw her aside like a discarded shoe and left her to self-destruct. In Freya's book, that amounted to murder.

'No one forced her to snort that crap up her nose.' His voice turned as flintlike as his uncompromising expression. 'Enough of Polly. This is about you. What are you doing here? I don't believe in coincidences and yet the moment you turn up, looking for revenge or fuck knows what, a friend of mine gets murdered and my name's in the frame.'

'Probably because you had more reason than most for wanting him dead.'

'Not to mention a large sum of money has gone missing.' He grabbed her upper arm in a vicelike grip. 'Who sent you? Who are you working for?'

'Let go of my arm.' She sent him a scathing look that miraculously had the desired effect. Freya walked to the other side of the study and stared at him with contempt. 'I took this job of my own volition in the hope of learning something to your detriment that I could take to the police and get you prosecuted for the lying, manipulative scumbag that you are. Unfortunately for Mr Irvine but happily from my perspective, his murder has done the work for me. I can now sit on the sidelines and enjoy seeing you crash and burn.'

Falcon's rictus smile was more frightening than his threats. 'Ain't you learned nothing yet?' he asked. 'No one gets one over on me and lives to enjoy the experience.'

'Kill people all the time, do you?' she asked with a derisive sniff.

'It's been known,' he replied. 'When they get my goat. You might wanna remember that.'

'Like Irvine did. Presumably, you killed him because he defrauded you. I can't think of any other reason why you'd take such an audacious risk.'

'Kill him? Me?' He shook his head. 'Nah. I can account for every minute of my time.'

'Except I know that you did it. I have proof.'

Freya had the satisfaction of seeing him look momentarily unsure of himself. 'What fucking proof?' he asked, an edge to his voice.

'If I had none, what you just said would be all the evidence I actually need.' She deliberately flashed a smug smile. 'An innocent man wouldn't have bothered to ask what I had on him because he would know there was nothing to be had.'

Aware that the room was still bugged and that Falcon couldn't do anything to harm her all the time the police were watching him, she decided to goad him further. A misogynist of his ilk always had to emphasise his position of strength, especially if it was a woman who dared to defy him. Then she recalled that the bug would only work if Greg was close enough with his gizmo to listen in. When Falcon briefly turned his back, she extracted her phone from her pocket and set it to record.

'Don't try and outsmart me, sweetheart,' he said, turning back a fraction of a second after she returned her phone to her pocket. 'Better people have tried and failed.'

She tilted her head and sent him a provocative look, astonished that it hadn't even occurred to him that she would record their conversation. Not so smart after all, then. 'Okay, so you'll get away with it, just like you seem to get away with doing whatever the hell you like.'

'Don't underestimate me, darlin'. The Spanish plod have got nothing on me and when they let me get the hell out of here, that will be the time for us to have another cosy little conversation about your grievances.'

She snorted. 'You think I'll carry on working for you after this?'

'Oh, I know you won't. I want you off this tub the moment the police stop sniffing around. But I don't like amateurs poking their long noses into my affairs. You need to be made to understand that so, like I say, when the time's right, I'll come and find you. And just so you know, there's nowhere you can hide. I'll find you.'

'Keep telling yourself that.' She sent him a challenging look. 'Rome burning springs to mind.'

'Er?'

'It's a quote. Look it up. It refers to the Emperor Nero playing his fiddle while Rome burned around him. A bit like you worrying about trivia when your personal empire is about to implode.'

'Ask Irvine if you think I'm losing it. Oh sorry, you can't, can you.' She had clearly rattled him, but had she done enough to make him boast about his cunning? 'Sure, I did Irvine,' he said, shrugging as casually as if they'd been discussing the weather. 'Bear that in mind the next time you get on your high horse with me. I am not the sort of man it's in your best interests to antagonise.'

Freya swallowed. 'To be clear, you murdered your friend?'

'The bastard thought he could run off with my money. He knows different now.'

Freya struggled to contain her euphoria. He had just been coerced into admitting what he'd done. All she had to do now was to goad the details out of him. 'You left your dinner guests for a while. It's the only time you could have done it. Risky though, I'd have thought.'

He gave her a slow, ironic round of applause. 'And the scrounging bastards didn't even notice I'd gone AWOL.'

'They were probably grateful to escape you for a while.'

Far from seeming offended, he actually laughed. 'That's what I was counting on.'

He'd said all she needed to hear. The police had been concentrating on finding the mystery woman who'd been with Irvine. Now they knew who to look for and approximately when, he would have been caught on a camera somewhere.

'Well done. You must be very proud.' Freya paused. 'But just for the record, why did you kill him if he'd taken what you consider to be your money? You can't find it without his help.'

'I don't trust anyone and like to keep them on their toes, so I turned up at his room when he wasn't expecting me.' Falcon chortled. 'You should have seen the look on his face when he opened the door and saw me standing there. He glanced over his shoulder at his tablet. He had the account open on it and I watched the funds disappear before my eyes. How's that for timing?' he asked bitterly. 'I hadn't planned to do him. You're right to say that it was too risky but... well, I saw red. My short fuse has always caused problems, I'll be the first to admit that much.'

'We all have a cross to bear.'

'Anyway, I threatened him with the knife I'd taken

with me, not meaning to kill him, obviously, at least not until he got the funds back for me, but he called my bluff, the fucking idiot. He stepped towards me at the same time as I moved towards him, the knife penetrated his heart and that was that. I scarpered before anyone saw me and now I don't have a sodding clue how to find the dosh.'

'I dare say you know someone who can trace it for you.'

'Won't do me no good if I don't have access to the account it's gone into.'

'Oh dear!'

'Don't worry your precious little heart about me, darlin'. I'm down but not out. Once I get rid of Inspector sodding Sanchez, I know someone who worked hand in glove with Irvine. His bit on the side who he was planning to run off with. She'll know his banking codes, I'm betting. She's a greedy little madam. It was probably her who persuaded him to do me over. Can't think why else Irvine would have done it. He's always been solid in the past but when a woman gets her claws into a bloke, he stops thinking with his brain.'

It all sounded rather tenuous to Freya. Not about Falcon killing Irvine. She didn't doubt that he'd done it but she did think that his plan for getting his hands back on the funds was a tad optimistic. Then again, if a woman was involved then his misogynistic instincts would work against him simply because he refused to accept that women could be men's equal in the cerebral department, often eclipsing them.

'Well,' she said, 'I'd best get back to work.'

'Not so fast!' He grabbed hold of her again and pushed her against the wall. 'Can't have you running around telling tales out of school.' He extracted his phone from his pocket with the hand not holding Freya and made a call. 'Eddie, get in here. Where is the useless tosser anyway,' he added after cutting the connection. 'He's made himself pretty damned scarce today.'

Eddie walked into the study and appeared to take the scene in at a glance. 'Turns out our pretty little hostess is Polly's big sister,' he said. 'Why the fuck didn't you tell me?'

Freya could see that Eddie was wavering. She gave a tiny shake of her head. She didn't want him to expose his part in Falcon's downfall. The short fuse he'd just referred to would explode in a whirlwind of violence and that would serve no purpose. Greg should be back imminently and then there would be no way out for Falcon.

'Didn't know,' Eddie replied casually.

'I'm surrounded by fucking incompetence,' Falcon growled, picking up a paperknife from his desk and flicking it idly between his fingers. 'You're a waste of fucking space.'

Eddie shrugged, unmoved. 'So you've said, more than once. Is there anything else or did you just call me in so you could insult me?'

Falcon's features filled with rage. Clearly, in his present state of simmering fury, Eddie answering him back felt like one betrayal too many. 'What did you just say, wanker?' he asked, his voice a threatening rumble.

Before Eddie had time to react, Falcon flew at him, raising the paperknife aloft. The man clearly didn't fight fair. Freya knew that Eddie had only defied Falcon in an effort to take the heat off her and she wasn't about to let him suffer the consequences. She simply stuck out a leg as Falcon leapt forward, ignoring her, all his fury concentrated on Eddie. He yelled as he tumbled over Freya's foot and fell onto the knife. Although blunt, the force of his fall caused it to penetrate the fleshy part of his arm and he howled, turning the air blue with his language.

'What the hell?' Greg stood in the open doorway, staring down at Falcon as blood poured from his wound. 'I heard the screaming and thought he was killing you, Freya.'

'You're dead men walking, all three of you,' Falcon said from his position on the floor, where he continued to clutch his arm and blood seeped through his fingers. 'Now get me a fucking doctor.'

22

A week later found Greg and Freya enjoying a drink in a pub garden in Surrey. Falcon's confession had been picked on Freya's phone, as had the man himself on CCTV in the lift going up to Irvine's room. He was now incarcerated in a Spanish prison awaiting trial for murder. The papers that Greg had taken from the safe were in the hands of the fraud squad and further charges would be forthcoming.

'We did good, all things considered,' Greg said, lifting his glass and clinking it against Freya's. 'Is retaliation all it's cracked up to be?'

'I think Polly can rest in peace now at any rate. I no longer sense her presence. If you believe that souls pass on to a better place once their business on this planet is resolved, then I like to think that she's in that place now.'

'I get you. I feel that I've laid my father's ghost to rest too.'

'Will Parker and Pyke be prosecuted?' Freya asked.

Greg shrugged. 'Not sure and don't really care. I can tell you that Eddie is away free and clear. Not sure that he deserves to be but that's another matter. Anyway, if there was any evidence of his involvement in Falcon's various scams in those documents then he'll have removed it before handing them over.'

'Falcon's mistake was putting him down too often and underestimating his intelligence.'

'One of many mistakes.'

'What I don't understand is why Irvine moved that money before meeting with Falcon. I mean, why not just take it and duck the meeting?'

'That was what Beth wanted to do but Irvine reckoned he'd never have felt safe. Falcon's reach is long. His empire would have been very badly damaged by the loss of those funds, but he'd still be in the game.'

Freya nodded. 'With a burning desire for revenge.'

'Right. Anyway, Eddie told Falcon that he thought Irvine was gonna double cross him.'

'He told you that?'

'He did. It's all down to greed. He wanted to cut

Irvine out of the deal and have all the funds for him and Beth. The vital thing is that he didn't know she'd be there with Irvine. She was supposed to be out of harm's way, waiting for Eddie somewhere safe and warm.'

'But she wanted to get her share and then take off with Sandy?'

Greg nodded. 'That's about the size of it.'

'Blimey, this is getting complicated.'

'Keep up!' Greg joked. 'I'll try to make it simple.'

'So that even I can understand.' Freya batted her lashes at him, making them both laugh.

'Irvine was supposed to move the lion's share, minus his generous fee naturally, to the account he'd set up for Falcon somewhere the banking regulations are looked upon as optional and to do it in front of Falcon at that hotel.'

'With you so far,' Freya said, grinning over the rim of her glass as she took a healthy sip of wine.

'My understanding is that those documents would have found their way into the hands of the regulators once Falcon was back on English shores, courtesy of Eddie—'

'Leaving Eddie and Beth free to ride off into the sunset, after removing the funds from Falcon's offshore account, naturally.' Freya shifted her position on the bench she shared with Greg and looked directly at him. 'So, my original question stands. Why had Irvine moved the money before Falcon got to his room?'

'Beth says they'd had a massive row. Irvine had a last minute fit of jitters and lost his nerve. He felt that Falcon would still get to him, even from a jail cell if he went down and the funds then disappeared. Irvine was happy with his 20 per cent and didn't want to be looking over his shoulder for the rest of his life. What Falcon saw wasn't Irvine moving the money out of *his* account; it was coming out of Irvine's and on the point of going back into Falcon's.'

'Irvine had already moved it?' Freya shook her head. 'My brain hurts.'

'No. Beth took matters into her own hands and did it when Irvine was in the shower. He noticed, got mad, and scared, and moved it back. That was what Falcon saw, and misinterpreted.'

'Irvine got murdered for trying to do the right thing. Well, the right thing if you discount handing millions of pounds worth of stolen money so I don't feel *that* sorry for him. Polly died, and your father too, and they did nothing to deserve it.' She smiled at Greg. 'Now my dull brain has caught up.'

'Like I said already, it's all down to greed.'

Freya took a sip of her wine as she watched a

family of ducks paddling across the river at the bottom of the pub garden. 'Any news of Sandy and Beth?'

'Nope, but I'm betting they're together some-where.' He chuckled. 'It's funny but Ray called me the other day. The police have received calls from several of the bitcoin fund victims. Seems they've had a healthy percentage of their losses returned anony-mously to their accounts.'

Freya smiled. 'That will be Beth's doing, I expect. I assume that not all the funds will be returned. If I was a gambling woman then I'd bet the farm that a few million will remain unaccounted for.'

Greg returned her smile. 'Enough for a decent chef and a gregarious hostess to open a restaurant somewhere exotic with relatively clear consciences.'

'Yep, and if we find out where it is, you are going to buy me a slap-up dinner, Captain.'

Greg picked up her hand and kissed her fingers. 'It's a date.'

ACKNOWLEDGEMENTS

My grateful thanks to the wonderful Boldwood team and especially my eagle-eyed editor, Emily Ruston.

ABOUT THE AUTHOR

Evie Hunter has written a great many successful regency romances as Wendy Soliman and is now redirecting her talents to produce dark gritty thrillers for Boldwood. For the past twenty years she has lived the life of a nomad, roaming the world on interesting forms of transport, but has now settled back in the UK.

Sign up to Evie Hunter's mailing list here for news, competitions and updates on future books.

Follow Evie Hunter on social media:

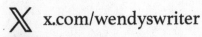 x.com/wendyswriter

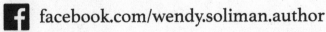 facebook.com/wendy.soliman.author

bookbub.com/authors/wendy-soliman

ALSO BY EVIE HUNTER

Revenge Thrillers

The Sting

The Trap

The Chase

The Scam

The Kill

The Alibi

The Takedown

The Hopgood Hall Murder Mysteries

A Date To Die For

A Contest To Kill For

A Marriage To Murder For

A Story to Strangle For

THE
Murder
LIST

THE MURDER LIST IS A NEWSLETTER DEDICATED TO SPINE-CHILLING FICTION AND GRIPPING PAGE-TURNERS!

SIGN UP TO MAKE SURE YOU'RE ON OUR HIT LIST FOR EXCLUSIVE DEALS, AUTHOR CONTENT, AND COMPETITIONS.

SIGN UP TO OUR NEWSLETTER

BIT.LY/THEMURDERLISTNEWS

Boldwood

Boldwood Books is an award-winning fiction publishing company seeking out the best stories from around the world.

Find out more at www.boldwoodbooks.com

Join our reader community for brilliant books, competitions and offers!

Follow us
@BoldwoodBooks
@TheBoldBookClub

Sign up to our weekly deals newsletter

https://bit.ly/BoldwoodBNewsletter